"The words escape me on how to really get across how exceptional this story truly was. A tale of woe, betrayal and forgiveness Courtesan is on my top ten list of books to read this year."

—Rachelle, *Enchanted in Romance*

"Louisa Trent's hardcore erotic tale dares to take readers on an enthralling journey of transformation through extremes. As I became involved in this tale, I was truly touched as the physical and psychological events escalated in the final chapters."

—Naomi, *Fallen Angel Reviews*

"The plot has enough astonishing twists and turns that you never really know what will happen until the scene rolls over you. I found the story would not have hit me quite so hard without the combination of the excellent plot and provocative sex scenes. Overall, I truly felt moved by Ms. Trent's latest novel and feel it easily justifies receiving the Gold Star Award."

— Francesca Hayne, *Just Erotic Romance Reviews*

"Why can't all historicals be this delicious?! Bondage, domination, and intensely erotic sex make this historical romance unique. I shivered. I bit my lip. I clenched my fist. I wanted. I love it when a book does that to me."

—*Joyfully Reviewed*

LooseId ®

ISBN 10: 1-59632-389-2
ISBN 13: 978-1-59632-389-6
COURTESAN
Copyright © January 2007 by Louisa Trent
Originally released in e-book format in September 2005

Cover Art by April Martinez

DISCLAIMER: Many of the acts described in our BDSM/fetish titles can be dangerous. Please do not try any new sexual practice, whether it be fire, rope, or whip play, without the guidance of an experienced practitioner. Neither Loose Id nor its authors will be responsible for any loss, harm, injury or death resulting from use of the information contained in any of its titles.

This book is an original publication of Loose Id. Each individual story herein was previously published in e-book format only by Loose Id and is a work of fiction. Any similarity to actual persons, events or existing locations is entirely coincidental.

Printed in the U.S.A. by
Lightning Source, Inc.
1246 Heil Quaker Blvd
La Vergne TN 37086
www.lightningsource.com

COURTESAN

Louisa Trent

Prologue

New York 1866

When the brass doorknocker fell for the third time, Margaret O'Sullivan left off her beeswax polishing and bustled from the Winslows' front parlor to the marble-floored foyer, her black bombazine skirts crackling with the heaving force of her stride. "Jesus, Mary, and Joseph, all the saints in Heaven, and Francis the ass in the stable, too. Sure and if 'tisn't enough I have to do with the cleaning and the cooking without having to meet and greet the bloody visitors, too?"

Still muttering under her breath, Maggie wrenched the door wide.

Ample hips fisted, she rolled her sharp Irish eyes at the dirty street urchin loitering upon the stoop. "Be you daft coming to the front door? Rag collectors use the servants' entrance 'round back." With a wag of her double chin, she pointed the way.

"No rag-picker am I, ma'am. No servant, neither."

Though visibly angry, the lad nevertheless removed his scruffy tweed hat, revealing fine manners along with a thick head of coal-black hair. Gorgeous hair 'twas, too!

And more than likely crawling with lice.

To put some space between herself and nit infestation, Maggie took a hasty backward step, where, from the safety of distance, her once-over of the vagrant continued.

She snorted. Imagine the scamp doffing his cap! Like him was a gent!

Tall and gangly, all limbs and cocky swagger, the boyo could have no more than thirteen years on his spare frame; for all that he comported himself more like a man than a boy, a telling lack of facial hair failed to support the boast.

Ah, but put some meat on his bones, give him a nice long soak in a tub, a strenuous delousing with kerosene, and he would charm the drawers right off the colleens, that he would. Why, even ladies-born would eat from this one's hand!

And go down lower, too, if he made the demand—

But Maggie had gotten ahead of herself. Today, he was only a young boy, short of wind from what must have been one hell of a good long run. Why had the filthy mite decided to darken Clearbrook's grand front door? If not a rag-picker come looking for castoffs, did the lad peddle gold trinkets, sure to turn grass-green in less than a fortnight? Or, perhaps he was a sweep on the lookout for a sooty chimney? God forbid he be a tinker, thinking to mend the household's metal utensils! Everyone knew gypsies would rob a household blind if given half the chance.

Hmm. Maggie tilted her jaw. With that wealth of coal-black hair and those flashing dark eyes, the lad might very well have Romany blood. A theft in the house, and her employer, Michael Winslow, would give her the boot—

"Well, speak up!" Maggie finally said, tapping her toe. "I haven't the whole blessed day to stand about dawdling. State your name and tell your business."

"No disrespect meant, ma'am, but I tell my business to the master of this here house, and nobody else."

Maggie's jaw dropped. *Why, would ye look at the arrogance on him!* Dressed in rags, still wet behind the ears, and yet the lad's confident bearing and self-possessed manner belied both his tender years and lowly station in life.

Impressed, Maggie gave the unlikely toff the benefit of her doubt. "And who shall I say is calling?"

"His son, Sebastian."

"Son?" Brogue thick as clotted cream and dripping with sarcasm, she scoffed, "The master of *this here house* has no son. Off with ye now, before I set the authorities on yer bony arse."

"Set whoever you like on me, ma'am. All the same to me, and neither here nor there what you do. I ain't leaving 'til I have words with my father!"

He lowered his eyes, and his belly grumbled. "My mother's last hope rests with Michael Winslow. Right now, all she has left is me."

Poor lamb! Maggie's heart went out to the brave lad. Dirty cap in hand, trying so hard to stay strong as his empty belly touched his backbone and the spit in his mouth leached dry, he fair choked on pride as he swallowed it down. Love for his ma had prompted this errand of mercy. How could she refuse love?

She never could. With a sigh of resignation for yet another lost housekeeping position, Maggie stepped aside for the boy to enter. "Wait here while I ask if Mr. Winslow is at home to his *son*."

As luck would have it, her employer chose that instant to bellow, "Mrs. O'Sullivan! I need you. What keeps you at the door?"

Maggie turned 'round. And gawked.

Saints be praised! There stood the self-important master of Clearbrook himself, a pink bundle held awkwardly in his arms.

As Mr. Winslow approached, Maggie's words stumbled over each other on the way out of her mouth. "S-someone h-here to see you, sir."

"I told you, no callers today." Her employer shook his head. "Will this brat's mewling never cease?"

Then, as if the wee little thing were naught but a big nuisance, Michael Winslow shoved the pink bundle at Maggie's matronly bosom. "Here, you take her."

Straight away, the fretting month-old infant rooted, tried to latch on.

Why, the babe is hungry! In need of a hug, too.

Plenty enough hugs remained in Maggie's beefy arms, but alas, no babe had suckled at her flat teats these past thirty years.

And what a sad state of affairs this was, indeed! Michael Winslow had demanded a son. Having received a daughter instead, he would allow no one to forget his bitter disappointment, particularly not his delicate new bride. As Mrs. Winslow had taken to her sickbed after the birth of her daughter, she would produce no heir anytime soon, if ever a'tall, a'tall. And so this innocent babe would pay for the mistake of her gender.

Margaret's Irish temper flared. *Fockin' housekeeper position be dammed!* Someone had to speak up to the tyrant, and it looked like the duty fell to her.

She glared at Michael Winslow. "This babe is starved. Without a wet nurse, she will not survive the week."

"Hire one," her employer replied, as if teats grew on trees!

As Maggie's brow furrowed, a voice chimed in as clear as a tolling bell, "There is Mrs. Thompson."

Hidden away in the corner as he was, not saying much—but not missing much either; leastwise, not as far as Maggie could tell—the lad had slipped from her attention. At his suggestion, she hearkened to him once more. "Mrs. Thompson?"

"A washwoman on the Bowery. Her baby came too soon and died day before last. She could wet-nurse the babe."

Maggie jumped at the proposal. "Tell this Mrs. Thompson to come over today. Otherwise, her milk will likely dry up. This little one's only chance rests with her."

"What is *he* doing here?" Michael Winslow blustered, finally noticing the observant boyo.

Worried over her new charge, Maggie dispensed with pomp and circumstance. "Your son, Sebastian, to see you."

"Son?" The master of Clearbrook's face turned florid. "What a preposterous lie! Boy, you are no son of mine!"

"Mother is sick. Consumption." Taking two paces forward, Sebastian grabbed ahold of Michael Winslow's morning coat. "Without your help, I fear she will d-d-die. Please, come with me now? Say yes!"

"If your mother has the wasting disease, she has one foot in the grave already. Naught I can do for her," he said with a shrug. "And what is more, stop spouting filthy slander about me! That woman was little better than a servant in this household. And you share none of my blood."

"True, by birth, I am not your son, but when Mother and I lived here, you told me to call you Father!"

The man who paid Margaret O'Sullivan's salary looked apoplectic. "Leave my sight, you bastard whelp, before you spread your whore-mother's putridity." Turning on his well-shod heel, her employer stormed away.

Outraged, Maggie had all she could do not to call after the sod and give him the dressing-down he so richly deserved.

This time, the tyrant had gone too far. Was the man blind? Resentment shone bright in Sebastian's jet-black eyes, the kind of resentment that smoldered for years and then ignited. Aye, Michael Winslow had made himself an enemy this fine day.

And then Margaret let righteousness go. In the here and now, she had more immediate concerns than a man's cruel indifference.

As the hungry babe in her arms squalled, she turned to the dejected lad. "Will you still fetch the wet nurse?"

"I said so, ma'am. And I always keep my word."

He could not lay claim to the lineage; still Sebastian clearly possessed a gentleman's honor. God help him, and Michael Winslow, too, if the lad also possessed a long memory.

Saying a silent prayer to the Virgin for the wisdom to accept what could not be changed, Maggie reached into the pocket of her apron. Pulling out a coin, she pressed the money into the grubby lad's palm. "For yer troubles."

To Maggie's astonishment, the lad refused the alms with a shake of his shaggy head.

And then she knew—'twas as bright as the self-respect shining on his too-thin face.

No beggarly soliciting for young Sebastian. No accepting of handouts, neither. And none of this asking for charity nonsense. He might not have come into life with a silver spoon stuck in his mouth, but he would find his rightful place, even if he had to steal it.

"Go on with ye now," she urged. "Pride is all well and good, but it makes for a poor meal. Do it for the sake of yer ma."

Peering down at the pink blanket, the dying woman's son fisted the coin. "Does the baby have a name?"

Maggie nodded. "Aye. That she does. 'Tis Miss Sarah."

"Sarah," the lad softly repeated.

Like a miracle, the wailing stopped. The infant's big blue eyes fastened on the boyo's grieving face.

"Not too close," Maggie said, setting things straight. "The likes of you are not meant for the likes of her."

Her warning came too late. Gurgling and cooing, Miss Sarah had already reached out her tiny baby hand from its pink blanket cocoon and latched onto the lad's grubby finger.

Incredulous, the housekeeper watched what ensued. The boy tried all manner of maneuvers to break free of the infant's fierce hold. He twisted. Squirmed. Even tried prying the dainty fingers off, one-by-one.

But no matter what Sebastian did to free himself, Sarah obstinately refused to let him go.

Chapter One

New York 1884

Sebastian Turner stretched out facedown on the velvet settee, his forehead laid atop his sinewy arms, every muscle in his long, lean body strung bow-tight.

"So tense," Michelle Beauvais complained, slapping his bare ass.

"*Ooo-la-la,* Chelle! I just love how you scold me," Seb teased the masseuse.

"*Mais oui!* I scold you, for you are a bad boy." A rubdown fit for a mule changed to a kittenish caress; a reprimanding nag turned to a seductive purr. "Mmm. A *very* bad boy."

Seb smiled in wry amusement. "Keep bullying me, honey," he drawled, his Western twang slipping into his speech no matter how hard he tried to keep it out. "Your Frenchie accent drives me plumb wild."

"*Alors!* You are one big, hard knot."

Not everywhere. A disappointing circumstance Chelle was bound to discover should he roll over to his back.

Hoping to keep his boredom to himself, Seb sank deeper into the plush gold pillows.

Chelle was a real sensitive type, with feelings quick to hurt; the last thing he looked to do was insult her. But hell and tarnation! A man has to be in the mood for humping!

"Allow Michelle to work her magic, eh?"

"Honey, I think—"

"*Non! Non!* You must not think! Thinking eez the very thing you must avoid."

That said, Chelle swung a limber leg up and over his hips. "Too much mind stimulation and not enough cock stimulation eez the entire problem. One moment, *s'il vous plait.* I must make—how do you say?—a minor adjustment."

A pink satin wrap fluttered past Seb's nose en route to the office floor.

Chelle meant well. And with neither the energy nor the inclination to rebuff her advances, Seb stoically suffered in silence. Offering not a word of reproach, he allowed her to work on him.

Without feeling so much as a tickle in his pickle.

Not even when sneaky female hands tunneled under his flat stomach, went for his groin, and closed around his limp—

Cucumber?

Dang! No man refers to his pride and joy as salad fixings, not even when that pride and joy is behaving a mite skittish!

"*Mon Dieu!*" She held him in her hand. "What has happened to you?"

Shit! Now that Chelle had found him out, there would be all Almighty hell to pay.

Hoping to ward off an imminent tantrum, Seb ducked his head into his arms. "Sorry."

"Eemposseeble," Chelle said, all Frenchie-like. Pummeling, rubbing, stroking...both hands running up and down and all over, she searched out his trigger.

"Honey, I appreciate the effort, but not even gifted fingers like yours can load my pistol today."

"This will never do! Always, you are full of vigor. Indomitable in bed. When did one of the girls last see to your manly needs?"

"Tough recalling rightly when," he replied. "A while ago, I reckon."

"Before we came back East, you were a four-times-a-day man. No release has wound you watch-tight. Theez situation eez bad for your health. Your animal spirits will suffer if theez continues."

With those words of wisdom, Chelle commenced to bumping and grinding.

"Let me take care of you," the bronco rider panted, bucking up and down. "I would like to. You always show a whore a good time. Allow me to return the favor."

"Thanks for the offer, honey," he wheezed, his backside getting saddlesore. "But not today."

"Give me a chance! Turn over for me, *s'il vous plait?*"

Seb genuinely liked Frenchie. And so, despite his wishes to the contrary, when she lifted up, he rolled onto his back.

"No reflection on you, honey," he quickly offered at her sad look.

Like a brooding French hen, she gave a cluck. "Such a glorious masterpiece as theez should never be allowed to go soft."

Before he could stop the descent, a pair of ruby lips paid him a visit south of the border.

After some intense effort, Seb raised a brow—the only part of his anatomy he could raise—and took the valiant Chelle by the shoulders. Kissing her rouged cheek, he put Frenchie away from him. "Thanks for the massage, honey."

Confusion, then hurt, flickered across her face. On her reddened mouth, Chelle wore a pout.

Thinking to give her a few moments to collect herself, Seb rose from the settee. He stationed himself at the window overlooking the back flowerbeds, and a slight figure walking amongst the plants caught his attention.

"How's the new gal getting along in the house?" he asked, looking over his shoulder.

At his question, Chelle vacated the settee and gave a languid stretch, both hands running over her nude body in a way meant to entice.

Seb sent a return look in a way meant to discourage.

In case his frown missed its mark, he added, "Sometimes, honey, a man just needs a friend."

The curtain came down on Chelle's performance. Crossing the room, she leaned back companionably against his chest, her backside melded to his loins.

"You ask about the new whore? Well, the unsuspecting patron who finds heez way into her starched drawers will have heez manhood frozen off for the effort. Best come to Michelle's bed. That cold snob will chill your ten inches to an icy stump."

Sarah—a cold snob?

Considering her parentage, no surprise there. "Thanks for the advice, honey."

No longer bored, Seb cast gaze eyes over Chelle's head to the gardens, where the "cold snob" had dropped to her knees. As her small shovel dug and scooped the soil, the tattered blue ribbon sticking out from under her straw bonnet dangled hypnotically back and forth from the end of her single black braid. Turned away to plant a row of orange nasturtiums, her features remained frustratingly outside his visual range. As to her shape...her homely—and childish—brown pinafore gave nothing away.

Why bother watching her like this? Spying on her did him no goldarn good!

Seb tried to come away from the window.

And failed.

Seemed like railroad spikes had his feet nailed to the floor. Not for all the tea in China could he move, not even when a hot course of blood rushing to his toes detoured to his groin.

Mighty tough concealing ten inches worth of interest, especially when a female has her nether regions backed up to it, but a gentleman at least makes the attempt. "See you tonight, honey. Save me a dance, hear?"

Chelle let out a sputter. "All that...for...for...her? That tall, skinny stick? Well, you will get no waltz from me tonight, Sebastian Turner. Go fuck yourself!"

In a Frenchie huff, she slammed from the office.

Now alone, Seb took Chelle's suggestion. Eyes narrowed on the window, he jerked his fist up and down the throbbing length of his hot misery.

"Sarah, Sarah, Sarah." He groaned. "I'm coming for you, Sarah."

* * *

Under the mellow glow of the ballroom's gas chandelier, Miss Sarah Winslow carefully negotiated the three-quarter time of the waltz. Though she assiduously counted off the intricate steps, and her timing showed absolute impeccability, her execution lacked both style and grace. And, yes, fluidity.

Not even four years of formal instruction at Mrs. Horatio Alexander's School for Young Ladies, where the dance master discouraged sloppy posture and heavy stepping with the sting of the cane, helped her stiffness. She feared she was utterly hopeless!

Her father had agreed. "Completely lacking in social accomplishment," he'd always said, when he bothered to say anything to her at all.

Though…she might have performed better on the dance floor this evening had she been able to properly inhale and exhale. As it was, she could scarcely breathe at all. No medical condition impeded her lung capacity. Truth to tell, she enjoyed almost ridiculously robust health. No, another source entirely constricted her respiration.

To not put too fine a point on it, the gentleman leading her in the waltz quite literally made her gag. Not a subscriber to the "less is more" school of thought, her dance partner had liberally doused his pate with perfumed pomade, then generously oiled his facial hair, too.

And goodness only knew what else.

As a result, whenever he opened his mouth to speak—done far too frequently in this instance—his moustache would slither across his upper lip much as a slimy black eel wiggles through a muddy river bottom. Thankfully, a leather mask covered most of his aforementioned error in grooming judgment. Would that it covered more!

Someone overhearing her thoughts might have construed her observations as rude, and she was never rude, not even in her most private inner reflections. Nor did she have anything against eels, per se. In fact, she rather liked eels, as she did all God's more maligned creatures. It was only that…well…when counting dance steps, an undulating sea serpent upon a partner's upper lip created a bit of a distraction.

And the eel was only the tip of the iceberg.

Apparently, her partner also suffered from a strange affliction—a rather pronounced and baffling twitch. This spasmodic movement would cause his hand to drop at the most inconvenient of times. Naturally, whenever the strange malady inopportunely occurred, she returned his digits to her upper back where they correctly belonged. Only to have his fingers twitch back down again—

To land on the region of her bustle—had she been wearing one.

Although ladies of fashion would wear such stylish accoutrements, as a lady of expediency, she wore none.

Without a bustle, his hand landed on her derrière, to be precise.

There, his fingers made what she could only describe as an odd gripping motion. Most peculiar.

"Sir—" she began, about to offer him a gentle rebuke for the discomfiture.

He craned his goatee at her—the stretch necessary due to his half-rule shorter height—and whispered a crude obscenity in her ear. Done whilst squeezing her posterior between two fingers!

This time, there could be no mistake. A pinch is a pinch is a pinch, and this was most decidedly a pinch. Not only foul-smelling, apparently her partner was also a masher.

What to do?

Her natural inclination called for lifting her limb and kneeing the odious reprobate in what must certainly be the most perfumed testicles in all of New York state.

This urge, she resisted. Barely.

She was a lady by birth, if not by present circumstance, and her knee would not stray anywhere near the profligate's inseam. More's the pity.

Sarah worried her lower lip with her upper teeth whilst considering the distressing quandary.

Obviously, the occasion warranted action. She must rectify this egregious breech of good taste! For naught would persuade her that off-color innuendos ever passed as genteel conversation or that groping should be tolerated in any circle, not even such a circle as this. Regardless that Mr. Dutton expected her to entertain the paying guests, she felt disinclined to suffer the offensive sea serpent's presence a moment longer. After all, even when employed in a house of ill repute, one must keep to one's standards!

"Excuse me," Sarah said, begging off in the middle of an orchestral downbeat. "I am feeling remarkably unwell of a sudden."

Her partner sniffed, lips pursed, slimy black eel moustache slithering. "I paid handsomely for this waltz, my dear, and you will finish the set."

Sarah drew herself up to her full five feet seven inches. "I think not. In fact, you, my depraved little man, have groped your last grope. Your mouth has uttered its last double entendre. Release me before your odious fragrance causes the contents of my stomach to eject. Let your coiffure be forewarned, sir!"

Fine words. Somehow, though, in the middle of her self-congratulations, her partner had danced her into a dark corner to the rear of the ballroom. In the small anteroom, the fronds of potted palms did very little to hide the fact that several couples eagerly sampled the pâté de foie gras canapés from one another's tonsils.

Screaming was out of the question. She detested scenes. Plus, there was the no small matter of her agreement to participate in the evening's activities.

Upon seeing what that participation entailed, however, second thoughts had crept into her mind.

Many of the surrounding couples wore far fewer clothes than they strictly should. "Naked" came to mind. And they were making guttural moans and grunts and high-pitched squeals, sounds one normally associates with animals in a zoo, perhaps emanating from a monkey cage.

Whilst her partner fiddled with the last button on his coat, then fidgeted a hand inside his trousers—perhaps an attack of dyspepsia required a loosening of the waistband—Sarah gawked at a gyrating couple energetically engaged in...well...an odd contortion of some sort.

Blinking, Sarah did a double-take. Heavens! Is that what doing *IT* looked like?

She'd thought she had a basic understanding of Mr. Dutton's requirements. She really did! But after observing one of those requirements in the flesh, as it were, the realization hit home that perhaps she had oversimplified her obligation and underestimated her knowledge.

All pretense of sophistication fell away. "Please, sir!" she cried in a panic. "Loose me! Aromatic considerations aside, I simply cannot do that with you!"

Chapter Two

In this swanky Park Avenue establishment, not everyone came to act out his own private fantasies; some members came to look at others enact theirs, and not so privately. What did Seb care if a voyeuristic patron masturbated while watching another man do the actual deed? The gal saved time, and the royalties still went to the house.

That would be him.

As the silent and, up until just recently, *distant* partner of Leonard Dutton, Seb held joint ownership of this exclusive brothel.

For protection of the gals, every room came equipped with strategically placed locked peepholes. The ones drilled in the walls of Seb's downstairs office provided excellent views of the ballroom, gaming room, and the front entranceway.

Seb squinted into the ballroom lookout and had the distinct pleasure of spying an oily gent put the squeeze on the new whore's rump. Sarah Winslow's already erect stance stiffened, sort of like a red-hot poker had just been stuffed up her ass. Both the pinching and poking fell well within the rules—so long as the house got paid first.

As this wily gent had neglected to grease Seb's palm *before* putting it to Sarah Winslow, he had violated house rules.

House rules also decreed that both patrons and prostitutes alike wore masks. Sarah's feathered creation prevented Seb from getting a clear bead on her eyes, but the uncovered portion of her features made her disapproval of her partner's antics pretty damned clear. Hell, could a nose get any further out of joint?

Seb's perusal moved to her lips, which she had puckered to lemon-sucking tightness. Prim. Prim. Her lips were tight-ass prim, like her drawers had just gotten bunched, then wedged up that tight, prim ass.

And her chin... *Mercy!* Her chin! The mulish jut of her regal jaw told Seb everything he needed to know about Sarah Winslow's character.

Seb chuckled to himself. Someone had better tell that gal real quick that the house paid her to be obligin'.

His mirth flattened out when the oily patron danced Sarah into a proverbial corner. Specifically, into an area set aside for guests with exhibitionist tendencies. There, amongst the potted palms, gentlemen who were so inclined could publicly woo similarly inclined partners.

Sarah Winslow did not look similarly inclined.

Her face first registered snootiness, then horror, and finally fear. By rights, Seb should have found this turn of events highly satisfying. Even amusing. But, personal vendetta aside, he ran a respectable establishment, and gents who forced their attentions on unwilling whores not only broke cathouse rules; they undermined profits.

Snapping the peephole shut, Seb raced from the office.

"Let-her-go," he said, dropping the three small words on top of the gent's shiny hairdo.

Apparently not looking to mess with the muscle behind the management, the patron reconsidered his breech of manners and snaked away, presumably to inflict his oily presence on the poker players in the backroom.

Sarah's gratitude shone through the eyeholes of her feathered mask, all that positive regard bestowed upon him. In a serious case of misdirected admiration, Sarah Winslow had evidently cast him in the role of Sir Galahad charging to her rescue on a fancy white steed. Too bad he always rode black stallions, and he never, but never, saved the damsel in distress.

"Thank you so, *so* much for coming to my assistance, sir," the deluded Miss Winslow enthused, flinging herself into his arms.

A first.

A lady looking to him for comfort had never happened to Seb before, no how, no way. Working gals, yeah, plenty of those, all ranting and raving, and weeping in their ale, their crying jags a calculated ploy to get their own way.

He dealt all the time with hissy fits over a broken nail or a missed dressmaker's appointment or an overspent monthly allowance, but nothing like this.

This was different. True, Sarah Winslow had him in a chokehold, but the underlying cause of her upset remained all bottled-up, her emotional upheaval trapped inside. She just 'bout vibrated with corralled sorrow. Seeing as how he had instigated her problems, his conscience should have been fretting him something awful.

Seb never felt a twinge, his inner judgmental voice having given up on him long ago. He had waited too many years for this moment not to savor it now. He reckoned gloating was due him.

"There, there." Seb patted Sarah's shoulder with studied sympathy, smoothing his palm over the glossy white satin of her ball gown, a demure Parisian confection he had personally selected.

Inside joke, that virginal apparel. The kind of twisted humor only a jaded bastard like himself would appreciate, preferably in a dark room over a double shot of whiskey.

Both laughter and liquor would need to wait for later—Seb had himself a crisis on his hands.

Out here in the East, where a man made his fortune based on the crispness of his tailoring, Sarah's embrace was not only putting a wrinkle in his suit, but in his bankroll, too. Already, her hug had rumpled the perfection of his pristine shirt linen and crushed the knife-straight lines of his black swallowtail coat, not to mention the unsightly creases her stubborn chin had made in his imported silk cravat. If she kept this up, he would be a disgrace to all gentlemen impersonators everywhere.

Seb eased Sarah away.

With an audible gulp, she pulled him right back. "But, sir, what shall I ever do if the eel returns?"

They came from two different worlds, but that made no never mind. Seb understood Sarah's meaning right off. "How 'bout this? You go outside, take a breath of fresh air, while I escort *the eel* to his carriage." Hell, he had to do something to save his expensive duds.

"But-but...Mr. Dutton expects the ladies in his employ to dance." Blue eyes peered owlishly at him through the holes in the facemask.

"A swooning gal on the dance floor is bad for business. Now scoot. You look 'bout ready to keel."

She dropped him a curtsey. "Thank you again for saving me, sir. Please forgive my precipitous departure." Pivoting on the heels of her white kid slippers, the prim and proper and oh-so-snobby Miss Sarah Winslow made her escape.

Seb looked after the new whore as she fled the overheated ballroom through the open veranda doors, the train of her fashionable white ball gown sweeping the black marble floor behind her. Before tonight, Sarah had represented nothing more than a vendetta to him; he'd never seen her as a real person, subject to feelings, who might feel pain. He had neither felt nor cared anything about her. Why would he? She was only an object, a *thing* on which he planned to retaliate.

After meeting her, Sarah remained only an object to him, though an exquisite one and one well worth collecting.

No facemask could hide the perfection of Sarah Winslow's features. Poets wrote sonnets to her kind of classical beauty, the sort of beauty that was about sculptured cheekbones, but also about poise and posture and pedigree. Compared to frontier women who worked hard, aged fast, and worried long over the return of their men from the range, she looked like she had spent her entire life under a frilly parasol in a framed painting—

Except for those unshed tears. He had never yet seen a portrait cry, not even silently.

As a snot-nosed street tough, Seb had acquired an appreciation for the finer things in life. His keen eye could easily distinguish between that which was precious and real and one of a kind, from that which was a fake. In a crowd, he could tell a born gent from a born phony, a genuine gold watch fob from painted tin, a purse made of silk and not a sow's ear. Gifted with talented fingers, a long running stride, good instincts, and even better senses—ten paces removed, he could sniff out a money pouch containing sawbucks from one stuffed with C-notes—Seb had quickly risen to a position of prominence amongst Bowery pickpockets.

Eighteen years later, he had changed in many ways and in some ways not all. Soap and water had rid his skin of the clinging stink of sweat. A tailor had spruced up his wardrobe. A barber kept his hair nattily trimmed. Except for the occasional slip of elocution—part lower Manhattan, part a drawl he had picked up out West—he mimicked a gentleman's refined patina pretty damned well. And when the convolutions of etiquette left him mystified, wealth generally forgave his mistakes.

He had money in spades. His holdings included several carriages, a stable of thoroughbred horses, and a country estate just outside the city's hustle and bustle. In the next year or so, he intended to buy himself a lady-bride. Some pretty and vapid young miss. A virgin, naturally, bartered at one of the flesh-pandering parties that passed as grand society in this town. No one would ever suspect him for the son of a discarded mistress. No one would know his polish rubbed off, the sheen a veneer. That he had paid for his class with wily intelligence and backbreaking toil. No one would guess his humble origins—

With one possible exception.

Sarah Winslow.

Seb had a sinking feeling that if he lowered his guard even an inch, the snobby miss who had just disappeared into the night would see right through him.

In her impatience to cleanse her nostrils of the eel's cloying perfume, Sarah almost took a tumble on the dark veranda.

Jeanette.

Her fellow boarder knelt before the open placket of a pair of pinstriped trousers, her red-rouged lips working feverishly. So as not to disturb the couple in a romantic moment, Sarah picked up her white skirts and raced past, running pell-mell for the glass conservatory—Mr. Dutton's nod and wink to London's Crystal Palace.

Once inside, Sarah concentrated on the rare collection of orchids she had nurtured over the past year. Soon, a profusion of delicate blossoms would pay her back for the Cattleyas' care.

Botany consumed her, especially the study of exotic tropical plants. After her mother's early death, her father had left her in the care of a succession of staid governesses. Much preferring the company of the family gardener, she had sneaked off to join him whenever possible—which was to say, all of the time. The kind and grandfatherly Mr. O'Sullivan had taught her everything he knew about horticulture. Before her tenth birthday, she had memorized the species names of most plants.

Unless her customers spoke Latin, a tremendous lot of good *that* would do her later on tonight when she lay flat on her back, her legs flung over her head!

How had she come to this?

As a child, there had been plenty of money. Old, inherited money. Nevertheless, her only privileges had been an education and involvement in charitable work at the village orphanage.

She had never felt the lack of society. The servants had kept her company, the orphan children gave her life meaning, and the gardens entertained her. She had been happy!

Unbeknownst to her, debts had started to pile up.

First bankruptcy and then a whisper campaign destroyed the Winslow name. Overnight, she became a social pariah. An outcast. An untouchable. Publicly disgraced. Her erstwhile friends were no longer at home to her! Their parlor maids refused her calling card. Her already scant social invitations dwindled to nothing, which destroyed her chances of resolving the family's financial difficulties through making a good marriage.

In New York society, the only condition more disgraceful than poverty itself was the acknowledgement that poverty existed. Her drastically reduced circumstances served as an ungentle reminder that some people actually went to bed cold and hungry at night. Like the orphans warehoused in a rundown shack on the outskirts of town, she served as an embarrassment, the reality of her situation far too painful for social acceptability.

To keep her father and herself fed, she had sold everything. The furniture and family jewelry went first at auction. A nearby livery purchased the horses and carriages, gone for a song.

Clearbrook had once shone like a magnificent jewel. But in the end, the house and grounds had fallen into a terrible state of disrepair. Having no funds to fix the leaking roof or to pay the servants, she stuck pots under the ceiling drips and, after paying their overdue wages, dismissed the household staff, undertaking her father's nursing herself.

A long death. Ten grueling months of exhausting, round-the-clock care, which left her physically and emotionally and financially depleted.

After his death, she learned her father had lived and died a rogue. A gambler. A womanizer. A cheat. The gossip said Michael Winslow's many tawdry affairs had broken her mother's heart. Unable to recover from the devastating blow to her trust, her mama had died much too young, before Sarah really even knew her. Afterwards, her father had rented a townhouse in the city, staying away from Clearbrook, the Winslow country estate, for longer and longer periods of time. A blessing, as her father's absences had sheltered her from much, but not all, of his philandering.

Genteel impoverishment rapidly deteriorated to destitution. When she was on the verge of starvation, her father's friend, Leonard Dutton, had approached her. Might he help her?

"Yes. Please, yes!"

When the creditors came knocking on Clearbrook's door, Mr. Dutton had handled the private sale of the estate, thus ending one hundred years of Winslow occupancy.

The property fetched very little. Not nearly enough to put a dent in the debt self-respect and family honor demanded she repay.

But how?

Mr. Dutton suggested making her a loan, an offer impossible to refuse. If in a year's time, she still had not married her way out of indebtedness, he would provide her with a lucrative means to repay him.

A godsend, she'd thought at the time.

Naïve, she now knew.

But with no place to live, no food on the table, and deeply indebted, she had moved into Mr. Dutton's guesthouse, with the agreement that she would landscape the surrounding property in lieu of room and board. The surrounding property included a prestigious gentlemen's club—another name for a gaming establishment. The crème de la crème of New York society frequented Dutton's card tables, with an occasional visit of European nobility thrown in, as well.

The stigma of her father's scandal had reached far and wide. After a year, she had received no marriage proposals, nor did she anticipate any in the future. As to gainful employment—she found none. Not as a teacher, not trimming hats in a milliner's shop, not even as a domestic. Not without references—which, of course, she had no way of obtaining. As she was a lady born and bred for marriage and charity work, no one anywhere would hire her.

She remained optimistic. Confident that somehow, someway, she would rise above her father's scandal and find a paying position somewhere.

Perhaps as a gardener. Patrons, who came and went at all hours of the day and night from the card tables, invariably stopped to admire the landscape; some had even offered her garden design commissions.

One after another, the offers fell through.

A crushing blow. Then, whilst she still reeled with disappointment, her note had come due.

During her repayment discussion with Mr. Dutton, she learned that more than gaming went on at the club. Those pretty girls fluttering about the premises like exotic butterflies in their silk wraps and colorful gowns? Well, they provided more than smiles of encouragement to the gamblers.

As it turned out, Mr. Dutton operated a den of iniquity. A fancy house.

In essence, when she had nothing left to sell, she had unknowingly sold herself. Her body had served as collateral on Mr. Dutton's loan.

Another crushing blow. She had placed her faith, her trust, her confidence...her very life...in a man's hands, and that man had unscrupulously used her to further his own ends. He had duped her! As she moved out of Mr. Dutton's guest quarters and into the second floor of the main house with the rest of the female "boarders," she vowed never again to place herself so fully under another's control. The only way to accomplish that goal was to gain her financial independence...

But first, she would need to pay off the note she owed.

Certainly, she was not a common streetwalker. However, for all that she wore silk, not garish rags, and leased her favors by the hour on prestigious Park Avenue rather than in an alleyway on the Bowery, she would still perform the services of a whore.

So far this evening, a patron had pawed her. Pinched her. Squeezed her about the bustle. He had whispered the most vulgar profanity in her ear. All that, and she had yet to earn a dime to repay her loan.

That would come later this evening.

Oh, she knew all she need do was lie there. And what she lacked in application she could always bluff—she excelled at pretense. But how would she tolerate the indignity? The loss of pride? How would she keep down the vomit when strange men used her body like a latrine?

What other choice had she?

With a blighted past, a reprehensible present, a bleak future, and every alternative considered and discarded—save for the one involving a lily, a shroud, and a pauper's burial—she had no other choice.

Chapter Three

Upon sufficiently composing herself, Sarah left the conservatory to wander the gardens, her mind a hopeless dark void. Through no conscious intent on her part, she found herself on the winding path to the gazebo. About midway to her destination, the masked guest who had come to her rescue inside the ballroom stepped out from behind a privet hedge and placed himself squarely in front of her.

"How are you?" he asked.

The words sounded innocuous enough, the phraseology polite, but the speech pattern itself bordered on rough. Definitely ill-bred. Coarse. He spoke with an artificial correctness, not a natural flow at all, as if weighing each word lest he choose the wrong one. And his vowels showed an odd and distinctive lengthening.

Oh, my, yes, she had read all about men like him. Her rescuer was not of her class, she decided. Not a true gentleman. Worse than a ruffian, the man was a Lower East Side thug with possible cowpoke affiliations.

Ordinarily, such a contemptuous and condescending thought would not have occurred to her. Or, if it had occurred to her, horrified, she would have pushed the patronizing thought right on through her mind. But after falling victim to duping by the unscrupulous Mr. Dutton and then, on top of that, only just narrowly escaping a potential masher, her usual equanimity slipped somewhere out of reach. With her dignity in shreds, her pride in tatters, she went up on her high horse and sat there looking down. At him.

"Sir," she began crossly, giving him the full brunt of her bitter mood, "do not assume because you came to my rescue inside the house you now have the right to detain me here in the gardens!" Picking up her voluminous skirts, she endeavored to step around him.

He sidestepped into her circumvention, essentially blocking her escape route.

Vexed, she offered him a scornful scowl of reproof. "Please allow me to pass."

He shook his head. "A gentleman never leaves a lady alone in the dark."

"A gentleman! You?" She gave a derisive laugh. "Sadly, I am unconvinced as to the merits of your argument!"

He cocked a dark brow; firm lips curved. "What gave me away—the cut of my trousers or my waistcoat's embroidery?"

"Neither!"

"What a relief. These togs cost enough to feed a family of eight for a year. But, if not the clothes, what led to your bad opinion of me?"

He actually sounded put upon. *Him!* Had *he* just had his nether quarters pinched? Had *he* nearly choked on smelly pomade?

Oh, no! He was not the injured party here, and he would not make her out as the villainess of this piece! "If you must know, sir, your presumptuous manner gave you away! Your forwardness is not at all the hallmark of a gentleman. Indeed, your familiarity, your very impertinence, denotes a much lower station in life. Now, you are standing in my way. Please move!"

She never, ever, gave way to petulance. But no longer the same naïve miss of the week before, she now understood the ulterior purpose this establishment on Park Avenue served. Bestial lust, not courtly gallantry, motivated this guest.

"Why not stay and talk?" he asked.

She fell back on decorum. "I cannot stay and talk because conversing with a strange man is not at all proper!"

"Proper?" He chuckled with an uncalled for merriment. "You ain't no debutante. This here ain't no coming-out party."

She held on to her stiff dignity for dear life. "But there are certain…well…conventions one must observe even in the lowliest of environments. Take ants, for instance."

"*Ants?*"

"Yes, *ants*. Even insects follow a social structure." She tsked, the same chastisement she used on the older, more exuberant orphan boys. "As the etiquette of this social structure seems to have escaped your attention, allow me to clarify the rules for you. In this establishment, the anonymity of both patron and...and..."

What to call herself?

Whore? Harlot? Prostitute? Wanton wench?

Sarah cringed at the plebeian terminology. None of those descriptions fit her. Rather, she was a lady who had fallen upon hard times, here to learn a trade in which she intended to excel. No slipshod mediocrity for her! She would take pride in her work as a...as a...

What?

Stroking her feathered mask, Sarah raised her chin. "As I was saying, sir, in this establishment, the anonymity of both patron and *courtesan* is guaranteed. Both parties wear facemasks to ensure neither recognizes the other, nor suffers the embarrassment of association, should their respective carriages happen to collide in Central Park. If you would like to...er...*see* me later in my chamber, you must first speak to Mr. Dutton to discuss...uh...*practical* matters."

"These practical matters presumably entail the cost of tossing your skirts over your head?"

"You are outrageous, sir!"

"And you, miss, are a prime piece of female flesh. Is your dance card filled this evening?"

"Of all the effrontery! This is a private club, with an influential membership. Obviously, *you* do not belong here." She muttered under her breath, "How such a person gained admittance in the first place is quite beyond the scope of my understanding."

"I bought my way in," he supplied.

"And that only goes to prove you are no gentleman. Only a shopkeeper discusses money. And a shopkeeper could never afford me. Now would you please just...just go?" She waved her hand in a shooing motion, as one would with a recalcitrant child. Or servant. Not that she had ever done so with either.

"Gal, looks to me like your seams are about to bust, and I can think of more pleasant ways of making you come apart than breaking a row of stitches."

At his suggestive remark, she trembled almost convulsively. Why did this man anger her so? And why, oh, why did she find the give-and-take of his argument so…so…stimulating?

Was it because he spoke the truth?

Because, of course, he could afford her. No one slipped past Mr. Dutton's stringent financial screening process.

Her waylayer took hold of the uppermost region of her arm. His thumb stroked the underside, where her long, white kid gloves met the tight-fitting bell sleeve of her gown. Horror of horrors, he touched skin—bare skin—in close proximity to her bosom, which had, quite remarkably, sprouted two hardening points. "Stay and talk," he cajoled. "Please?"

"Quite impossible, sir."

"You little baggage! Money makes everything possible."

"But I…I have no knowledge of you," she stammered, her heaving breasts aching at his closeness, her hardened nipples uncomfortably poking her chemise. "W-w-we have not been formally introduced. *I have not made your acquaintance!*"

"So? What of it? Will you know who crawls between your thighs later on tonight?"

At her gasp, he shook his head, as if in aggravation. "Listen, right now the only thing on my mind is conversation."

"I am not a dimwit, sir. I know full well you wish more!"

"All right. I do. May I be frank?"

"I much prefer frankness to flattery."

"As do I." He paused, then added, "A male has needs."

"These needs are of a carnal nature, correct? That is to say, you wish to p-p-place your male reproductive part inside me and deposit your viscous secretion. We *are* talking about a spermatozoa emission, are we not? "

Her rescuer coughed. "What an unseemly question for a lady to pose! And your tone! Tut-tut. You exhibit an inordinate amount of unsavory relish about a remarkably indelicate subject! I tell you, I am quite, *quite* scandalized."

His affected speech pattern poked fun at her. Did she really sound like such a priss?

Her chin jutted. "Do you, or do you not, wish to procure me for an evening's entertainment? Physical intercourse, not intellectual discourse—is that not what this conversation is about?"

"Yes, procurement is what this conversation is about. But where is the harm in teasing you first?"

A drooping feather from her mask tickled her brow, a brow she was quite sure must by now be scrunched in a furrow, regardless of her repeated attempts to present a placid expression. "Teasing? Ah, I see. As in foreplay! In preparation for tonight, I have done extensive research in the subject of sexual intercourse."

"Research? What the hell kind of research?"

"The prudent kind. The kind derived from books."

"Books?" He laughed.

At her expense.

Pride wounded, she climbed back atop her high horse. "Yes, books," she said in a pique. "You have heard of books, have you not?"

"Well, shucks, ma'am! I sure have heard of books," he drawled. "Tarnation! Reckon, I might even have read me a few." He laughed some more. "What a little snob you are!"

The man belonged on the stage; he altered his manner of speaking at whim!

Notching up her own voice, to be heard above his ill-mannered guffaws, she continued with her lecture. "I shall have you know, I am quite knowledgeable about any and all positions, deviancies, and orifices involved in male ejaculation. I can expound on oral, vaginal, or anal penetration. Or any combinations thereof," she said, warming to the academic subject matter. "In regard to the benefits of one position over the next, let us take...oh...fellatio for an example. I should think that—"

His bellowing laughter changed to another fierce bout of coughs.

"Are you all right?" she queried. "Shall I thump you between the shoulder blades?"

"No thumping!" His voice sounded strangled. "Instead, tell me about the gardens."

"Gardens? Sir Richard Burton just published the *Kama Sutra* and will soon publish *The Perfumed Garden* as well! Is that the book to which you refer? Fancy you knowing the treatise. At any rate, you know, I should think, in regard to Eastern versus Western philosophy, that—"

"Damn and blast! I mean *these* gardens." He gestured rather wildly to the raised beds. "Not some damned gardens in some damned erotic literature."

"You wish to discuss flowers?" Her question carried a hint of incredulousness.

"Why not? As it so happens, white nicotinia are a favorite of mine. The landscape designer did an excellent job on these gardens."

She flushed with pleasure. "Thank you. You are entirely too kind, really."

"Are you saying *you* designed the gardens?"

It was difficult not to preen. "Why, yes."

Not only had she designed the gardens; she'd dug them, hauled horse manure from the stables to fertilize them, and weeded them on hands and knees. Which explained why tonight she wore heavy, elbow-length kid gloves, their lacy counterparts little help in disguising her callused hands and broken nails. Everyone who saw the gardens loved them. Why had all her commission offers fallen through?

She bit her lip, so as not to cry.

"Something wrong?" the man asked.

At first, Sarah shook her head. Mr. Dutton was paying her to project a pampered image, to laugh, to dance...to sleep with the patrons. Not cry on their shoulders. But for some perverse reason, this guest struck a responsive cord within her, both good and bad, which caused her to blurt, "If you must know, I am somewhat financially embarrassed. I owe a large sum of money to creditors, which forced me to seek out a loan, which I now have no means to repay."

The man offered up a very male grin. "Oh, those milliner's balances! How they do tally up. But, I suppose, beautiful ladies must wear beautiful clothes."

Not in years had she bought so much as a hatpin! Her gown tonight was a prop. Window dressing. Worn to please the male clientele of this establishment. She had never owned anything pretty. And this man's reference to her as beautiful amounted to empty flattery. Clumsy and not much to look at—her father had hammered both truths home often enough for her to know them by rote—

"Can we go someplace private?" the patron asked, once again interrupting her train of thought.

When she made to protest, he held up a large, tanned hand. "Just to talk. Naturally, I agree to pay for your time."

Pay for your time...

That last stinging dart pierced what remained of her pride. So difficult to think of oneself as a commodity, whose time, whose company, whose body a man might purchase.

Rallying, Sarah straightened her shoulders. No more would she stick her head in the sand like an ostrich. She must accustom herself to the financial aspects of these sorts of arrangements, or she would never repay her debts.

She forced herself to nod. "Very well. You may discuss the cost of my time with Mr. Dutton." She cleared nervousness from her throat. "Actually, if you must know, I was on my way to the new gazebo when you jumped out of the bushes at me."

"'Leap first, apologize later' is my motto."

"You are brash, sir."

"And you are a most perceptive young lady." He drew her hand through the crook of his elbow. "Now tell me—did you also design the gazebo plantings...?"

Chapter Four

As a Bowery tough, Seb's survival had depended on his ability to size up prospective marks. He had built a lucrative career on watching people, and so, as they strolled side by side down the boxwood-lined walk toward the gazebo, he studied Sarah Winslow.

Using a conman's grifts and charm, he sought to put her at ease. Hardly a chore, as beauty pleasured him in all of its many forms. He appreciated a beautiful garden on an equal footing with a beautiful painting. Though he enjoyed beautiful women most of all.

Sarah Winslow was very enjoyable company.

The evening air filled his nostrils. "Nothing compares to the scent of white nicotinia."

The lady at his side nodded her agreement. "Garden visitors often overlook the blossoms in sunlight, but come evening, the white variety show at their best."

As they chatted on about various plants, Sarah's rigidly controlled composure slowly relaxed. Lost in conversation, she lowered her guard; her reserve grew less pronounced. She even smiled up at him once or twice. She was still spoiled and still a snob, and yet Seb found he liked Sarah Winslow. Since her father had cold-bloodedly allowed his mother to die, it was hard to countenance that liking, to explain the pull he felt.

She amused him, he supposed.

Dang! The *Kama Sutra* and spermatozoa emissions—talk like that took the pleasure clean out of fornication.

After her inspection of a rose bush—"checking for mildew"—they continued along the path. Occasionally, one or both of them would make some innocuous comment about a plant, her conversation growing lively when expounding on, of all things, root rot and leaf fungus.

Sarah's animation abandoned her inside the gazebo's white latticework. She crumbled against him, her complexion a sickly shade of gray.

He helped her to a bench beneath the hanging tendrils of a wisteria. "Head between your knees."

"Oh, a lady never strikes such an indelicate pose."

Ordinarily, her convoluted manners would have had him roaring, but nothing about illness made him want to laugh.

He pressed her stubborn chin to the gazebo floor. "Where will your overblown sense of dignity be when you upchuck the buffet dinner?"

"I used that very threat to thwart the attentions of Mr. Eel when he tried to spawn upon me."

"Good for you." *Now* he bit back a chuckle. "And for your information, I would have lopped off Mr. Eel's slimy head before letting him spawn on you."

"More gratifying if you had instead lopped off his..." Her chin tilted in thought. "Goodness! Does an eel even have a penis?"

"I assume so. Shall I return to the house and dispense with his? A very *small* loss, I should think."

"Not necessary." She giggled. "Enough for the castration to remain a fantasy."

Proper Sarah! Full of starch, but surprisingly free of vanity. With tutoring, she might become almost human—

Seb nipped the wayward direction of his thoughts in the bud. Snobby Sarah would never understand the wants and needs of a person from his lowly social class.

Thrown off his game plan, Seb asked, a little too sharply, "When did you last eat?"

"A lump in my throat made swallowing a bit difficult today. I believe I did have some dry toast yesterday at tea, though."

"Dry toast! Is that all you have in your belly?"

"I work to offset my room and board, sir. Eating too much will only sink me deeper in debt."

Seb would not delude himself about the part he had played in either her present or past discomfort. He had caused her missed meals, her hunger...her homelessness. The blame for her swoon fell to him.

"The housekeeper will bring a tray to your chamber before my visit. I have no patience for a listless lover in my bed."

With a toss of her head, she threw off his restraining hand. Straightening to sit upright on the bench, she snipped, "It is *my* bed, and I am not at all sure you will be visiting it!"

Seb supposed pride dictated that the snobby miss cling to the illusion that she had a choice over who came and went in her bedchamber. And having himself lived on nothing but pride for years, he supposed he understood. "You sound just like the virgin you are."

Sarah Winslow's gray complexion took on a rosy hue. "And *you* took *me* to task for speaking indelicately!" Her jaw tilted again. "And how are you privy to such intimate information about me?"

"I made it my business to know."

Whether trafficking in explosives or prostitution, Seb kept a running tally of who owed him what. Michael Winslow had owed him plenty. Tonight, Sarah would begin repaying her old man's debt, but the thought of physically hurting her during the collection made Seb a mite testy. He had never hurt any female, especially in bed—which explained why he steered clear of virgins.

Seb squeezed in behind Sarah, between bench and latticework, and gazed at her profile.

She looked wilted, like a stomped-on flower blossom. And she looked frightened. He had done that to her. He had put that cornered look on her face. Seb knew that look well. His own mother had worn a similar expression when a wealthy man had discharged her from his home, young son in tow, with no way to support either of them, save one.

While he drowned in sad memories, Sarah whispered something that sounded an awful lot like "Forgive me" to him.

Seb assigned forgiveness to the pulpit on Sabbath mornings. Weak people forgave; strong people evened the score. He never turned a cheek, never backed down from a fight, never apologized afterwards. The path begun at his mother's deathbed had brought him here tonight, with eighteen years of rage seething inside him. He had lived those eighteen years for only one thing—to bring down the Winslows.

Only, Sarah Winslow was different than what he had expected.

Hell, yeah, she was a prissy, tight-ass snob, but not mean-spirited. Spoiled, but not spoiled rotten. And for some reason, the thought of other men touching her, caressing her...defiling her...filled him with revulsion. He knew firsthand how men treated women who sold their bodies. Knew how those women ended up dead inside. A damnable shame, destroying beauty that way, especially seeing the beautiful lady had just asked for his forgiveness—

Seb shook his head. Was his mask on too tight? How come she had just asked for his forgiveness? Was he hearing things?

"What did you just say?" he finally asked Sarah.

She made a small choking sound, her breath coming in shallow gasps. "Such a nuisance! Forgive me. I—I—cannot breathe."

Shit! While she squirmed, her breathlessness no doubt on account of her recent run-in with the eel, Seb tugged at the endless row of tiny hooks and eyes fastening the back of Sarah's gown. "Sit still! Ravishing you is the last thing on my mind right now. No fun a'tall debauching an unconscious female."

When the satin edges of her gown gaped to the waist, he gaped, too—in disgust over the killer whalebone stays on her corset. "Why are you laced so tight?"

"To create the illusion of a bosom where a bosom, lamentably, does not exist," she said, speaking with less effort than before. "The stays push up what little I do have and turn me into a femme fatale."

He attacked the whalebone monstrosity. "No sense suffocating over an illusion."

Twisting around, she grabbed hold of his wide laborer's wrists at the shirt cuffs. Ladylike horror laced her steadily strengthening voice. "You must not undo me! Illusion is all I have."

"Fine," he muttered. Giving up on the tug-of-war, he reached for the ribbon that encircled her upswept black hair and held the mask in place.

"Do not! The house rules!"

His hands dropping away, Seb took a backward step. Then another. Until his spine hit the latticework. "I forgot about the rules."

He had forgotten a hell of a lot of things, like the purpose of this little tête-à-tête. "I only thought you could breathe more easily without the mask."

She gulped a shaky breath and said disjointedly, "But the mask makes it easier to...to..." She looked down at her lap. "...to receive a gentleman."

She said *receive*, but Seb knew the lady meant something else. Another one of those snobby illusions of hers—

Tonight, Sarah Winslow would lose her virginity. Not in love. Not in passion. Not even in lust. Tonight, she would serve as a receptacle for one man's revenge. Afterwards, a line of anonymous customers would impersonally use her body. And so it would continue every night, until she paid her debt. The cancellation of her loan could take years. How would a conservatory-grown flower like her survive?

Seb stepped out from behind Sarah, his gaze on the tight blue line of her lips, a lush mouth that should have reflected the shallow gaiety of a young society miss. His words mirrored what he felt inside. "Looks like you could use a good scream."

Her chin lifted. "Oh, I never scream, sir."

"Well, maybe you should. Plenty of women do. Pitching a fit seems to help."

"I beg your pardon?"

"Let it out. Yell. Say a few choice words. Go ahead, before you burst."

"Another veiled reference to my split seams? La! What is this concern of yours for the stitching in my gown?" She shook her head. "I am not paid to scream, sir."

Such innocence!

Faking orgasm was part of a whore's job, and that usually involved screaming. Sarah must have skipped that chapter during her "research." He chuckled.

"You laugh, sir! Why? I made no jest."

No way could he explain the joke to a virgin. "Forget about impressing me," he said instead. "Just be yourself."

"Oh, I certainly cannot." Spreading her white skirts around her neatly crossed ankles, she folded her hands in her lap. "My real self would simply never do."

His lips lifted again, this time in a half-smile of sympathy over her overblown sense of propriety. At the tug on his heartstrings, his jaw dipped to Sarah's ladylike mouth.

"Please, sir," she said, her pupils widening inside the mask's eyeholes. "This is not allowed. You will most certainly aggrieve Mr. Dutton."

"Such an obedient lady," he crooned. "Do rules always govern you?"

He kissed the corner of her lips. Tenderly.

"Do you always do as you're told?" He breathed in Sarah's light floral scent. "Hmm?" he prompted and took her plump, moist, slightly blue mouth.

No way could Seb have prepared himself for that first contact with her lips. Sure, he'd thought her lips would taste sweet. And they did taste sweet. Very sweet. But he had always before preferred salt to sugar.

Not this time. Where had this urge to drown in her sweet mouth come from?

Seb was a virile and healthy man of thirty-one; his arousal reflected this. But the strength of his erection came as a shock, and at the same time, left him vulnerable.

He never left himself unguarded. Not as a thieving lad in the Bowery. Not as an ambitious man out West. And nothing had ever gotten in the way of what he wanted.

Until now.

At the first brush of his lips, at the initial soft stroke, the lady trembled. Heedless of her reaction, he kissed his way to the shell of her ear, where a pearl earring dangled from a gold chain. She reminded him of what taking a breath of fresh air felt like after working in a long, dark, musty railroad tunnel, the kind of underground cavern out West where he had routinely performed backbreaking labor seven days a week, in sixteen-hour shifts. Her innocence seduced him now as revenge had seduced him then.

He drew back. "Surely, someone has kissed you?"

"No. Never." She touched two gloved fingertips to her sweet lips. "Not until you. Not until tonight."

"But you must have attended parties, social occasions—"

"Very few."

"No necking under the apple tree?" he asked, trying to lighten up the dead seriousness of this discussion.

"Other than Mr. Dutton, a dear friend of Papa's, I have never before been alone with a man." She averted her face. "And I should not be alone with you now. Such behavior reeks of dishonor."

"And selling your maidenhead on the open market is not dishonorable?"

Sarah's proud jaw jutted. "I had once thought to give my virginity as a gift to the man I loved, as virtue is all a woman really has of her own to give. After tonight, I shall no longer have even that small gift. Puff! Gone, and my honor with it."

Though her beautiful blue eyes sparkled with unshed tears, she rallied and charged. "Society is of the opinion that a thin membrane is all a lady has of any real value. That a heart and brain and loyalty count for naught." Her shoulders squared. "I know differently. Even after tonight, I shall have worth. Even after I am used and discarded, I shall still be worthy of love. Someday, a gentleman will agree. He will not care if I am a thousand lovers past my virginity or ten years past my youth, for he will love me for who I am inside. And regardless of his past, I shall love him the same."

Sarah folded her hands in her lap. "After everything I have seen to the contrary, after all the unbearable pain I have witnessed to contradict its existence, I still believe in love."

She sounded wistful, and innocent, and idealistically hopeful...and damn fucking idiotic...all at the same time. To think this romantic claptrap fell from the lips of a young woman who would tonight begin her career as a prostitute!

And yet, he found himself admiring her—she stuck up for her beliefs!

When was the last time he had believed in anything?

Frenchie had gotten it all wrong. The young Miss Winslow was far from cold. Spitting angry, she radiated enough heat to warm his blood. This was no weak miss; this was a worthy opponent. When jabbed, she jabbed right back. For a gal raised-up sheltered and cosseted, he reckoned she had a lot of pluck. Those shiny stars in her eyes blinded him to his plan—

Seb dropped his lids fast. "Where will you find this noble hero?" He forced out a chuckle. "Here?"

"Perhaps not. But perhaps *he* will find *me* elsewhere. Perhaps in church. As far as I know, whores are still allowed to pray on Sundays."

His mouth opened, then slammed shut. What could he say in the face of such flagrant sentimentality?

No way could he respond to her immature romanticism. No way for him to argue against her youthful idealized notion of love. But, so as not to offend or frighten her off—or give his vulnerability to her away—his hand tunneled under his coat, where he made a discreet adjustment to his trousers, pushing the painful engorgement to the side, away from her notice.

That bit of housekeeping accomplished, Seb took her shy, untutored mouth again, not as delicately this time. Parting her lips, he made his way inside. Patiently.

For all that his tongue was eager to push down her throat.

As a tribute to his forbearance, she responded to him as a romantic and sheltered young miss of eighteen would respond.

Then, something happened, something plumb loco. Without his comprehending why, the kiss deepened. Dangerously deepened. And he quickly lost control. For Sarah, innocent Sarah, *wanton* Sarah, had jumped from her seat on the bench, wound her arms around his neck, and pressed her belly to his erection. Knowingly or accidentally, she cradled his hardness, refusing to allow him to play the part of a gentleman.

Groaning, Seb attempted to slow it down. "Wait," he said, breathing rough. "Not here. Not outside, not where a voyeuristic patron walking by might see."

"I care less than a whit for the surroundings or if anyone sees. Do not stop. Please?" After begging him, she began placing hot little kisses along his jaw, his throat, and back to his lips again.

Seb felt himself fall into the promise of Sarah. Her prim and prissy yet, at the same time, lush mouth. Her chaste but wholly passionate kiss. The inexperienced yearning of her voice that contained the seeds of womanly wisdom. No coital sophisticate could have won him over as she had won him over.

He had not intended to desire her. But he did desire her. Had desired her from the moment he had set eyes on her toiling on hands and knees in the gardens. Desire had caught him as unaware then as it did now.

Meanwhile, the dregs of his weakened conscience paid Seb a mighty inconvenient revisit.

He had already hurt the snobby virgin. Missed stature in society, missed opportunities, a missed marriage...missed meals. He had ruined Michael Winslow's name and his daughter's chances—he could spare her the final indignity. Even now, he could modify his plan.

Something sharp wrenched inside him. Then ripped away. The plan, borne of hatred, nourished on revenge, dropped from his body like an amputated limb. Though withered from lack of blood, though diseased and rotten with decay, still losing a piece of himself hurt. Like any man who has ever lost an arm or a leg will attest, he still felt that gangrenous member, still wished for its return, foulness and all. It had belonged to him for so long, its corruption had become a part of him. How would he go on now that he no longer had a leg to stand on?

Removing Sarah's entwined wrists from around his neck, Seb pulled back and stumbled down the gazebo stairs. Lest he lose his remaining control and interfere with the virgin right there in the gazebo, he skulked off into the darkness, leaving the innocent miss alone and untouched. His plan had changed.

Now the hell what?

Chapter Five

Sarah removed her gloves and placed them neatly on the bureau before her second-floor bedchamber window, her gaze straying to the darkened garden path that led to the gazebo as a scream of hysteria rose up within her. She could easily rend her clothing, pull out her hair, claw at the embossed silk walls of her Park Avenue debtors' prison, cry out in frustration...rail against her fate.

Melodrama. An exaggerated display of emotionalism. Her nannies had schooled her against just such selfish carryings-on. And so, she closed her lips against the scream, preventing its melodramatic escape.

The man in the garden gazebo had told her to scream. Little did he know that causing a scene would prove quite beyond her capabilities, as would loud outbursts of any type, particularly in public. Always correct, her emotions wrapped in the etiquette of proper deportment and sealed in desperate politeness, she'd had a team of paid employees who'd raised her to keep all the ugly stuff inside, to fear being one of those ugly things.

She had never felt so afraid.

Or despairing. Everything seemed so bleak, especially now, after meeting that rough-spoken man.

His courtly kiss had moved her, made her breasts ache and swell, and the womanly place between her legs throb. His gentle kiss neither rushed nor coerced, demanded no more of her than she had wished to give. Held loosely in his arms, she'd allowed him to guide her into passion, allowing her desire to build gradually. Naturally. She was the one who had strained to get closer, who had deepened the kiss, who had forced the intimacy.

His realness! Goodness, the honesty of his realness!

Her thoughts had centered only on obtaining some of his honesty. When he'd slanted his mouth over hers, when he'd offered her his tongue, she had taken it hungrily. Boldly. Greedy for the knowledge of that oh-so-heavy thrust against her throat. Languidness seeping into her limbs, lust warming her blood, she had surrendered to a nameless man whose face a mask had partially obscured. In a completely uninhibited release of all her former restraints, she had moaned against his lips.

For his part, he had tried to allow for space between them. In a misguided effort to keep his arousal a secret from her, he had tried to hold her off.

She would have none of that!

Arching into him, she had felt his erection prod her, a hard ridge against her belly, an arousal impossible to hide. Thrilling! And real.

Concerned for their location, he had put her away from him then.

What matter the location? she had thought at the time. A bedchamber or a church, their pairing witnessed by none or by many, in her emotional transcendence, she could not bring herself to care.

Sarah touched her bruised lips. The realness of his kiss still lingered.

She liked the way her mouth felt. Liked the way he had made her feel. That rough-spoken man had drawn her. She thought she might already have fallen in love with him. For how else to explain this awful yearning, this betraying need to touch him and have him touch her?

Sarah ruefully shook her head. Why bother thinking about him, mooning over him?

A life of prostitution awaited her. She was about to sleep with patrons for money. No question of feelings, of genuine emotion. Only pretense. Only the bastardization of lovemaking. Only business. Only illusion.

Outside in the hall, footsteps came and went. Suddenly, a pair stopped. Someone knocked at the door.

"Come in," Sarah called over her shoulder.

Leonard Dutton's housekeeper lumbered over the threshold. "My lands, Miss Sarah, here you are! I have been looking all over for you!"

The crisp, polished chintz curtains fell through her fingers, and Sarah turned to the tray-carrying servant. "So sorry to have inconvenienced you,

Mrs. Brown." Well used to putting a false face on her feelings, she pasted on a smile. "I took a stroll through the gardens and then returned here to freshen up."

Poise fixed in place, showing the world—in this instance, the housekeeper—a serene expression, Sarah left the window and proceeded to the middle of the bedchamber. As polished as the floor under her footsteps, she faced the servant. Unflappability, after all, served as the hallmark of impeccable breeding—

At four or perhaps five years of age, a particularly diligent governess had found her under the bed linens with her finger stuffed up her nose. "A lady is a lady whether anyone watches or not," the dour Miss Rogers had lectured and then proceeded to beat the lesson into her charge. The memory still lingered—along with a jagged white scar on her wrist, a souvenir received during the finger extraction. She had never picked her nose again...nor done anything else smacking of unladylike behavior.

Until this evening.

Mrs. Brown placed the black enamel tray, undoubtedly imported from the Orient, atop the mahogany nightstand. "No harm done. Now eat, before your first suitor arrives."

Sarah's eyes bugged at all the food. Before she could savor the feast, the servant handed her a demitasse of coffee. "For you, dear."

"What is this?" Sarah took a sniff, and her nose wrinkled. "Brandy? I never drink liquor, Mrs. Brown."

"All the ladies take a little something to help them relax."

"No, thank you. I do not partake of harsh spirits."

"You will take partake of these harsh spirits, dearie." She forced the cup to Sarah's lips. "Bottoms up." The housekeeper winked.

Sarah had no idea what that wink meant, but she did know the spirits burned her throat as the liquid went down. Once she had drained the nasty stuff, she placed the cup back on the tray, her gaze drifting longingly out the window toward the gazebo again.

The pull of her rescuer was just too overwhelming to refuse. "Mrs. Brown, please tell Mr. Dutton I have changed my mind about tonight. Tell him I cannot go through with this arrangement, after all. I shall find another method to repay my debt. Perhaps hawking flowers on the street corner. No reference is required for that position."

Sarah sidestepped toward the door. "If you will excuse me? I really do need to leave. Right away. Tonight."

Somehow, Mrs. Brown managed to block her exit. "Only nerves talking, luv."

"No, truly." Sarah endeavored to reach around Mrs. Brown for the sculpted glass knob. "I must go. I believe in love, you see—"

"Not to fret, dearie. You are fortunate in your first suitor," the housekeeper divulged. "All the ladies here love him."

"Well, I shall certainly not *love* him. Someone else has quite taken over my heart."

During her protest, an attack of wooziness struck and threatened to turn her upside down. The dizziness felt peculiarly pleasant.

A few seconds later and that had altered, the pleasant euphoria changing to something else, something a great deal more sinister than a mild intoxication, something that felt remarkably strange indeed.

Whilst Sarah reeled and swayed, the housekeeper stepped around behind her.

Knuckles clicked on her spine. Fingernails tapped. Hooks and eyes pinged. Tiny buttons popped. White satin exploded.

So noisy! Sarah had all she could do not to cover her ears.

Far too early to retire for the evening. Why had the servant undone her, after Sarah had only just finished tidying up?

That question, the one she wished to ask, *meant* to ask, refused to take shape. Though she must have said something, for when Sarah glanced over her shoulder again, the housekeeper's mouth moved, as though in reply.

But wait! Did Mrs. Brown speak in a foreign language?

No matter how Sarah concentrated, the strange contortion of syllables and phrasing defied interpretation. All gibberish to her! And then it was too late to comprehend; like a chubby cherub, the servant drifted away on a purple cloud.

A completely inappropriate urge to giggle bubbled up inside Sarah. Giving in to the irresistible need, she laughed merrily. Aloud! To herself! My, she really felt quite tipsy!

This changed, too. And rapidly. Sarah went from laughing gaily to yawning hugely. Then, her mood shifted into something else entirely.

She tingled. All over. Her skin burned red-hot. Oh, God, her body was afire! What was happening to her? What was wrong with her?

Air whispered across her bare shoulders. But the faint breeze from the open window did nothing to temper her fever. For that, she would need a winter's snowstorm. Oh, how she wished she might remove her gown! Take it off altogether, and rub her—and rub her—

Throbbing breasts!

Dear Lord! What an unbecoming thought!

Regardless of the inappropriateness, the terrible urge grew and grew until Sarah could no longer forestall it.

Her hand strayed to a nipple. The nub, once girlishly soft, had grown womanly hard and elongated. About to expire from longing, Sarah pressed both hands to her pulsating nipples, pretending her rescuer caressed her breasts, that he took the ache away.

She ached somewhere else, too. Between her legs. How would she bear it?

That man from the gazebo would know what to do, what she needed. Not a true gentleman, he would understand her base urges. He would know where to wedge his hand, how to quench the illicit fire raging within her. After rescuing her once, would he come to her aid again?

* * *

When Sebastian was a small lad of three or so, his mama had taken him to live at a country estate outside Manhattan, a magical place where clouds of pastel flowers nestled within large expanses of manicured lawns. He would often laze on those rolling green lawns, his gaze on those sweet-scented flowers, and imagine how wonderful life would be if the owner of the estate would only wed his beautiful mama and they would all lived happily-ever-after in the splendid surroundings.

Less than a decade later, the owner of those flower gardens and that fine house up on the hill had discarded his mistress, thrown her out like a cast-off shoe, and replaced her with a much younger, pedigreed lady-bride. Mother and son went to live in a cold and damp tenement in the Mulberry Bend block of the Bowery, where only weeds grew and the stink of the tanneries and the rancid smell of cooking onions permeated the air. His once lively mama no longer laughed. Strange men came and went into her sheet-partitioned sleeping space, at all hours of the day and night.

Hunger pangs always nagging, the sun never shining, barely eking out a living, his beautiful mama had soon sickened with a cough, a wracking congestion of the lungs that persisted no matter how many cups of hot tea and honey he made for her. When her breathing grew rattled and shallow, and the coughing fits produced specks of bright red blood on the coarse gray linen, not knowing what else to do, Seb had stolen some money from a rich gent's back pocket—the fee for medical treatment. Up the four flights of stairs to the tenement room, Seb had dragged the drunken doctor who treated Bottle Alley whores.

Standing several feet away from his patient, the physician had made his diagnosis with very little solemnity.

"Consumption," Doc Peterson belched.

A death sentence.

Determined to save his mother, Seb had turned stealing into an art form. But no matter how many watches he pickpocketed on the city streets, no matter how many bobs he lifted from marks in Bandit's Roost, no matter how great his success in obtaining food and medicine, paid for with stolen money and goods, his mama remained ill.

And so he had made his way back to the fine house up on the hill, past the manicured gardens and sweet-smelling flowers to the front door of Clearbrook. To beg, to plead, to cry for charity.

Only to have the man Seb had called Father for over nine years turn him away. Michael Winslow's bride had just delivered a baby girl, and he no longer had any use for a bastard, a boy not of his blood.

His mama had never kept Seb's wrong-side-of-the-blanket birth a secret. While accepting his illegitimacy, he had nevertheless harbored the sneaking suspicion that Michael Winslow had sired him. Learning he had not, and in such a callous way, had sent him reeling. After the revelation, he no longer knew how to think of himself. If not Michael Winslow's by-blow, then who was he?

As only the very young can hate, Seb had hated Michael Winslow, his bride, and, yes, even their daughter, Sarah. Under different circumstances, he might have called that baby his kid sister.

When his mama died, Seb had known just who to blame.

Everyone generally, and one man in particular.

With a bellyful of hate raging inside him, by the age of thirteen, he had already turned into a hardened criminal. On the run from the authorities, he had left New York City to make his fortune out West. Eighteen years of backbreaking labor later, he had acquired enough wealth to bring down the man he held responsible for his mother's death. With the help of Leonard Dutton, his New York business agent, Seb had put his plan into action.

Everything Michael Winslow had once owned now belonged to the son of his discarded mistress—the estate, furnishings, heirloom jewelry, horses...daughter. Sarah's obligation amounted to a figure impossible for a young, destitute girl to repay—

For all intents and purposes, he had forced whoring on Sarah Winslow, as her father had, long ago, forced whoring on Seb's mother.

Full circle.

A cycle of revenge he intended to break.

Tonight.

Chapter Six

Seb turned the gold key in his hand, and the peephole to Sarah's second-floor bedchamber opened without making a sound.

Inside, the snobby miss tottered on her feet, weaving back and forth like a sailor in search of her sea legs. Eyes unfocused, head thrown back, white virginal gown hiked up around her waist, she clawed frantically at the lacy drawers that covered her mons.

She was not exactly an expert at self-gratification, her innocence precluding a high degree of skill. But what the lady lacked in experience, she more than made up for in enthusiasm.

Unless—was he witnessing enthusiasm or something else?

Something else, Seb quickly decided. Her frenetic activity was symptomatic of a young woman half out of her mind in sexual excitement.

Damn Leonard, anyway! His business partner must have taken it upon himself to drug the virgin. A stimulant of some sort. In her very aroused state, Sarah would gladly fornicate with a stallion.

Snapping the peephole shut, Seb stormed the bedchamber

"You," she murmured sluggishly upon seeing him burst through the door. "But why are you here?" Dazed, she blinked in rapid succession. "Surely you are not my first customer, as my first customer is a gentleman, and you, sir, are no gentleman."

Even drugged, Sarah Winslow retained her haughty snobbery and excellent perception—she had seen right through him, as he had predicted she would, and knew him for what he was: not a gentleman.

Her honesty stung.

"What can I do?" he asked as she writhed and her palm rubbed against the slit in her lacy drawers.

"You can tell me what ails me." Her answer came out slurred.

"You must know—"

"Would I ask if I knew?"

He took hold of her arm, looked directly into her dilated eyes. "Keep a civil tongue in your head when you speak to me. I am not your servant. Now tell me, did you drink something before my arrival?"

"A small brandy." Her heavy tongue clubbed the words, her formerly precise elocution coming out flat and fuzzy.

"An elixir, more likely."

"W-what kind of e-elixir?"

"An aphrodisiac. A draught to make you sexually crazed." He released her to rake both hands through his hair. "How the hell should I know what you swallowed?"

Her head tilted. Had her mind registered what he said?

Doubtful. Whatever the drug, the potency had started to distort her reasoning abilities. In an opiate haze, from here on out, she would act on instincts, as an animal would, with no real understanding of her actions.

Less than a blink later, she bore out his theory.

"I ache," she said thickly.

"Where?" he asked, though he already knew.

Her mouth gaped as she struggled to put the ache into ladylike words. "In my...in my..."

He might have come to her aid. After censoring his thoughts, he might have substituted euphemism for realism, prettied up her need in a suitably flowery phrase. But, to his mind, politeness substituted for honesty always equaled a less than favorable exchange. "Cunt?"

"No, here is where I ache." In demonstration, her ungloved hand jerked in and out of the slit in her lace-trimmed drawers, the front panel of which rapidly dampened, turning the fabric transparent.

Her cunt.

If not for the elixir, the prim lady would never have responded so graphically. But in the throes of her hallucination, Sarah cared only about physical release.

"Use a lighter touch," he instructed, eyeing Sarah's midnight-black pubic hair, the curls glistening with the dew of her honey, the pretty triangle a dark, womanly shadow under the moistly transparent drawers. *Mercy!* But the juice-drenched, pouty folds within mesmerized him.

"Pardon?"

"A rough stroke bruises. Allow me?" He lifted her hand from between her splayed thighs.

Just like his, calluses lined her palm, the skin work-thickened. He drew his thumb over the lifeline, then kissed the center before licking the cunnycream from her fingertips, one by one. "Mmm. Delicious."

She shook her head. "But I want. I want… What is it I want?"

"Poor baby. Too innocent too know," he commiserated. Lucky for her, he had no problem figuring out what she wanted.

An oblivious Sarah no longer impeding him, he removed first his mask and then hers.

Her face was perfect, more beautiful than even he had imagined. Symmetry meets poetry, her features even and sensitive. She was all rosy cheeks, big eyes, and plump lips, a sheltered child-woman, too young and idealistic for a cynical man like him. But she needed him, for what he could do for her, for the relief he could provide.

Understanding his preferences, which included an impatience for gee-gaws and fripperies, the housekeeper had already undone Sarah's tiny buttons and bows.

While the lady fidgeted, he slid the white satin over milky shoulders, past a non-existent waist and narrow hips, a pervasive sense of something weighing him down.

Despite the figure-revealing linen chemise, bosom-shelving corset, hip-padding petticoats, red-gartered hose, and grown-up slippers, Sarah resembled a lost little girl.

Seb dropped his gaze to the polished floor, his pervasive sense of something more clearly defined. That heavy something felt like a big ol' grizzly. The weight of that bear's furry rump sat on his chest.

Guilt.

While true that Sarah needed the relief he could provide, the lady was not fully cognizant of her actions. Reprehensible to take advantage of her innocence in a fugue state...or twilight sleep...or whatever the hell else the influence she was under was called. Only a bastard would bed an eighteen-year-old virgin when she had taken leave of her right senses.

Then again, that pretty much described him.

Michael Winslow had agreed. Tough to forget his words...

Sarah moaned. "Help me."

His mouth set in a hard line. "What do you say?"

"Please?"

"More like it!" His turn now to have the upper hand, to laud his superiority over a Winslow.

"Everything off," he decreed. She would cast off her innocent undergarments and strip for him. To the skin. Out in the open. In full light. No changing screen. No place for her to hide her blushes. He would come to her aid, give her surcease, but that diseased part of himself also demanded satisfaction. His plan had changed, he swore it had, but the poison in his system remained. He could not discard eighteen years of unrequited revenge so easily. His plan had changed, but his disease hung on; corruption ate away at him even now. What would he have left if he cut away his revenge?

"My unmentionables too?" She visibly trembled.

"Yes," he said tersely, the childlike innocence of her question shaming him.

Sarah's elegant neck rounded. "What have I done? Why are you angry with me?"

Seb's voice turned gruff. "This here ain't personal."

"But your stern tone says otherwise."

He had always considered justice a simple concept. Revenge, too. But with Sarah, simple had grown complex.

For years, he had lived for only one reason—to ruin everything Winslow-connected. But a kiss in a garden gazebo had altered his plan. No longer sure of himself or his motivation, he settled on the uncomplicated truth as he knew it in that fleeting instant.

He stepped behind her. "My voice is stern because I desire you more than I have ever desired any woman."

"You do?"

"Yes." He worked on removing her loosened corset.

Though weaving on her feet, she nevertheless managed to swivel around and hold on to his wrists.

To steady herself?

Or to wordlessly try to stop him?

She stroked along his jaw. "I desire you, too."

Her corset slipped through his fingers; the whalebones fell with a *clunk* to the floor. Freed of the restrictive lacing, Sarah now filled her lungs with ease.

Unlike him. He could barely breathe at all, a surprise that took him aback and then some, considering his cool-headed handling of even the most temperamental explosives.

Sarah's titties. Sarah's small and pretty titties, clearly outlined under the chemise. Perfect in every way. Set high, the shape conical, the nipples pointed to fit a man's mouth.

Not any man's mouth, Seb modified. *His* mouth.

"I hurt," she groaned, plucking at perfection.

Christ! The way she did that, the way she pulled the pink tip, like making taffy.

Sweat popped on his brow. He knew why she hurt. Her nipples— distended, enormous in their arousal—butted against her chemise. Even the thin layer of linen would abrade Sarah's drug-sensitized skin.

"Shh," he crooned. "I can make the hurting go away." With unsteady fingers, he peeled back her chemise.

Pink-tipped nipples poked out at him. "Oh, thank you. That is ever so much better. But, please, sir." She batted her lashes. "Would you touch me?"

What a hoot! Inside the virgin Sarah, a seductress fought to get out.

Playing hard-to-get never even entered his mind.

Not at first.

Then, edginess crept into his thoughts. "Where shall I touch you?"

He would make her work for her relief. Make her grovel. Not a lot. But a little. She need not prostrate herself. A minor subservience would satisfy him. After all, she owed him a little servility.

Sarah appeared not to share his point of view.

Withholding her answer, she stubbornly refused to name where she needed his hand. Once again, her overblown sense of propriety conflicted with her physical urgency.

He had to say, he understood. Staying in control warred mightily with the undisciplined urges of his cock.

"Tell me," he insisted.

Only to back down when her dilated eyes filled with unshed tears. "All right," he mumbled. "No need to speak. I know where you need me to touch you."

He thumbed a huge areola.

She jumped, her small tits bouncing within the gaping chemise.

"Tender?" he questioned.

She shook her head. "Heavenly. But a gentleman is never to touch a lady where you are touching me. What a tremendous imposition to have requested it of you."

She bit her lip. "Of course, you are not a gentleman."

"Correct. So, feel free to say whatever is on your mind." At her bashful nod, like a physician asking a patient for a list of ailments, he said, "Now tell me, where else do you hurt?"

Her chin dropped as she directed him to her cunt again.

"*Hmm.*" His brows lifted. "Inside there, eh?"

"You must certainly not respect me now." She pushed away.

He pulled her back to him, tilted her chin. "You asked for my help, now let me help you. Better to get relief from me than from some mangy pervert masquerading as a gentleman. Just keep your fingers crossed that I have the stamina to keep it up. Otherwise, you might go from cock to cock, until you end up out on the streets, begging for it from passersby."

At his strong words, his harsh tone, she whimpered.

"Hush. Let me take care of you. No imposition."

Unable to help himself, he drew a fingertip down her shallow cleavage. Unable to help himself, he backed her up against the wall. What she did to him!

"Pretty," he told her in a hushed tone, unable to help himself. "So pretty."

Her big blue eyes went saucer-wide; her thick sooty lashes fluttered. "Me?"

Entranced, intrigued, rational thought left his mind and lust took over—inconceivable that no one had ever told Sarah Winslow that her unique loveliness put the flowers she loved in the shade.

Seb pulled the pins from Sarah's blue-black hair, scattering them everywhere in his rush to see the midnight cloud drift against a sky of pearl—her pale shoulders.

"Blessed Virgin," he prayed.

The contrast of light and dark fascinated him. Which exemplified Sarah? Which true nature did her prim, ladylike airs hide?

As a result of long hours spent in dark tunnels, Seb's normally swarthy skin had lightened up a bit; now he looked merely tanned, like Sarah would after some sun exposure. And, like her hair, his competed with a moonless night. On the inside, he was every bit as dark. Was Sarah dark inside, too?

In proof of his dark nature, nostrils flaring, he pitched forward, burying his face in the perfumed black wealth of Sarah's hair, breathing deeply, rapturously, of the young lady he had once vowed to destroy.

Holding her upright, he sampled her drug-slackened mouth.

In heady response, she offered up her tongue, which tasted of aphrodisiac-laced brandy. And passion. So much passion! All of it directed at him.

He ate at her mouth, and her conical-shaped tits shifted slightly against his chest.

What he had in mind to do to her! What he *would* do to her before this night ran its course! And what transpired between them would have nothing to do with revenge, destruction, or hatred for the Winslow name.

What started out complicated had suddenly turned simple.

Because Sarah vibrated with hunger. Hummed with appetite. Looked to him for appeasement of both. *Him*, Sebastian Turner.

This had to do with them. Nothing else. Nobody else. From this night forward, the past would stay in the past.

Chapter Seven

Seb kissed Sarah's regal jaw, licked her sluggish pulse, lapped at her enlarged nipples, his teeth clamping around one rigid point.

"Oh!" Her back bowed. "Mmm. Yes."

He suckled her good and hard, until she came up on her toes, moaning deep in her throat. When he finished with one little tittie, she offered him the other. He sucked that one too, pulling and drawing on the tip until both nipples turned red and swollen, as red and swollen as her full lips. Afterwards, he cupped and fondled and squeezed the dainty, wet-from-his-mouth mounds, kneading and pinching, his fingers closing possessively over the small bounty, until panting, he broke it off. "Arms over your head."

Like a good little girl, she raised her hands high, and he nuzzled the fine black hair of her underarms, revealed in the sleeveless chemise. Lips to the hollow, then his nose, he absorbed her perspiration. Tasted her saltiness. Sniffed her scent. Wore the sweet, feminine perfume of Sarah on his flesh. Christ! He might never wash again.

"Let me in, let me in, let me in," he chanted and wheezed and shook, working the ties on Sarah's voluminous petticoats until the yards of lace plummeted to her ankles, leaving her now in split drawers, stockings, and gaping chemise.

Inside the split linen, her raven-black pubic curls looked wicked and mysterious against the paleness of her skin. He investigated the plump pleasure bud with the tip of his baby finger, groaning appreciatively. "Lush and luscious."

"Coarse and common," she pronounced aloofly in return, condemning him to a lifetime sentence of inferiority. As further punishment, she clawed the side of his face, scraping away stripes of flesh.

Seb touched a gouge. Common and coarse? Maybe so, but her truth contained only half his story. He was also powerful and wealthy. More importantly, he was dangerous. He had a reputation he richly deserved, a long memory, and he fought dirty. His kind of retaliation left men quaking in their boots and women begging for more.

"Act the lady in the drawing room, if you must, but not in the bedchamber," he growled and turned her 'round to face the wall. Pulling her drawers down low over her round buttocks, he leaned her upper body in, yanked her lower body out.

His hand came down. Five times. On the fullest portion of her winsome ass.

"I misbehaved," she mewed softly, just like a little kitten. "I should not have struck you. I deserved the spanking."

He propped her stubborn chin up on his bent index finger. "True, but I disciplined you for another reason." He kissed her swollen lips, then whispered in her ear, "You needed some of your female tension released, and the pain of the spanking let the knot inside you go. You need something else, too. Do you know what that something is?"

"You. I need you."

No question about it—she did need him. Tonight. But what of the morrow? How would she feel tomorrow when her opiate dream ended and she recalled that the man who had eased her torment was not of her class, not of her station, not a true gentleman? Would she think he had substituted one form of punishment for another? Revenge for—

What? What motivated him now that his plans had changed?

Seb floundered. Beyond alleviating Sarah Winslow's carnal distress, he no longer followed a charted course.

He dragged her down to the floor, placed her on her back, and slid her drawers down to her pretty, *pretty* knees.

Murmuring incoherently, she gave herself over to him, her inhibitions—as well as her laced drawers—lowered.

Not quite low enough.

He pushed her drawers lower, down her shapely legs to her ankles. Never once losing sight of that dainty pelt of blue-black curls, a neat thicket at her body's center that pleasured his eyes, he drew her moist underpinnings over her high-arched feet. Keeping her garters and silk hose purposefully in place, he splayed her thighs to get at the notch, that mysterious cleft gentlemen and thieves alike crave.

Bottom lip aquiver, head rocking back and forth on the floor, breasts heaving, Sarah denied her need. "No, no, no, you must not," she cried, propriety and passion warring. "Sir, this is not nice."

"Oh, all of it is very nice." He petted the plump pubic lips, circled the clit. "Let me?" he coaxed.

"Mmm," Sarah murmured. Then, "No, you must not!"

"Do as I say," he replied sternly.

With a docile nod, obedient Sarah, needy Sarah, spread herself wide for his delectation. In the dregs of her chemise, garters, and hose, the lady made for a delightful sight.

He wanted a better look.

Seb removed a decorative red pillow from a nearby chair and stuffed it under her hips to hike them up a mite, and the succulent pink passage, soft as wet silk, tantalizing as sin, lay open before him.

He breathed across the folds. Inhaled her musk.

One lick, he thought. Just one slow, luxuriant lick with his agile, thieving tongue.

He went down on her. Lapping at the lady's spread thighs, circling her plump, virginal pubic lips, slipping inside to taste her essence, swallowing her pearled honey as it dripped onto his taste buds and trickled down his throat. When he sucked on the excitable little bud at the top of her cleft, she bucked like a wild thing. Granted, Seb had never done a lady before, but he knew the difference between a female who genuinely liked it and a female who would just as soon not.

Sarah genuinely liked it.

Shocking, how much she liked it.

Pussy passion, he mused, and smoothed his tongue over the bud again and again, until her thighs tightened and she came, her juices filling his mouth.

Well, hell. She went off like a stick of dynamite.

Grinning a dirty grin, Seb licked his lips, the hollow of Sarah's belly serving as his resting place while she calmed. He would give her a moment, then introduce a finger—

Waiting proved impossible. Less than a moment later, he slipped a digit inside, up to the virginal membrane.

Another first. He had never felt *that* before.

When he got through with her, she would have no innocence left to steal. But if not him, then some other man would get on her—this was a whorehouse, not a hotel bridal suite. And though he might not know his way around gentlemanly pursuits, he did know his way around fornication. He would show her the kind of consideration a virgin deserved—more than Sarah could expect from a patron.

Seb turned Sarah over, the pillow beneath her belly propping her bottom up high; the exposed roundness of her fine ass totally engrossed him. Breathing hard, shaking with unquenched excitement, he eyed the deep and seductive demarcation between the two perfectly symmetrical and now glowing-pink cheeks.

He owned Sarah's ladylike ass, had paid for it many times over. Why not investigate his property?

Seb let his palm roam. Up and down and underneath. He yearned to survey in between. Just one finger. Just to see her reaction. Just to gauge his own. Just to ease the hurt he had inflicted.

With all those reasons in mind, Seb applied his mouth to the seductive seam that separated the two perfectly shaped bottom cheeks. He nuzzled her, then plied his tongue up and down the crevice.

"Hold still," he instructed when she wiggled.

She held still for him, and he slipped his tongue inside, licking her deep, delving into the demarcation again and again. Savoring her. Kissing the hurt away.

"Oh, my," she slurred. "This is not at all proper, sir."

"Proper! I am many things, but never that," he told her, his jaw sliding up and down her flank before he bit into her roundness. "I was born on the wrong side of the blanket, and on that wrong side I'll remain 'til the day I die."

His bites sharpened. Deepened. Already her skin had started to passion-bruise. And ladylike Sarah, a scream removed from coming again, rammed her fist in her mouth to stifle the sounds, those husky, unladylike noises he very much wanted to hear. Some women—like Sarah—needed a little hurt to find their release. And some men, like him, eagerly complied.

He continued biting her bottom, pushing her closer and closer to the edge, taking care that this time she remained hovering at the precipice, a freefall away from toppling.

Taking full advantage of her extremity, he returned her to her back. "Tell me you need my cock inside you."

In answer, she spat up into his face.

Not bothering to wipe her contempt for him away, he systematically undid the front of his trousers. When his heavy cock jutted, he said quietly, "Tell me."

Her body thrashed wildly—her discomfort had quickly gone from minor to acute. If she kept this up, she would hurt herself.

To subdue her, Seb crawled over Sarah until her small body lay naked beneath his much larger one.

And still she fought the very relief she needed.

Damn her virtue anyway! Sarah refused to give in, whereas he had come to the end of his endurance. That he would *eventually* get inside her was a foregone conclusion, but her fighting him would undermine his ability to take her gently.

To spare her his weight, he hung suspended on his elbows above her. In a last desperate attempt at reason, before he resorted to physically overpowering her, he grated, "Give over!"

Seb had only ever begged once before. For the sake of his dying mother, he had pleaded with Michael Winslow to come visit. The swine had refused, turned him away at the door. Now he pleaded with Michael Winslow's daughter to save what remained of his bastard's soul. Would Sarah turn him away, as her father had done all those years ago? Would she condemn him to a different death? Would the remainder of his humanity die this night?

He had never forced a woman. Had never done rape. But to mitigate the results of the drug, he might have to do both. "Please, Sarah. Tell me yes," he pleaded.

Sarah ceased struggling; her body went limp. Reaching up a hand, she stroked his face. "I—I acquiesce."

At best, her answer represented passive compliance, a token consent.

He would take it.

And then he would give. And give. He would keep giving Sarah what she needed until his cock quit on him. Because sparing himself would mean agony for her.

Picking Sarah up in his arms, he carried her to the velvet-covered bed.

All his life, he'd had to settle for less. This was no different—if not for the drugs in her bloodstream, Sarah would never have accepted his attentions. But right now, his feelings were neither here nor there; only Sarah's feelings counted. And a hard floor is no kind of proper place a'tall to take a virgin.

As though she were a bride, he placed her gently in the center of the soft goose-feather mattress.

Though a bastard thief will settle for less, the same would not do for a well-bred lady.

Chapter Eight

Hiked up on one bent arm, Seb took himself in hand.

Pre-come dripped from his cock and anointed Sarah's lower belly, the natural lubricant glistening like tears on her pubic hair. With every nerve in his body centered on that weeping part of himself, he nudged her.

And gasped in torment.

Gone without a man's relief for far too long, his ten-inch iron spike needed a good hammering. Unfortunately, a virgin—no, *Sarah*—required care.

Groaning, mouth agape, his body beaded with sweat, Seb moved the bulbous crown slowly into her.

Both arms locked around his neck, vise to metal, Sarah drew him close. Hugging him to her as though she would never let him go, she moaned deep in her throat.

Only the smallest degree in, and already she was having a hard time of it. And he asked himself, if she struggled to accept the blunt top of the head, how the hell would she accommodate all of him?

Never before had Seb wished for a cock a few inches shorter and a whole lot less wide, but he did then.

"I know it hurts." Unwilling to shy away from the brutal truth, not even to spare himself, he corrected the prior statement. "I know *I* hurt you."

In the past, and in the present, too.

No altering old history or his make, he pulled out.

The house provided love toys free of charge. He reached for the top drawer of the bed stand and started rummaging around inside for the small bottle of oil that working gals used to simulate desire where none existed and to provide moisture when the passage had grown dry from overuse. Patrons never used the oil on virgins, because the club only employed the initiated— this policy was a major bone of contention between Len and himself.

Virgins will make us a bundle of money, his business partner had protested. *Every patron wants to pop a virgin.*

Regardless, the rule stayed. A man's cruel indifference had forced Seb's mother into prostitution, and so he understood the unhappy necessity that drove a decent woman to the streets. But he had to draw the line somewhere, and virgins fell on the wrong side.

Elbowing the drawer shut, Seb turned back to the bed and proceeded to lube his near ruler-size length, coating the head twice for good measure. That done, he went back to stretching Sarah with his fingers. With his erection gleaming oil-slick and Sarah murmuring her enjoyment, he began again. This time, thank you, Jesus, he slipped easily into the lips of her vaginal passage.

In a romantic move that plucked at his heart, Sarah laced her fingers with his.

No sense—or kindness—in delaying the inevitable. He thrust.

Her muscles tensed as the membrane tore, and he pushed inside.

Seb went still, savoring the pulse of her, the joining of her body with his, the blood-silky wetness of Sarah.

Even the savoring was not without conflict. Warring with the urge to complete the act that would make her his own was the low-down, self-protective instinct to escape while he still could.

At least, Seb told himself he could still escape. He reckoned maybe that might have been wishful thinking on his part.

So as not to break the connection of their interlaced fingers, Seb used his tongue to lick Sarah's silent tears away. "You should have screamed," he told her, between kisses. "No need to lock your pain inside. No need to keep to your ladylike manners with me. Now tell me, does my cock still hurt you? Am I in too deep? Shall I pull up? Move to one side or the other?"

She gave him a confused look.

Yeah, he understood. In fact, he suspected his face wore a similar expression. He grappled with a lot of confusion, too, and that was before counting his shitload of ambivalence.

Lordy, Lordy! What a time for soul-searching.

Even with all her naughty reading, Sarah proved that when it came to fornication, experience was always the best teacher.

To eliminate some of her confusion, he moved, rolling his hips but keeping the motion reserved.

The blue eyes staring up at him went wide.

"Better?" he asked.

She scowled. "No."

Someday, Sarah would prove herself a sensual lady. But no virgin anywhere would have taken kindly to having ten inches shoved up inside her.

With that in mind, Seb kept it shallow. Forcing himself to climax on the third gentle stroke, he squirted hot and fast within Sarah's tight clasp.

A mistake. Having long ago decided no child of his would carry the taint of illegitimacy, he had intended to ejaculate outside. But Sarah had felt too damned good to leave.

Damage done, he stayed put. Only when Sarah slipped into a drugged sleep did he make a reluctant withdrawal.

Once, Seb had expected to feel a sense of triumph, of jubilation, or, at the very least, vindication at seeing Michael Winslow's daughter spread naked atop a gaudy whorehouse bed. Upon seeing Sarah's virgin blood mixed with his spent semen, both rolling down the inside of her thighs, he felt neither triumphant nor jubilant nor vindicated.

Sickened, he turned away.

Christ Jesus, what had he done?

Chapter Nine

The peephole clicked.

Leaving the cold compress between Sarah's open thighs, Seb yanked the velvet cover up to the dozing lady's chin, then turned to face his business partner as he entered the bedchamber. "I never gave the order to drug her."

Len tucked the door's gold key into his pocket and approached the bed. "She pass out?"

Usually he and Len agreed on just about everything, their long and beneficial relationship based on a shared past of thievery, but this time his boyhood friend had gone too far, taken too much upon himself. Drugging Sarah was lower than low.

Seb's voice hitched a notch. "You got eyes in that thick skull of yours? Yeah, she passed out!"

Len held both hands up in the air. "Hey, cowpoke, no need to bust my balls. I never interfere in your concerns. Mrs. Brown must have administered the opiate."

"See that it never happens again," Seb shot back.

"Will do." Len grinned, his lids heavy and slumberous. "Our Sarah must have given you a ride for your money, eh? So, tell me already, how was the little virgin? Any good?"

From time to time, Len and he would share a gal. Seb could tell his business partner assumed this was one of those times.

Len assumed wrong.

Seb let another shout go. "None of your damn business how she was."

Len played with his diamond stickpin. "Cowpoke, our split is fifty-fifty. That goes for the girls, as well as the profits." Taking another step closer to the bed, he reached out to stroke Sarah's hair. "Unless—are you looking to change things?"

Seb's innards clenched at Len's stroking fingers, at the unspoken challenge in his words. Equal owners in the establishment, they also owned half rights to the gals. The arrangement had always worked that way. *Was* Seb looking to change things?

"You should see the line of gents downstairs, all waiting to take their turn on the new whore," Len said conversationally.

Seb exploded. "Everyone in the line can go to hell!"

The only thing Len ever took lying down was fucking, and so he returned the volley. "Tell our clientele that, and we stand to lose thousands tonight."

"Do I look like I give a shit how much we lose?"

At the raised voices, Sarah roused. Sitting up on the bed, she rubbed her dilated eyes. "Is it warm in here?"

Feeling a might hot under the collar himself, Seb nevertheless tucked the covers tight around Sarah so as not to reveal any of the prim and proper lady to Len's prurient stare.

As misfortune would have it, Sarah had a mind to get herself in trouble. Shaking free of the velvet, she flung her arms over her head in a stretch that left her pretty tits exposed and pointing to the ceiling.

She smiled at Len. And Len, the prick, smiled right back at her.

Seb gave a warning growl.

"You say something, cowpoke?"

Out of her senses, Sarah purred seductively. "Ohhh, cowpoke, show me your spurs."

Len turned his roguish gaze on him. "You heard the little lady. How about it? Up for a threesome?"

Seb was up, all right, but in no mood for sharing. "Not tonight. The lady is soused. She might fall off the damn bed."

"Soused," Sarah repeated with a drugged giggle, "on the *damn* bed." She crooked a finger in a come-hither kind of way. Not at Len, in particular. Not at Seb, either. With the drug in her system, she would flirt with any pair of trousers.

"A threesome, a threesome," she sang like a nursery rhyme. "Let's do a threesome."

Seb groaned.

Offering him an I-told-you-so look, his randy partner fingered the buttons on his trousers as he raised a brow. "Unless...do you care for her?"

Care for Michael Winslow's spoiled brat?

Seb had shared plenty of bad times with his partner—plenty of good times, too—and the same amount and variety of women. What would one more matter?

"Care for Sarah Winslow?" Seb shook his head. "The gal means nothing to me. Just another lay."

"Good. Glad to hear it." Len removed the velvet cover from Sarah's lap, leaving her naked and smiling from ear to ear. "Woo-hee! Lookee there. She wants me!" His partner sent him a wink. "Come on, cowpoke, you can see the lady is willing. Join the fun."

Seb hated Len seeing Sarah naked, hated that his partner had an equal right to touch her soft skin—

What the hell was he thinking? Seb gave a snort. *Soft skin!* That was nothing but pussy-talk. What better way to prove Winslow's daughter meant nothing to him than to go along for a three-way ride?

Seb nodded his agreement. "Got me no place to be, so I reckon I will."

Len went back to fiddling with the buttons on his trousers. "Bow-wow, all right? I get her mouth." He chuckled. "You play a hand of backroom pok'er."

"Come on, honey," Seb said, helping Sarah up onto hands and knees, her lush mouth directed to Len.

Naked, up on all fours in the doggie position, her legs spread wide, her titties delicately swinging, her long black hair snarled and covering most of her face, Sarah no longer looked so prim and proper.

His partner edged his prick towards Sarah's smiling mouth. "Open up! Len is coming in."

Before he made contact, Seb decked his childhood friend.

Sprawled on the floor beside the bed, Len gingerly touched his jaw. "You scurvy dockrat! You nearly broke my face. Why not tell me you changed your mind instead of trying to knock my teeth down my throat? I live by my good looks, asshole."

Seb turned a deaf ear to his partner's whines. Everything but Sarah had faded away.

"Please?" She moaned. "I ache so."

Seb made a swift decision. "My half of the club is yours. Take it as full payment for Sarah Winslow."

Len struggled to a stand. "You want her all for yourself? Fine with me. Take her. No need to pay me."

Seb shook his head. "Payment now prevents a property dispute down the line." Walking around behind Sarah, he smoothed his hand down her spine, petting her between the legs while Len looked on.

"Last time I checked, cowpoke, we still had us a friendship. Since when does a friend cheat a friend? Since when does a friend move in on a friend's woman? You should have said you felt that way about the cunt." Len's voice held reproach.

Something had to get said. Taking a deep breath, Seb got it off his chest. "You got it all wrong—I feel nothing for Sarah. But it is high time I went respectable. Moved into legitimate businesses. So, take the club. The gals, too. All but this one. "

Seb moved one finger, two fingers, three fingers inside Sarah's notch, pushing relentlessly up into the passage, a thumb applied to the clit.

Straightaway, Sarah came on a lusty wail.

Len's rapidly discoloring face split in a grin. "Crissakes, cowpoke! Now I see why you wanted to buy me out."

Disrespectful to comment. But to himself, Seb conceded that the piss-and-vinegar Sarah Winslow had just about worn him out in bed. The drugs, of course. She felt nothing for him. And he felt nothing for her.

To prove he felt nothing, Seb settled his new purchase onto her back and let her go without a cover. "Knees bent to your belly and legs open," he instructed in the stern voice Sarah had shown she responded to right well.

The obedient Sarah performed a lewd split, and Len gave a wolfish whistle. "Trained and prime pussy, too! Hey, I got the short end of the stick here."

Moving out to the hall, the two old friends shook hands on the deal. Then, giving Seb a clap on the back, Len asked, "You planning on marrying up with her?"

Marry Sarah Winslow?

Sugar was sugar, but matrimony was something else again.

"Stop looking at me like I just grew a second head, cowpoke. Our little Sarah has blood blue enough to match her eyes. If you intend to climb to the top of New York society, a bona fide lady will grease the way."

Seb laughed so hard tears rolled down his cheeks.

His former partner said suspiciously, "What the hell are you guffawing about?"

"I do need to wed me a bona fide lady. But since I just finished making Sarah a bona fide whore, that description no longer fits her."

Seb slung an arm over Len's shoulders. "C'mon, you no-good, thieving coyote. I hear the bar calling. Whiskey is on me."

Chapter Ten

In the dim bedchamber, Sarah lifted her dizzy head from the pillow.

Goodness! The room spun like the carousel on Coney Island, the one she had always longed to ride. Her governesses had all forbade the excursion—far too risqué for Michael Winslow's well-bred daughter!

Her body felt most odd, too. Heavy. Her leaden limbs seemed to belong to someone else.

And good gracious! A numbing stupor had descended over her mind, her thoughts clouding over much like the sky before a storm. What had happened to her?

Lifting a weighted arm, she swept her wildly disordered hair back from her forehead. Was this disoriented fuzziness how the aftermath of inebriation felt?

Hard liquor might explain her scattered thoughts, as well as the torpor and lethargy, but alcohol would not explain her terrible urge to…to…

Do unspeakably carnal things.

Blushing, Sarah looked down at her sprawled body. Her *naked* sprawled body.

Her knees were raised, her legs open. Unnaturally, *spread* open on the bed. A wet spot puddled beneath her. Had she lost control of her bladder and peed the linens?

No. The fullness of her bladder reminded her she had not voided of late.

But if not an accident, what had made the bed wet? Sticky, too.

Whilst sluggishly sorting out an answer to her question, an instinctual awareness made itself known to her. She hurt. A unique rawness not easily identified.

Where did she hurt?

As an impartial observer might, outside and apart from her inner self, she craned her neck up from her flattened perspective and dispassionately examined the hills and valleys of her torso.

Her breasts looked swollen, the nipples reddened. Chafed. Bruised. Small indentations—teeth marks?—ringed the perimeters. But though sore, her nipples did not precisely hurt, causing her to speculate that the pain originated somewhere else.

Removed from all emotion, her dulled thought processes informed her that the pain stemmed from between her thighs.

Shifting her splayed limbs, she gave an involuntary gasp.

With some difficulty, she raised the dead weight that masqueraded as her hand and moved the uncooperative appendage to the center of her body. Numbed fingers probed a hitherto untouched area of her anatomy.

Wetness.

Between the legs. A sticky wetness. The same kind of wet stickiness that puddled the bed linen. The stuff saturated her pubic hair. So much so, her fingertips actually slid into her privates.

She winced. A tear slid down her cheek. Just one. She would allow herself no more than one. Self-pity never accomplished anything.

Her gift to her husband was a thing of the past. She had lost her virginity.

The certainty of her deflowering pierced her confused haze without a compensatory remembrance.

Dropping her legs to the floor, Sarah wobbled to a standing position. Clutching the bedpost for support, she noticed the horribly twisted and obscenely stained bed linens. Seminal fluids. Her virgin's blood. Who had taken her virginity?

The door opened, and a man crossed the threshold.

Her rescuer from the ballroom.

His swagger gave him away. She would know that stride anywhere. Much like a cocky rooster struts across a barnyard, he took everything in, as though he owned the place. And her.

"You," she said tonelessly, dispassionately, unable to muster the outrage for his trespass on her privacy.

He placed the basin he carried atop the bed stand. "Are you feeling more yourself now, Sarah?"

"I am at a distinct disadvantage here. You obviously know my name, but who are you?" Too dull-witted to cover her bare breasts and loins, she hung her hands aimlessly at her sides. "I mean, I know we met earlier, but...but..."

Assembling even the simplest statement proved too much for her. Having not the vaguest notion of what she had been trying to express, she left the remainder of the sentence dangling.

"Let me introduce myself." He dipped at the waist. "My name is Sebastian Turner, and I own your note."

Her tangled hair flopped into her unfocused eyes. She impatiently pushed the mess back and away. "My note?"

"The amount you owed Len. I paid it. You are no longer indebted to him."

"Instead, I am...I am...indebted to you." She shook her head at the gibberish of her speech. "Instead, you own me."

He smiled. "Exactly."

She used the bedpost to steady herself once more. "I can see your face. You removed the mask. Why are you not wearing a mask?" A touch to her own face confirmed her mask had also gone missing. "The rules! We are breaking the rules."

"The house rules no longer apply. You are free of this establishment, Sarah."

"But how? How did this come about? Why? And...and how is it that you know my name, that you gave me your name? None of the patrons are privy to my name, or I theirs. This is not allowed—"

"I know everything about you, Sarah. Leonard Dutton filled me in on all the pertinent details when I purchased you from him."

That high-handed pronouncement sparked a glimmer of outrage. "I am not a...a pet! You had no right to purchase me."

"I had every right. And you are my pet, my pretty, obliging plaything."

Dear Heavens! What madness did he speak?

Sarah stared at the man, this stranger, whilst trying to comprehend the insanity of the situation, and understood only her wanton attraction for her new owner.

If only she were properly groomed! Clean and dressed, her hair neatly arranged—every woman feels more in charge when tidily coiffed—she could cope. Or, at the very least, she would feel more like a human being instead of a...*pet.* But neither clean nor dressed nor coiffed, her thoughts scattered at sixes and sevens, she felt overwhelmed. And soiled. A soiled dove. A soiled pet dove.

She giggled. And, helpless not to, rubbed the jutting end of her swollen breast. So funny, absurd really, to find herself standing naked and sticky before a man richly dressed in evening attire!

My, but he looked clean and neat. Neat as a pin. His immaculate toilette showed nary a rumple—

Save for that rather conspicuously large rumple directly below his waistcoat.

His cock. His big, luscious, thick, *hard cock.*

She licked her lips. For a certainty, the owner of her note owned a splendid member. She still felt its imprint inside her. He had pushed his hardness so far in! Deeply in. Hotly in.

From his outward appearance, one would never know that now.

He acted coolly toward her, as though they had never indulged in such prolonged heated intimacy.

She rubbed her bare bosom, and Mr. Turner scarcely lifted a brow. The epitome of respectfulness, he bore himself with rigid formality, deferring to her as if she were a lady in a drawing room, for all that she stood naked and sticky in the lust-scented bedchamber of a whorehouse.

He gestured to the basin. "I thought you might like to bathe. Please use caution, as the water is extremely hot. We take our leave as soon as you finish your ablutions."

"Leave?" she asked stupidly, trying to make a cohesive unit from his unconnected words. "Where are we going?"

"Only a small journey. To my estate."

Her throbbing temples made logic quite impossible. "No! I cannot go with you. No! I dare not go with you."

"Why?"

Too disoriented for sound argument, she fell back on the ridiculousness of propriety. "I cannot go with you because I—I hardly know you. We are not properly acquainted."

"To set you at your ease, let me *acquaint* you with part of my background. Born ambitious, but poor, I made my money in the railroads out West. Explosives."

"How nice. You make holes for a living, much like the Irish ditch-diggers do."

His eyes turned hard. "I am wealthy by anyone's standards. And as I have no wife, I have chosen to pay, rather than seduce, to have my needs satisfied. I hope that sums up my background and my requirements without sounding overly boorish."

She digested this information.

In the dark nooks of palatial homes, female servants often found themselves intimidated into having intimate relations with their employers, only to find themselves later dismissed for arriving in a family way. Nowhere else to go, nothing else to do, they walked the streets.

In light of that sad circumstance, paying a willing whore rather than seducing an unwilling housemaid seemed practically honorable. Why, some "true" gentlemen only pretended to the kind of integrity this rough man actually possessed. Only a small person, indeed, would dwell on his brusque manner rather than look below the surface.

Upon recalling what delights he hid beneath his surface, she tingled all over. "May I speak?"

"Go on. Shoot."

Shoot? My, he certainly did come from the West! "Since you have given me leave, I think I shall...er...shoot. And directly from the hip."

At that last bit of rustic colloquialism, she twittered. Then she turned serious. "I would prefer you return my note to Mr. Dutton."

"Downstairs, some dozen gentlemen await their turn on you. Leave with me tonight, in my carriage, and you avoid their pawing hands. Stay, and you will service those customers and more before dawn. Is that your aim?"

Customers pawing at her body—her aim?

No! That was not her *aim!*

Was it?

Strangely, she felt absolutely no horror at the prospect of pawing hands. She needed the void between her legs filled. With cock. With huge, hard, driving, pounding cock!

Twelve customers? They might do for a start. An army of cocks, all coming at her, one regiment after another, a vanguard battling to put out her body's urgency—now that sounded more like it.

"I just purchased an estate," he said, seeming to rush out the words. "The grounds have gone neglected for some time. Weeds overrun the flowerbeds and will require the services of a full-time gardener for re-establishment. Thinking about building me one of those new glass conservatories, too, like the one Leonard has here. Maybe I'll keep orchids, to show off in the rooms."

Sarah's hand fluttered to her heart, the pounding so loud she thought for sure he must hear it. "I can design your gardens!" She panted, her small breasts rapidly rising and falling in her agitation. "I can manage the construction of the glass conservatory. I can do it all, from start to finish. All I need is a few helpers for the heaviest labor."

"You?" he scoffed.

"Yes! Me! Did I not tell you that I designed the gardens here? Nothing grew here a short while ago, save rock and mud. I did all the creative work, practically all the digging, too. I—I nursed Mr. Dutton's orchid collection back to health. I planted every flowerbed. I did it!" she boasted. "I did it. Me!"

"A lady of refinement, on hands in knees, digging in the dirt?"

"I assure you, I am often on all fours."

For some reason, he grinned, then said, "As it so happens, I have a proposal to make you—"

Sarah clapped her hands together. "Say no more. I agree to accept the position of gardener."

"I proposed nothing of the sort."

Sarah's brow furrowed. "You offer me marriage, then?"

"Hell, no! I need me a mistress."

For all of two seconds, she remained perfectly still before drawing back her hand and slapping his handsome face. "You, sir, are no gentleman. You are naught but a…but a social upstart."

"If you stay here and work off your debt, what do you think will happen later on tonight when one of these *real* gentlemen visits your bedchamber? Think your fancy suitor will set himself down a spell and discuss Shakespeare with you?

"Not likely!" he answered for her, and with more than a vestige of cruelty. "Your fancy suitor will shove his not-so-fancy cock up your ladylike privates. And after that fine gentleman finishes up, another fine gentleman will take his place. Your legs will open to any fancy prick whose purse is fat enough to pay for the entry to this club, while my fat purse purchased you outright for my own exclusive use."

"No need to keep reminding me of how low I have fallen," she said, grandly.

"Oh, I think there is every reason to remind you. Say it," he demanded, giving her no quarter. "Tell me. What position do you hold in this club?"

Her shoulders slumped; her chin dipped. "In my thoughts, I call myself a courtesan," she whispered. "But I know others will call me a prostitute. A whore."

"And why is that?"

Her bottom lip trembled. "Because that is what a woman who engages in illicit congress for money is called." Her chin raised; her glance lifted; her spine straightened. "But that is beside the point. I believed we're conducting a business discussion."

"We are. Out West, a man can make it with just his brawn and his brain. Here in the East, a well-bred lady at my side will open otherwise closed doors. This is one class-conscious town. Which is why I mean to wed me a lady. Until I find a suitable candidate, I need a woman to satisfy my manly urges."

"Sir, you insult me! I would rather starve than accept your proposition."

"How are you insulted? I offered you a degree of respectability. I wager none of these *gentlemen* will offer you as much tonight." He raked both hands through his abbreviated hair. "Listen, every streetwalker in Manhattan has more than likely said at one time or another that she 'would rather starve' than sell her body. But hunger ain't pretty. Starvation gnaws at the belly until a body will do anything, with anyone, just to buy a loaf of moldy, week-old bread."

Her breath went shallow. "You have been there, have you not? You have known hunger."

Roughened knuckles skimmed along her jaw. "The past is in the past. In the here and now, you interest me. Carnally. I reckon we would make each other happy. In bed."

She remained statue-still whilst he caressed her throat, not daring to move lest she do something extremely forward, like tackle him to the floor. Wave after wave of unspeakable carnal hunger had started to move over her, like the ocean moves over the sands, and she could not stem the ache inside her. For that, she needed him.

"I paid off all your debts," he rasped. "I would take real good care of you. At the end, I would settle an agreed-upon amount on you, a nest egg to ensure your independence. You could pick and choose clientele at your discretion."

"So hard," she murmured as his fingers played lightly upon her shoulder. "How does a person get so hard?"

"I am hard. And ruthless. But this here is a sound business deal."

Swallowing a licentious groan, Sarah let go of the bedpost and stumbled away from him toward the door. To find those cocks? Or to escape her own promiscuousness?

She wanted him desperately again...

"Where are you going?" he called after her.

"Somewhere. Anywhere. I know not where." Picking up one leaden foot after the other, she continued her slow retreat.

"Come here to me, Sarah."

She shook her head back and forth, the action sending tangled black strands cascading over her face once more. She must look the harlot!

"Now, young lady."

She turned. Made her way back to him. Looked up at him bashfully through her knotted hair. "Yes?"

"Back up to me."

Without questioning the directive, she performed a dizzy pirouette, the turn ending with her leaning against him.

"There's a good girl. Only a little more now."

A little more?

Very well. She aligned her bottom to the front of his trousers. When her derriere melded to his bulge, she stopped.

"Go on," he said. "Make use of me. Pretend my hands belong to a marionette and you control the strings."

How did he know what she needed? How did he know how much she ached?

No matter how he knew, like a puppeteer she brought one of his big hands to a breast; the other she carried to the aching void between her legs. As she rubbed her bottom against the front of his trousers, the give of her buttocks encapsulating the hardness she found there, her bare breasts bobbed up and down with her frenzy. "Pinch my nipple," she directed.

"Like so?" her own personal puppet replied.

"Harder! And press the heel of your hand into my privates." Depraved excitement burned in her belly as she continued to use him like a cat at a scratching post.

"Like so?" he asked again.

"Yes. Lovely." Her head fell back against his chest, her throat arching, as a glimpse of memory returned. "You punched Mr. Dutton. Why?"

"To prevent him from coming in your mouth."

"No!"

"You will permit any man anything, Sarah. And not only will you permit anything, you will beg for more."

"I absolutely would not do anything so undignified."

His hands fell away. "Bend over, Sarah. Present your bottom to me. I have a hankering for your little hole."

Oh, God, she ached! How could he do this to her? How could he take her relief away?

She rounded a bit. "Like this?"

"Not nearly enough. Touch your palms to the floor."

Did he actually wish her to raise her buttocks up as a female animal does in mating?

She bit her lip. "Will you see to me then?"

"I own you, Sarah. No bargaining. Do as you are told."

Desperate for relief, any sort of relief, she dropped all the way down.

"What do you say, Sarah?"

"Please?" she begged.

"Please what?"

"Please see to me, sir!"

A finger slid over her rump, penetrated the crack. "Oh, yes," she cooed when the same finger circled her back opening.

"Are you giving this to me?" he asked.

"Yes." Anything, anything at all for relief.

"Let me get this straight—you just begged me for sodomy, right?"

"That is correct."

"Another time, perhaps," her owner said tightly.

"But you said..."

When his palm came down hard on her backside, she gave an undignified yelp of pleasure. "Oh, yes, yes, yes—"

"I think I proved my point about you doing anything with anyone," he said, smug as can be. "Stand up now and we can leave."

As Sarah straightened, she posed the sensitive question, "With Mr. Dutton—did I—?"

How does one delicately ask if one has accepted the advances of two men at the same time? How does one go on after one has learned the truth?

She tried again. "Did I do *it* with both of you?"

"Only I had you tonight. Only me," he said softly. "I would have killed Len to prevent him from having you. I never share what is mine, and I always protect my investments."

"Is that all I am to you...an investment?"

"Yes. Now, admit this is preferable." A big hand cupped her loins. "Admit you would rather have one man own you outright than have many different men rent you for a night."

Unable to dissemble, whatever it was coursing through her system loosening her tongue as well as her carnal appetites, she surrendered her pride to the owner of her note. "I will admit to whatever you like, so long as you make the ache go away." She bit her lip. "Though, in my current state of dishabille, I can understand why you would refuse me. I must look most unappealing."

He laughed. "You have a lot to learn about men, even more about what they find appealing. Look at your reflection and see how I see you."

Without her knowledge, he had purposefully posed her before the cheval looking glass, situated across the room. Obeying him, she stared into the mirror.

A nude woman with widely spread legs stared back at her. Was that really she?

Impossible!

But true—for in the glass, a dark male hand stroked between the woman's open thighs, whilst another dark hand cupped and squeezed and pulled the nipple of the woman's small, up-tilted breast, and her owner currently performed the same lovely activity on her.

"You make for a very appealing sight," he said

"I wish you owned more hands," she shamelessly replied.

Chuckling, he set her away. "Come and bathe." He brought her back to the bed stand. "The sooner you finish, the sooner I can bring you home."

The last word stung like a whip, its bitter bite lashing through her mind's fog.

Home.

Sarah had never known such a place.

Chapter Eleven

Mr. Turner dropped the folded bathing cloth into the steaming water. After wringing out the linen, he held the square out to her.

His black brows arched. "Unless—Sarah, do you need help?"

A heated blush suffused her skin. All of her burned in shame, in humiliation, in offended modesty. Not because of her nudity, but because of her naked desire—

For his hands on her flesh, and without that square of linen.

As penance for her wicked thoughts, she said, "No, thank you, sir. I can manage." Picking up the basin of water, she started for the dressing screen.

"Stop!" he called after her. "As we start, Sarah, so we shall proceed. You will keep no secrets from me, bathing included."

He had bought and paid for her. In exchange for paying her debt, she belonged to him. She had no rights anymore, no prerogative over her own person. He could do with her body as he pleased.

The prospect excited her.

But she intended to keep the excitement to herself, regardless that he told her she may not have secrets from him.

"Sir, there is a shallow reservoir behind the screen. I stand inside the pan and thus avoid water spotting the floor."

"Remain here," he said.

How calmly she waited for her owner's return. How calmly she lifted one foot, then the other, and stepped into the shallow reservoir he had brought back to her. Like a placid lamb going to the slaughter, she proceeded to wash, thinking no further than that the water no longer felt scalding hot, but comfortably tepid. Without benefit of privacy, she cleansed her face first, moving the cloth 'round and 'round, before applying the wet linen to her throat. Next, she washed her breasts. Cupping each in a hand, she circled her distended nipples. Done there, she opened her legs, displaying to him that secret part of her anatomy that made her a woman. Rather than blush, she enjoyed the exhibitionism so much she lost her balance.

Mr. Turner caught her. "Allow me to finish bathing you." He removed the cloth from her hand.

Unable to suppress the longing, the aching desire, she blurted, "Would you please—"

She lost courage. Raised never to ask for anything, certainly not something that would bring her delight, she clamped her mouth shut.

"If you have something to say, speak up!" he ordered.

Stuck between a rock and a hard place, her owner's reprimand ringing in her ears, she could either divulge her wanton need or suffer the consequences of his impatience.

But what if he found her request disgusting? What if, in that disgust, he turned away from her? Or, worse still, ridiculed her?

She recalled that he had not turned away from her in the gazebo, and that memory gave her the necessary daring to say, "Would you please dispense with the cloth?"

He dropped the cloth forthwith.

At his calm acceptance of her need, her eyes smarted.

Naturally, she refused to allow even one self-pitying tear to fall when, treating her need as his own, the ruffian tenderly bathed her.

Perversely, she found herself wishing for a harder touch. A rough penetration, to put her wish in more graphic terms, and with something longer and thicker that the two moistened fingers with which he cleansed her.

Finished with her front, he started in on her backside.

"Ouch!" She turned, and her eyes widened at the site of her bottom cheeks.

Bruises decorated both halves.

"Five spanks," related the man of few words.

Then, "Semen," he explained, trickling bath water between her buttocks.

"Oh." She nodded wisely. "Discipline and buggery, too." With a giggle, she covered her mouth with both hands.

Buggery. What a rude word. Ladies never thought such things, never mind spoke such things.

"I have yet to sodomize you," he said matter-of-factly, his finger gliding up and down the seam between her buttocks. "But I did take you from behind, stallion to mare. Withdrawing to prevent conception, I ejaculated onto your buttocks." Helping her out of the reservoir, he led her to the bed.

"Do you find that unspeakably scandalous, innocent Sarah?"

Scandal? Where was the scandal?

"Not particularly," she replied with a shrug. She needed relief. How he accomplished that goal mattered very little to her.

He pressed her down on top of the velvet coverlet. Would he penetrate her now?

"To prevent a fall while I dry you," he explained.

"Oh, bosh." She threw her arms up over her head; her disappointment knew no bounds. "I thought you might have something else in mind."

His chuckling rolled to a merry laugh as he wiped her down with a clean, dry cloth—face, torso, limbs. When he came to the juncture of her body, he said straightforwardly, "Open your thighs, legs apart, heels at the edge of the bed."

She complied enthusiastically.

He patted her folds dry. "Fortunately, because of the drug, you experienced less than the usual amount of a virgin's pain."

So—she had been drugged!

"Did you do it?" she asked. Please, God! Make him say he had not!

"You have no memory of it?"

"My recollections are draped in fog. At times, the sun burns through, but not for long."

"Well, just so you know, I have no need to ply my women with an aphrodisiac. I manage fairly well all on my own."

The conceit of the man...

Still, relief flooded her mixed-up mind. "But if not you, then who—?" She gasped. "I remember now! Mrs. Brown. She thought me tense. Whatever I drank, it worked." She twirled a strand of hair around a finger. "I have never felt more relaxed. You may consider that an invitation."

"Which, lamentably, I must refuse until you heal."

Did he think to punish her?

"Thank you for your concern, but you need not abstain on my account."

"Because you want me? Or because I paid for you?"

He slipped a long finger inside her vagina, and she purred lustfully. "What matter the reason? Come into me!"

"Too soon." His finger retracted.

Unfair! How did he stay so cool when a fire burned inside her?

He placed something colder than even his voice upon her belly.

"Lock these bracelets around your wrists and ankles, and you will have the relief of my hand."

Pretentious popinjay! Regardless of his affected speech and stiff mannerisms, he was still no gentleman—

That suited her. And it suited her too to wear his silly shackles, because they mattered not at all. He said he owned her, but he did not! He owned only a piece of paper, an obligation she must fulfill. He would never own her—

Not until she also owned him.

Rising up to sit at the edge of the bed, she picked up the four lustrous rings, gold, very beautiful, and engraved with a rose motif.

"I have never owned anything as fine." She eagerly slipped the bracelets around her wrists and ankles.

"To lock them in place," he said softly and inserted a tiny key in each.

With each *click*, the ache inside her grew. "Please, sir, I need you so."

"Where do you need me?"

"Between my legs." She reclined again, prepared to show him. Exactly.

Before she could, teasing fingers moved low on her belly. "Here?" he asked.

"Yes."

"Tell me why you wish me to touch you here."

Her fists clenched at her sides—either that, or strike him. Was the man such a dullard as all that?

She gritted her teeth. "To give me pleasure, of course."

"Aha! So you admit I give you pleasure?"

"Yes," she grated out. "Pleasure me again."

A single finger—though an extraordinarily large single finger—sawed her swollen folds back and forth.

Hurry! Could he not see her agony?

After a moment, pleasure took agony's place. "Oh, yes."

"Feel nice?"

"Nothing so bland as 'nice.' 'Decadent' is a more apt description."

When he rubbed the sensitive nub at the top of her sex, her hips shot up off the bed. A thousand sunbursts exploded within her, and she came on a desolate wail.

He was not a dullard, after all. Indeed, she must confess her owner possessed quite talented hands. Even gifted hands.

"Again," she commanded. With a lazy stretch, she repeated the order. "Again, I say."

Quick as lightning strikes, he rolled her over onto her belly, much as a dockworker rolls a gunnysack of turnips down a ship's plank. A hand came down hard on her already bruised posterior.

She yelped. Her body going rigid, fingers clawing the coverlet, her bottom brazenly rose up to meet his palm.

Nothing followed.

Her lips pursed in vexation. Only one smack? Surely, her bratty behavior was deserving of two?

"I am not your love slave, Sarah Winslow. You are mine. Keep that in mind." His palm descended again.

Oh, joy. Oh, unbridled, unrestrained bliss. She could grow accustomed to this sort of punishment. In fact, the punishment could prove habit-forming.

The knot inside her evaporated, and with a tremendous screech, she came again.

Her uninhibited response might have provided Mr. Turner unlimited fodder with which to humiliate her. Fortuitously, her owner seemed not the sort to judge. If anything, he seemed to approve. At least, his grunt sounded as though it held approval.

"Up you go, Miss Winslow." He lent her a hand to rise. "Let's find you something pretty to wear."

Rubbing her derriere, she dragged her heavy body from the bed to the wardrobe, where she reached inside for her one and only gown, a modest navy blue left over from her former life as a modest young lady. Neither modest nor a lady anymore, she declared both a small loss. What had either ever gotten her?

Her owner looked down the aquiline pitch of his nose at the worsted gown in her hand. "I said, something pretty."

"I sold everything I owned. Not that the clothing brought much, you understand. Years old and not at all fashionable, my gowns went to the ragman. I have always dressed plainly. All I have left is this navy gown."

Next, she removed her set of mended undergarments from their separate hooks, placing both the unadorned blue gown and the white cambric underclothes over his outstretched arm.

"These are little better than rags," he muttered. Making a scornful face, he shoved the lot back into the wardrobe. "Have you a cloak?"

"Yes. My good gray wool." She motioned. "There. In the far corner."

His sensual mouth tightened. "Not even the moths will have that hideous thing."

As she had sewn that eminently serviceable *thing* herself, she glared up at him.

A glare he overlooked. "You will use my cape. I left it downstairs in the cloakroom." He made to leave—to retrieve it, no doubt.

Frightened of what she might do if left to her own devices, she cried after him, "You are not to go!" She wracked her aching brain for a solution to the quandary of her nudity. "I know," she said brightly. "I shall wrap myself up in the bed linen, toga style." She laughed at her own wit and daring. "Who knows? I may start a fashion trend."

"Suit yourself," he said coolly. "As long as you have a proper cover when we leave this chamber and go downstairs."

Proper.

She sniffed in disdain. She had left that virtue behind when she entered this establishment. Now, she had no virtue and but one concern.

"Between my legs, s-sir," she stammered. "The urgency—when will it leave?"

"Aphrodisiacs can last twenty-four hours, longer in a person of slight build."

"I cannot bear it." Her thighs clamped together to stem the compulsion.

The pressure helped, but not nearly enough. She needed more.

She needed the rough man who owned her.

Chapter Twelve

"I fear I am depraved, sir."

Mr. Turner picked up her fallen chin. "Depraved? You?"

"Yes," Sarah answered. "Depraved."

"Not even close. And once again, those are the drugs talking." He jerked his jaw to the changing screen. "Is there a commode behind there?"

"Yes, sir."

"You have my permission to use it. Voiding might help rid you of the drug's hold. "

She would try anything!

Feet clumsy, she rushed to the screen, stumbling before reaching her destination.

He helped her finish the seemingly endless journey. Helped her squat over the chamber pot. Helped spread her legs. Wide. Wider still, presumably so she might hit the dancing target.

She danced, too. Wiggled, actually. She really did have to make water, and the pot refused to hold still. Would she further disgrace herself and tip over?

In the very ultimate of humiliations, Mr. Turner stooped to her level. Two hands about her waist, thumbs stroking the undersides of her breasts, he steadied her on the commode.

"What are you waiting for?" he asked.

Too, *too* much. The man had absolutely no reserve whatsoever!

"I am not often called upon to piddle on demand in a less than private situation. What, pray, is the etiquette?" Her shoulders went up, then down. "You must forgive me, sir, if I am at a loss as to how to proceed."

"Sarah, I have already seen you at your worst."

"In this bedchamber?" she asked in a huff.

"No. On the way to the gazebo. What a little snob!"

Once, perhaps, but certainly not anymore.

She let go, the gush sounding as loud as a waterfall as the stream hit the porcelain pot. Could she sink any lower?

He patted her dry, proving, yes, she could sink lower.

"You will wear a pessary," he said.

"Pardon?" she asked, not quite meeting his eyes.

"A contraceptive device. I prefer a Dutch Cap."

She plucked at her knobby knees. "Then, by all means, you must wear this hat from Holland, the one which you prefer. I certainly have no such inclination myself."

Ignoring her vented spleen, he continued. "To determine the best fit, I ordered the cap in several sizes."

She looked up, curiosity pushing embarrassment aside. "W-where does it go?"

"Inside here," he said, fingering her privates. "Before its installation inside the vagina to cover the cervix, the device is dusted with powder, boric or bicarbonate of soda."

"I would never know how to install such a thing inside me."

"It's a simple enough device—a cap of rubber on a watch-spring, worn to bed each night in anticipation of intercourse, and at other times when coitus seems imminent. In your case, you will wear it very nearly all the time. And I shall install it, not you."

"I would rather not wear something lodged inside me. Other than you, of course." She twittered.

"But you will wear it, all the same. Now, hold tight a little longer. You need a douche before we leave."

Whilst she clutched the rim, he squirted a vinegar-and-apples-smelling solution between her open legs.

"It stings," she complained and squirmed.

"Sit still. Are you looking to get a big belly?"

"A baby," she said wistfully, going very still indeed. "Someone to love."

The squirting stopped. "The first time, I gave you my seed. A mistake."

She hugged her middle. "A sweet baby, a mistake?"

Her owner stood over her as she straddled the pee-pot. "Any son of mine will have a lady for a mother, not a whore."

"You—you think me a whore?" She closed her legs.

"You are to keep open until I tell you otherwise."

Naked, legs spread wide, she sought to set him to rights. "I have decided, after all, to call myself a courtesan." A small but necessary distinction of elevated status that she would strive her utmost to achieve. "You are wealthy. I am destitute. An entire social class in Europe, the demimonde, abides by such financial arrangements."

"Still hanging on to your snobby airs, are you?" He pointed between her thighs. "Open that up some more, darlin'. Use your hand and pull up on the folds. Stretch it out all the way."

She did as instructed; he could now view her entire genitalia at one glance.

"Good," he said, sounding odd. "Real good." He loosened his collar. "This here ain't Europe, sweetpea. This here is good ol' America. And here, if you fornicate for money, you get called a—"

Her shoulders rounded.

He sighed. "Call yourself whatever the hell you want. To a bastard, a name makes not a damn bit of difference." He looked at her soulfully. "No reason to act like a wet hen cutting teeth. I asked you to become my mistress, and you slapped my face. I should take offense here, not you."

"We both must live with our respective and abiding hurt, then, mustn't we?"

"Abiding hurt?" he asked, sounding vexed indeed. "What hurt? I just looked you over good, and though the passage is swollen, there are no rips, no tears. You will recover."

"You asked me to become your mistress, as though the arrangement were a cut-and-dried business proposition, as though you were shopping for waistcoats at a tailor's shop, as though you could dispense with me when I grew frayed or you tired of me. That hurt!"

He raked both hands through his hair. "Are you saying...are you telling me...you would rather service a line of waiting gentlemen than become the mistress of a man not of your class?"

"I am not a dither-brain, sir! Only a fool would reject your proposal, and I am not a fool. However, I request a slight but significant modification in the terms."

"What sort of modification? If you want more money, fine—"

She waved his settlement offer aside. "A mistress implies a relationship of tacit affection. In our situation, that would make a mockery of love, something I refuse to do. Instead, I shall stay with you as long as it is mutually beneficial. *To both of us.*"

To her mind, this was the more honest course. For a woman who became a mistress under a false pretense of affection lived a lie. At least a courtesan assumed no such pretension. Servicing a man for money seemed less dishonorable, less mercenary, less *cold* than going into a relationship assuming beforehand it must end.

She would make no such assumption. Affection could spring up in the most unlikely places...

Was she mad for believing in the possibility of love?

Most likely. Affection prompted few society marriages; money formed the basis of most vows said at the altar. She held her own parents' marriage up as just such an example. Now *there* was a society marriage founded on profit!

Not so the passionate marriage of the O'Sullivans. The gardener at Clearbrook had loved his wife dearly. Even after her death, right before Sarah's fourth birthday, Mr. O'Sullivan continued to love his wife until he himself had departed this green earth. As a child, Sarah had listened raptly as Mr. O'Sullivan recounted the details of his romance with the young Maggie. The stories outlined a relationship built on admiration and respect, a union of hearts that had lasted forty years. His love story had taught her not to settle for less.

"Do you agree to my contractual change of verbiage?" she asked her owner.

"Courtesan. Mistress. All the blasted same to me."

Then, as if she had a choice, she said solemnly, "I agree to go with you."

She said no more as he applied an unguent to her privates. Who could speak in profundities whilst he did that?

Not she. She had all she could do to breathe. The salve felt cool, his finger hot. Burning hot. Searing hot. His finger slipped in and out of her in long, torrid strokes for an impossibly long duration, until her hips rolled and her bare, pointed breasts bounced up and down, and she moaned and groaned, and yes, oh, yes, came. Again.

The despicable beast! He had done that intentionally.

"That should hold you awhile," he said, sounding very smug indeed, as he helped her up off the pot and across the floor to the bed, where, with a theatrical flourish, he pulled the top linen free. He handed her the same. "Make your haute couture creation from this yardage."

A challenge she accepted with aplomb. Having grown up with very little, save a good name—since sullied—she had learned at a young age to make do with very little. Granted, she had never had to resort to filling an empty belly with stone soup—not until recently anyway—but she knew how to take one respectable gown and dress it up to fit whatever the occasion. Poise and posture hid the moth holes—

In a bind, she reverted to Miss Sarah Winslow again, a lady of impeccable lineage, a serious-minded horticulturalist of lofty ambition. Though she had assigned both her virtue and aspirations to the dung heap, she could pretend with the best of them.

With a jaunty tilt of her chin, she wrapped herself up in the lamentably soiled and wrinkled linen, one end tucked in at the bosom. Allowing a scant amount of cleavage to show, she tossed one end back over her shoulder in a fashionable, Romanesque style. "There!" She preened. "How do I look?"

"Charming. Like a goddess."

Neither charming nor goddesslike, she took his remark with a large grain of salt. Still, buoyed on his insincerity, she gave a pirouette. Never had she executed one better, her grandeur and confidence owing to praise, she supposed.

Her new owner scratched his jaw and smiled. "Ever play poker?"

"Hardly."

"I rightly think I should teach you cards."

She looked at him askance. "Whatever do you mean?"

"Your expression. How you mask your feelings. Except when I was inside you. Everything showed right there on your face then."

"Your meaning escapes me." Her nose hiked to the ceiling. "Now, shall we away?"

He placed a mask over her face, one over his own, and opened the bedchamber door.

An audience awaited them in the hall.

A tad cavalier, her declining the offer of Mr. Turner's cape—

Not allowing her misgivings to show, she pasted on a smile and swept down the treads like a sovereign. Like Queen Victoria herself, minus several chins and layers of black bombazine.

"No one will touch you," Mr. Turner told her, wrapping an arm about her shoulders.

Though he was less than a gentleman—or perhaps *because* he was less than a gentleman—she felt quite safe with her owner at her side. Without whale-boned corset and stiff petticoat—the armor of a lady—she felt well defended.

And warm. His protective gesture gave her reason to hope that more than crass business governed the terms of their liaison.

"Are you enamored of me, sir?" she playfully asked, exploring both flirtatiousness and exhibitionism for the first time.

"I thought my adoration obvious."

False front in place, she laughed gaily. Other women inspired adoration in men, not Sarah Winslow, a hunk of plain bread in the cupboard, ignored in favor of fancy pastry. Mr. Turner must have decided to poke fun at her. Fortunately, the drugs in her blood cushioned the barb.

Downstairs hummed with business, the house a beehive of activity. Patrons and prostitutes, all fully and elaborately dressed in the latest of fashions, talked animatedly, probably negotiating who went upstairs with whom. Suddenly, her attire bothered her not at all. In fact, she found the stares she received from gentlemen rather titillating. Even a hunk of plain bread will show off its merits when a safe opportunity presents itself...

Outside the cloakroom, her libidinous impulses grew stronger. "See to me, sir!"

Her new owner ignored her imperial command.

She sent him a quelling stare. "Did you not hear me?"

"I heard you." With delicious deliberation, he kissed her.

A lovely and gentle kiss upon the cheek, a chaste and circumspect kiss a gentleman would bestow upon a lady.

Regardless of the milling crowd, she openly, wordlessly, taunted him. With a boldness only a hussy would employ, she urged him to enter her. A coy smile, a raised shoulder, a languid posturing—all conveyed, and in no uncertain terms, that she was his for the taking.

Without so much as a backward glance, Mr. Turner left her to go inside the cloakroom.

The nerve! She would teach him not to ignore her!

She doe-eyed any and all gentlemen who eyed her. Tit for tat. Like a tart, she lasciviously wiggled her hips at one full-of-himself dandy.

Just as the fop made his approach, her owner returned.

"Enough of that, young lady!" Her owner scowled at the approaching patron, who ran off in the opposite direction, coattails between his legs. "Apparently, I cannot leave you alone more than a minute."

She offered up a saucy grin. "Apparently, that is correct, sir."

Her new owner held his cape out to her. Thick with fur, its voluminous folds would cover her from head to toe. She would look quite respectable in that cape.

"No, thank you. I am perfectly fine as I am." She tossed her head.

"Have it your way, then. Just see you behave yourself until I can get you in my covered carriage. No more solicitation. And, for decency's sake, keep your legs closed!"

Decency. Such a vastly overrated commodity. Just look at her. She had played by society's rules, done the right thing, the *expected* thing, and she had ended up in a bawdy house. Time to rethink societal rules, time to look out for herself, time to hang decency.

She left the club wearing soiled linen from a whorehouse bed. Considering her new station in life, her attire seemed entirely apropos.

Chapter Thirteen

Sarah awakened ensconced in a plushly upholstered carriage, snuggled close against a hard and masculine body. A blanket covered her lap, a warm cape wrapped her shoulders in fur, and a linen sheet thwarted her nakedness—and a recently acquired taste for exhibitionism.

In the dim light of a quickly encroaching dawn, she slanted her eyes up at the dashing profile of the man who held both her and the reins with utmost panache. Deep ruts marred the road, but his vim and verve cushioned her from the bruising bounce of the wheels.

Her owner reeked of handsome virility, but in no way or manner of speaking might one classify him as well-bred. A tan proclaimed his life as an adventurer, not a scholar or an ascetic. For all that he possessed a refined, patrician bone structure, his sensuous mouth gave away his appetite for corporal pleasure, even excess. As did certain other endowments, which she would not dwell upon...

Not whilst riding in a moving carriage.

Sarah clenched her thighs together. Why had she allowed her thoughts to stray *there?* She must concentrate on only his face.

On a clean-shaven cheek, three scratches showed red and angry. These marks lent Mr. Turner a somewhat wayward look. The rakish scratches also made one wonder about the caliber of individuals with whom he associated. No doubt he had a story to tell there, and no doubt that story involved a woman.

A woman with a temper, she would say.

His tale would also involve hot, passionate, throbbing, libidinous activity. Perspiration-soaked libidinous activity. The kind of libidinous activity that made a woman wish to...

No, she must not think about *that,* either. Not whilst riding in a moving carriage.

Mr. Turner's nose was almost, but not quite, aggressively large; most assuredly his proboscis dominated the rest of his features. She thought his thick black hair easily his most beautiful asset, though he could have made more of that gift with a more deliberate grooming. He kept the wavy strands clipped short. With neither the icy glint of blue nor the warmth of red lighting the strands, his hair contained all the dark elements of a moonless night. Midnight at its most determinedly black. She would dearly love to reach up and run her hands through his hair. Mess it up a bit. Comb the strands into a stylish disorganization. Perhaps take his head between her legs and...

No, her imagination must not take over. Not whilst riding outside on the open road in a moving carriage.

Her owner carried himself elegantly, gracefully, for all that he possessed the powerful build of a man used to hard work—a laborer's hard body, a laborer's callused hands, a laborer's dark skin. Heavens, but she wished he would labor over her...

But not now and not here. Open road. Moving carriage.

Sarah squeezed her thighs together.

Mr. Turner's arm muscles, ill disguised within the confines of his formal black evening coat, came into hard prominence as they swelled and tensed at the reins; his shoulder muscles bunched as he shielded her from the worst of the road's bumps and jolts.

She bit her lip. He wore his trousers tight. Incredibly tight. Not skintight, but nearly. Or did they only seem tight because he required a fuller cut in certain places? Was that bulge a fixed protuberance? Did the swelling never go away? And more importantly, would he use that tumescence on her, on the open road, in a moving carriage?

Under the blanket, Sarah crossed her legs. Ladies never did, but what of it?

Though she had no way of knowing for sure, she sensed this rugged man would have little tolerance for the effete and simpering males of New York society, those indolent gentlemen whose only occupation entailed the making of witty drawing room conversation. The intuition also struck her that he would despise affectation of any sort. Yet, he dressed in rich evening attire, and obviously he had chosen his carriage for beauty as well as utility.

And the matter of his speech confused her. At times so Western, at other times so precise, and underlined always with the distinctive flavoring of desperate poverty.

How was it that he contained so many divergences whilst she contained none? All lines pointed to her hot, wet, central core.

God help her! Under the cover of the wool blanket, her hand crept to that central core.

Mr. Turner seemed protective, rather than threatening. Yet his underlying roughness excited her. In truth, everything about her companion excited her. Who was he *really?*

Who was *she* really?

Writhing on the luxurious leather, unable to control her unspeakable carnality, she rocked back and forth against the carriage's seat for relief.

"Fuck me!" The statement just slipped out, though its harsh boldness aptly described her need.

Her owner's features exhibited no outward shock, but his hands did clench on the reins. "The house is only up the drive—"

Their surroundings? Unimportant! Only the hot, wet, throbbing void between her legs held any significance.

Throwing off the wool blanket, shrugging her shoulders free of the confining fur-lined cape, Sarah sat straight up on the seat, a fire positively burning her loins. "I fear I cannot wait. If you are disinclined to do the deed yourself, stop here and I shall alight from this vehicle and seek out someone who is so inclined."

He yanked the horses to the side of the lane.

"Sarah," her owner began, offering her an unreadable scrutiny. "You are still under the influence of the drug."

Had she asked for a lesson in pharmacology?

Blast him! She desired this man, but she had long passed fussiness—any functioning male genitalia would do her.

With one last rock of her hips, Sarah jumped to the ground—careful not to clumsily trip over her shrouding sheet—determined to find some man, any man, rough or well-bred, she cared not which, to put out the fire in her loins.

In the predawn fog, Sarah raced in the probable direction of the stables. Two or three randy stable lads? Eminently doable. Even a horse, sixteen-hands high, would present her no problem. Like Catherine the Great, she would take all comers...

Sloppy mud squished between her bare toes as she ran. Whilst she slept, rain must have fallen, a hard downpour that turned the ground oily underfoot and splattered ooze up onto her linen tunic.

Always clumsy, she slipped on the sludge underfoot.

A pair of strong hands caught her about the waist.

He handled her like a piece of fine crystal, a fluted wineglass stored in spun batting to prevent breakage. Oh, if only he knew her unwholesome thoughts, could read the dark desires of her flesh, he would not think her in need of swaddling then!

"Allow me to escort you back to your seat," her owner offered. "This weather is perilous to your health."

What cared she for a little damp?

Shaking him off, she raced ahead.

Two steps, and he had grabbed her once again.

"Let me go!" she yelled, swinging her elbows, kicking her feet. Why had he turned cruel? Did he wish her to beg?

His voice lowered to a whisper. Laced with the poison of sympathy, he said, "Any further, and you run the risk of observation. My staff rises early to stoke the fires."

She could not bring herself to care. Not about those big, chilly rooms, not about servants gazing out the windows at her. She cared about only one thing.

"Please," she finally did beg. Over the bedraggled sheeting, she cupped her mons, her fingers grinding, rooting, trying to stem the horrible ache there.

"Sarah, there is a big, comfortable rosewood bed up at the house and a door we can close against the world. Let me take you there."

"I cannot wait."

Facing him, she lewdly tilted her pelvis, pantomiming the push and pull of mating. "You would put an animal out of its misery, would you not? I beseech you, sir, put me out of mine."

"The house is straight ahead." He spoke to her in a quiet and gentle tone, the civilized and soothing manner an adult employs with a child.

She would have none of his reasoning. None of his studied gentleness. Beyond civilized, past soothing, only a rough handling would put out the bonfire raging within her.

In the semi-darkness, the immediate environs enclosed in a pea-soup fog, her mind a confused turmoil, she had difficulty pinning down her location. The muddy expanse might once have been lush green lawn. Lacking any sort of attention, weeds now clutched the area; tenacious thorns and brambles and thistles ran rampant. She felt just as wild, just as neglected as her surroundings.

"Do me hard," she canted, clawing at her linen-covered breasts. "Rut on me like an animal. Hurt me," she cried, stomping the muddy ground in her frustration. "Punish me. I deserve a beating. My behavior warrants a sound thrashing, a strenuous…a strenuous…"

"Christ, Sarah," he rasped. "Not like this. Never like this. I never wanted this." He shook his head. "Listen, I left the blanket back in the carriage." He walked away from her.

The blanket served as an excuse, and a poor one at that. She disgusted him, her unladylike needs disgusted him, and so he had left her. What had she expected? Everyone abandoned her in the end.

Damn him anyway!

The rising sun cut through the fog, the light of a new day dissipating some of her drug-induced confusion. Like a curtain being lifted on a stage production, slowly, revealing not all the set at once, her senses cleared and she recognized her location.

Clearbrook!

Within yards of the Winslow ancestral front door, where awakening servants or anyone else might see or hear her, she had just begged a man to rut upon her like a sow in the slops. What a pretty picture she must make, delivered straight from a whorehouse, wrapped in mud- and semen-streaked bed linen!

Of all the places on earth, why, oh, why had her owner brought her here?

Chapter Fourteen

Seb ripped the blanket from inside the carriage. Sarah's skin had felt like ice. Women suffered the cold; warming her would stave off illness. He had to start force-feeding her, too—her thinness worried him. *Damn!* Had she eaten the tray of food Mrs. Brown had taken to her room that night? He had never asked.

He had to start checking up on Sarah more often, making sure she was warm enough, that she did more than just pick at her grub...that she laughed...

Despite him stealing coal for the stove, their dingy tenement room had remained freezing, and despite his best attempts to improve their lot, his mother had remained cold and hungry and sad.

He could have done more. He *should* have done more. Maybe then...maybe then his mother would have licked the wasting disease...

A high-pitched sound diverted his attention from the past.

Had Sarah called out to him?

But no. A hawk circled overhead, screeching after a breakfast mouse. Sarah had too much pride to call out to him—

Except to relieve her aphrodisiac-induced urgency.

That damn drug! Who knew what it would make her do?

The blanket clutched in his hand, Seb whipped around.

Shit! The headstrong miss was sprinting for the copse of trees that surrounded his newly purchased estate.

Hoping against hope she would hear him, he cupped his hands around his mouth. "Sarah, no," he yelled. "Not that way! The rain! The stream is high due to the rain."

Having grown up on the estate, Sarah had to understand the river's treachery. She must realize the terrible chance she took crossing the dilapidated bridge to the gardener's little cottage on the other side. Why go there? Unless—

She deliberately sought out jeopardy.

Did she intentionally think to place herself in harm's way?

Bloody hell!

Seb gave chase, his boots covering the muddy earth with speed born of fear, a strangled shout leaving his throat—"Sarah, no!"—as she plunged over the side of the bridge and disappeared into the bloated river.

Not waiting to see if she would resurface, Seb dropped the blanket, threw off his boots, and dove in after her, searching the churning muddy water for a trace of her.

On the fourth attempt, he spied her slender body wrapped in the bordello sheet, the linen glimmering white in the underwater darkness. Her streaming hair had caught on a submerged tree branch, the rotting debris trapping her in a watery grave.

Reaching into his pocket for the alley knife he never went anywhere without, he clicked the blade open with a flick of his thumb, thrust the knife between his teeth, and sliced through the current to reach her. A cut near her scalp freed her long hair, and he kicked for the surface, an inert Sarah in his arms.

On the muddy riverbank, he prayed. Made promises. Struck bargains. Offered up his soul to Deity and devil alike, to whichever would have it. He cared not what happened to him in the next life; he cared only about what happened to Sarah Winslow in this one.

"Breathe," he demanded, on his knees, his ear to her pale, unmoving chest.

Once before, he had done battle with death. And lost. Not this time. Not this woman. This time, he vowed he would win.

His mouth to Sarah's, Seb forced his life into her.

Three puffs later, she coughed up the river. Then, shuddering, gasped air into her lungs.

Seb picked her up in his arms. Staggering up the riverbank's deep gullies, he scooped up the discarded blanket on the fly and wrapped her, wet and shivering, in the woolen folds.

Every minute counted. Rather than head for the house, he crashed through the overgrown landscape for the gardener's cottage a few yards away. Lifting the latch, he pushed open the door and carried Sarah inside.

In advance of hiring a new groundskeeper, he'd had the leaking roof fixed, the mice trapped, and the fireplace cleaned. A veritable army of servants had scoured the single room from top to bottom, turning the humble residence into a dry, cozy, and clean private retreat, the things Sarah needed most.

He stripped her of the wet linen and placed her under the coverlet of the made-up bed.

Her chattering worsened.

Seb gathered kindling and split wood from the outdoor lean-to. Carrying an armful inside, he started a fire in the hearth. When the seasoned oak sparked and flared, he removed his own soggy clothes and climbed in with her under the covers. Holding Sarah close in his arms, Seb fell into an exhausted sleep.

Sunlight streamed through the windows, the golden ribbons tickling Sarah's closed eyes. Resisting the seduction of a brand-new day, she refused to open her lids.

All night long, in her sleep a man had whispered to her in an uncultured voice. In a garden gazebo, he had kissed her lips softly, then roughly, and she had melted into his arms. But more, so much more, than carnal attraction pulsated between them. Beneath desire hovered the possibility of love.

She rarely dreamt, but when she did, her dreams never led her astray. Their relationship, though founded on practicality, would blossom like a spring flower into something beautiful—she just knew it!

Optimism flowing through her, Sarah cracked an eye to her surroundings.

The gardener's cottage at Clearbrook.

Hmm. Who had tucked her snug as a bug in Mr. O'Sullivan's big, comfortable bed?

Brow furrowed, she tried to piece together what had happened.

And drew a blank.

The angle of the sun told her morning had just barely arrived. However, naming the day of the week proved quite beyond her grasp. How much time had gone missing from her memory? An hour? A day? A fortnight?

Another blank. A year might have passed, for all she knew.

No need to panic. Yet. First things first. She would simply take halting baby steps backward in her mind, starting with the present moment and with her present environment.

The one-room gardener's cottage sparkled. A new coat of whitewash shone on the lath and plaster walls; the pine floors gleamed; the windows were so spotless, birds flying by could spy themselves in the glass.

Sarah breathed in a hint of beeswax and lavender and soup.

Soup?

Her taste buds watered. Her belly growled. She looked to Mr. O'Sullivan's woodstove. On top perched a big black pot, from which emanated the most divine aroma.

She came upright amongst the goose-feather pillows.

And noted her attire.

Not hers, she decided. All the same, the night rail, yards too wide and feet too short, felt wonderfully clean. In fact, all of her felt wonderfully clean, as if she had just left the tub, though she had no corresponding recollection of bathing.

As she fretted over her baffling memory loss, the cottage door opened. Quietly. Obviously, her visitor did not wish her disturbed.

A man skulked across the threshold.

Now *him*, she remembered.

The obvious care he took to tread lightly—much akin to a bull in a china shop—looked so ridiculous, she smiled despite herself.

He caught her in the act. "Finally awake, I see."

Her smile wavered. Unaccustomed to receiving a visitor, particularly a male, while in a state of dishabille, she drew the freshly laundered bedding up to cover her breasts.

Squaring her shoulders, she asked the unavoidable. "Why am I here?"

A fleeting expression of *something* flashed across her owner's tanned face before he turned his back, stalked to the stove, and began stirring the delicious-smelling contents of the black pot.

After a time, he looked over at her, ladling spoon in hand. "You took a toss in the river."

The river. Of course!

"If you thought to escape, give up on the idea," he growled, like a hurting little boy. "Run, and I come after you. Escape, and I hunt you down. I paid a fortune for you, and I expect to get my money's worth."

Why, he worried after her! Fear for her safety explained why he behaved like a lion with a thorn wedged in his paw. His caring concern, couched in anger, gave her cause to hope.

She tilted her head. *Cause to hope?* For what? To what end did she hope?

Recent events left her bewildered, but she had one certainty. "I did not think to escape you."

"Crashing through the trees, trying to cross a rain-swollen river, throwing yourself against the rotted side of a bridge—was that fool stunt an attempt to take your own life?"

"Take my own life!" she said, indignantly. Life was a gift, one of the few she had ever received. Why would she throw it back, especially now, when her dreams told her she had so much to live for?

Unable to face the censure of that house or the disapproving ghosts of its former inhabitants, she had simply turned on her heel and taken off for the wooded glen that abutted the property. There, she had raced over the small footbridge that connected one riverbank to the other. Woozy, she'd tottered. At the halfway point, where rapids below churned brown and frothy, like a venison stew coming to a boil, her hip hit the planks. The old timber cracked, the wood finally splitting and letting go from the post, and she had fallen, spiraling downward into the swollen river. Before the turbulent waters had closed over her head and rushed into her lungs, her mind had revisited a kiss. A deep and passionate kiss shared with a masked man in a garden gazebo…

"I assure you, sir, ending it all never entered my mind. It was just…facing the house, garbed in only a mud-splattered sheet…the untenable realization that I would have gone to any man…all of it shamed me."

"You have done nothing to be ashamed of. What you did, the drugs made you do."

"Very chivalrous of you to say so."

"We need to get this straight, once and for all—I am not chivalrous. I bought you fair and square, and I protect my assets."

"So, you always look to protect your own ass—" She coughed. "Forgive me. I meant, of course, to say ass*ets*." She slanted her eyes mutinously away.

She had given up much, but she would harbor her romantic notions about him. The bombastic lout. The insensitive nincompoop.

The hurting little boy.

"I ran to the cottage for solace," she continued, staring at the far wall. "For asylum, if you will. This dear little place holds much of my affection. But as I raced across the bridge, the timber side gave way, and I fell in. I certainly would never have thrown myself in."

"Are you sure?"

"Of course I am sure! Deliberately tossing oneself into the drink is hardly something one is likely to forget." She shot him a grievous look. "Did I swim to shore?"

"You tell me."

He seemed to take great pride in irritating her with an almost chronic evasiveness, which made her even more determined to ferret out the truth.

"Everything is foggy," she whined pathetically, and completely artificially. "Reasoning tires me so."

"You did not swim. Now, rest."

Hooked him! Now to reel him in. "Then, how did I manage?"

"I am not quite bastardly enough to let you drown, Sarah," he said curtly. "I dove in after you."

She let his self-derogation pass. No matter how she longed to correct him, words, no matter how well-meant, always proved inadequate to the task of bolstering love of self. So, too, did the giving of empty compliments and false platitudes. She had learned the folly of that notion through her work at the orphanage. One must show people they are good, that they are worthy of love. What in Sebastian's past, she wondered, had prompted his poor regard of self?

"Well, then, you came to my rescue again," she said briskly, unsentimentally. "That is twice now. I really should thank you."

Her owner scooped some of the contents from the black pot. Putting the wooden spoon to his mouth, he took an inordinately loud slurp. At least, the slurp seemed loud to her.

"So, when do we go at *it* again?" she asked, getting practical matters out of the way. "Do you have some sort of schedule in mind? Never having worked as a courtesan before, I shall need guidance in the area of fucking."

Her owner made a small choking sound.

Something must have gone down his windpipe the wrong way. Perhaps a piece of stewed venison. Or a lovely aromatic slice of carrot. Even some pungent parsnip. Charitably, she tried not to think choking was what he deserved for eating in front of her.

"Are you all right?" she inquired.

"Fine," he sputtered. "The soup is hot."

"Speaking of which—did I have a fever?" she questioned the red-faced soup-stirrer, hoping to keep from drooling. Hoping the saliva would stay in her mouth where it belonged, rather than dribble down her chin. Hoping he would not hear her noisy stomach. Lord, nothing brought a person lower than hunger.

He looked over at her. "A fever? Why do you ask?"

She touched the uneven curls that fell onto her forehead, all that remained of her singular vanity. "I am shorn. Since this is done in sickbed, I assumed I had taken ill."

Much akin to a little boy caught doing a bad deed, he hunched his shoulders. "You did have a fever, but a fever is not why you are shorn." His mouth tensed. "I found you in the river, trapped beneath a fallen tree. By the hair. I cut you free with my knife."

She clicked her tongue. "How very thoughtless of you! My hair would have looked ever so nice on my corpse."

"Pardon?"

"Shorn hair is a small price to pay for life, sir. I am truly grateful to you."

His dark eyes squinted, as if in pain. "I am undeserving of gratitude. Anyone would have done the same, and most likely would have saved your hair, too."

Why, he actually believed his action might have angered her! He must think her a spoiled debutante, concerned more about her appearance than anything else. How did he come by these misguided opinions of her?

She would find out!

But not today.

Chapter Fifteen

Sarah pinned her owner with a look she used on the recalcitrant schoolboys at the orphanage. "You have disregarded my question, sir."

"What question?"

"About the fucking."

"Sarah, for the last three days, you have lain unconscious in that bed. You wear a bump the size of a goose egg on the back of your head. Give me some credit here. During that time, humping your bones held a low priority in my thoughts."

"Oh, too bad. I rather liked the image of you pining away after my bones." She sent a sunny smile his way. "Only teasing, sir."

His abashed expression actually cheered her. To her mind, any reaction was superior to cold indifference. She had encountered enough of that in her childhood to last through her dotage.

"No demands, not of any kind, until you have fully recovered," Mr. Turner blustered. "And for your information, I neither think of nor call what we did *fucking.*"

He turned back to his stirring. "Would you care for a bowl of soup?"

About time he asked!

"A lady should never admit to base needs. But, as I am no longer a lady, I may now freely declare that I am positively famished! Forget the bowl! Simply hand me a spoon and make way for me at the cooking pot."

She swung her legs over the side of the bed, plunked her feet on the floor, and clumsily stood upright.

A step, and she swayed. "Drat this lightheadedness!"

Mr. Turner rushed to her side. "Allow me to help you." He moved with her to a chair before the table, one muscled arm around her waist, supporting her.

Her borrowed nightgown, though huge, was made of gauzy stuff which in no way disguised the pronounced peaks of her breasts—a result of Mr. Turner's proximity. Like a ninny, she felt herself blush.

"Has your fever returned?" the silly man asked.

"No," she murmured.

"I am well acquainted with the sickroom, Sarah. No cause for embarrassment, not about anything."

"I am not embarrassed!" Far too tepid a description for her current state of humiliation. Mortified unto death—now that came closer, but still understated her wretchedness.

She quickly changed the subject. "Whom did you care for in the sickroom?"

"My mother."

She negotiated the chair, wobbling onto the seat. "You lost her?"

At his nod, she whispered, "I am so sorry for your grief. At a very young age, I too lost my dear mother. One never fully recovers from the sorrow."

After settling her at the table, he returned to the bed, picked up the quilt, and draped it modestly over her shoulders. Only to leave her again, this time to ladle soup into a crockery bowl, which he then placed before her.

Food should have held her sole attention. Unfortunately, it did not. For some reason, she stared up at Sebastian's enflamed cheek. "Your face is scratched."

"I know."

"A cat?"

His lips quirked, but he kept his silence.

"Cats prone to jealousy often spit and claw," she offered.

"This little pussy spit and clawed, all right, but not from feline jealousy. More like confusion. After setting her straight about who was the master and who the pet, she purred real loud."

She had just discomfited him. Now, turning the tables, he had returned the favor. She fingered the collar on her oversized nightie. "Was it I who scratched you?"

"Yep." He smiled. "How much of that night do you remember?"

"I know I am no longer a virgin. I know we fucked several times, but the details remain rather sketchy. My clearest recollection is of the garden gazebo. But the rest..." She shrugged. "It is as though the events of that evening happened to someone else, not to me."

Mostly, she remembered feelings. Never mistaken about feelings, she relied on them faithfully, and spoke of them not at all. Her feelings about her patron perhaps explained her present lack of fear.

She picked up her spoon. "After eating, I should like to dress."

"You arrived without a valise."

She laughed. "No matter. I have no clothes to fill one, anyway." She sipped from the spoon. "Mmm. This soup is absolutely scrumptious!" After taking another dainty sip, she gulped the rest down.

And belched. Loudly. A locomotive came to mind.

In horror, both hands flew to her mouth. "Pardon me," she whispered through her raised fingers.

"For what?" he asked.

"For my departure of manners, of course." Her chin fell. "I fear I am terribly disgraced."

"And here I took the burp as a compliment to my fine cooking."

Naught she did or said seemed to offend this man.

With a full belly came renewed energy. Replacing her spoon neatly alongside the bowl, she tottered to her feet. "Mr. O'Sullivan kept a trunk..."

She looked around the cottage. "Ah, there it is. Over by the wall."

Dragging the quilt with her, she made her way there and opened the lid. "And here are his clothes, all nicely folded. When our gardener died, I could not bring myself to part with any of his things. He was like a grandfather to me, you see. In his waning years, Mr. O'Sullivan grew quite thin. I should fit into his shirts and trousers."

In her enthusiasm, the quilt fell to the floor. Unmindful of her nearly transparent nightgown, she bent over the trunk. "There are boots here, too.

On the bottom," she called from inside the interior, her own bottom sticking ignobly up in the air.

"Sarah, I am a generous man. Whatever gee-gaws you desire are yours. Fancy gowns. Fine jewelry. Satin hair ribbons—"

"What need have I for hair ribbons, satin or otherwise, now that my hair is shorn? As to jewelry, these bracelets and anklets are fine indeed." She held out a gold-banded arm. "And, as I plan to make you a most excellent courtesan, I imagine I will spend most of my time naked. The rest of the hours, I am content enough to borrow these trousers and shirts."

"You intend to wear a dead man's clothing?"

The incredulous voice came from directly behind her. "Whyever not? I am sure Mr. O'Sullivan would not have minded. He would have said, 'Miss Sarah, gardening is dirty work, fit for good, sturdy garb. Go on, wear my shirts and trousers.'" She popped her head up out of the trunk.

And promptly lost her balance again as blood rushed back to her feet.

Mr. Turner held her against his unmistakably male body. "Careful."

Too late for that warning! His hands spanned her waist, big masculine thumbs brushed her already tight nipples and a certain unforgettable hardness poked her derriere.

"You ain't performing manual labor, Sarah."

His voice sounded hoarse, his tone coarse, his grammar of a much lower class. All thrilled her. "I quite understand. I am here for you to fuck. But you see, sir, gardening is a labor of love. I derive a great deal of long-lasting pleasure from sticking my hands in the soil. Whereas, when you stick your hands and, well, *other parts* into me—" She shrugged. "Well, the pleasure there is transitory at best."

She looked up at him guilelessly. Lest she scare him off, she could not give away her romantic hopes for the future. Better he think his attention left her unstirred. "Please, sir? I would so enjoy the outside work."

"You might fall ill."

"Nonsense! I am as healthy as a horse. Shall I take off this nightgown and prove it?"

Though trumpery, the question sounded quite authentic. Owing to her recent bout of illness, she most assuredly lacked the wherewithal to oblige him in bed. But needing to prove her worth, she sidestepped his support and made her woozy way back toward the bed-tick. Before she swooned from weakness, she reclined hastily—on her back, nightgown buttoned up to the chin, thighs tight together. "All set," she called gaily.

My, but her owner was in for a rude awakening if he thought she would give up her dreams! He had ambitions; she had ambitions, too—

Though hers came in a smaller package than his.

Essentially, they both wished to make something of themselves. She had her gardening and he had his investments. Whilst he wanted to scale society's walls, she wanted to scale the walls around one man's heart. They both longed for acceptance—he from the world, she from just one person— and conversely, they both had an independent streak.

At Michael Winslow's instruction, her governesses had raised her to obedience. But because her father had left her alone at the estate much of the time, she had also enjoyed a fair amount of personal freedom—behind the backs of her caretakers. Unthinkable, to give up her freedom now.

"Sir, allow me to garden," she wheedled. "And in return, I shall please you in any manner and way you may wish."

Joining her at bedside, her owner thumbed along her jaw. "Any manner and way I wish, eh?"

Having slept off most of her false courage, at present she found the idea of total nudity a wee bit daunting. She hardly looked or felt her best. And though wildly attracted to Mr. Turner, she felt jittery about her courtesan duties. But with too much at stake here to lose her nerve, she determinedly showed him her mettle. "Yes, allow me to garden, and you may have me in any manner and way you wish. Unless—does that present too much the challenge for you?"

"I think I can handle it."

"Such a tremendous relief."

Her bravado was all showmanship. In actuality, clammy perspiration moistened her underarms. Faint she might, but she would not back down.

His dark eyes crinkled. "Spread those long legs of yours. Raise your arms over your head."

Good Heavens! Was this caveman rhetoric the usual thing?

Sighing, she supposed it was the usual thing amongst brash men like Mr. Turner. Chest-thumping, knuckle-dragging males preferred a dominant approach in the bedroom as well as the drawing room and, for that matter, everywhere else.

Well, so much for showing him her true self—

Doing as instructed, she submissively spread her legs and raised her arms over her head.

"I have a yen to play a little game." He cocked a black brow. "You like to playact, right?"

Not *liked*. For a strong-willed woman living in a society that expected females to behave like witless chattel, playacting was a necessity.

"And you respond mighty fine to discipline," he continued.

Oh, is that why her bottom stung? Had he spanked her?

He *had* spanked her! Now she remembered. And she also recalled squealing in delight.

She demurely dropped her gaze. "Thank you, sir. One does what one can."

"I wonder—how will you take to bondage?"

"Naturally, in my research, I came upon the topic. Although, in theory, I must say bondage seems a tad silly, I am certainly not opposed to exploring various diverse personal fantasies." She licked her lips. "Leather or rope?"

"Leather and rope are for tethering heifers, not females." He removed a slender chain from his pocket. "How about we use this?"

"Gold is an extremely malleable metal. That chain is hardly strong enough to hold me against my wishes, sir. "

"Bondage is not about force, but about voluntary compliance."

Then why pursue a pointless exercise?

She was about to argue the logic of restraining a willing subject, but lost sight of the more erudite points of her debate when he attached the gold chain to her left bracelet, which he in turn clamped to the bedpost.

Perhaps bondage had its merits. After all, one should never make mock of another's inner imaginings.

Feeling herself go liquid between the legs, she handed over the other wrist.

"No, thank you," he said. "One will do for now." He stepped away from the bed.

"B-but what of my ankles? Also, you neglected to spread-eagle me. I do not feel at all vulnerable, sir." She tsked. "I really think if we are going to do bondage, we should do it correctly."

Mr. Turner headed for the door.

"Where are you going?" she called after him.

"Out."

"Out where?"

"Just out. Cover yourself up with a blanket if you get cold."

"But I thought you wished to fuck?"

"Naw," he drawled. "Not in the mood. Sit tight 'til I return, hear?"

Chapter Sixteen

As Seb let himself into the green taffeta-appointed bedchamber, the curvaceous redhead seated at the befrilled dressing table smiled into the oval mirror.

Not in all the years of their acquaintance had the generously endowed, generously natured woman smiling into the glass ever turned him away. A hunch told him the same would apply now.

Pacing the floor behind her, he said, "Molly, I need me a favor."

"You got it, sugar, whatever it is," answered the former saloon madam.

He had never doubted it—though his regular visits to Molly's bed had stopped five years before, she still always came through for him.

They had met in a dusty hellhole of a town out West, and had hit it off right from the very first lay, a sweaty carnal session that had lasted, unabated, for one full week. The round-the-clock humping had eventually petered out, but their friendship hung on just as strong as ever. At thirty-six, she remained unbelievably beautiful, both inside and out. Molly had stayed with him through thick and thin, and now more than ever, he depended on her loyalty. And her understanding.

Seb took the bull by the horns. "There's this young gal—"

"You mean the one holed up in the cottage on the river? The one who put those scratches on your face? That one?"

"Yeah." He touched his healing cheek. "That one. Keep an eye on her for me, would you?"

No questions asked, Molly nodded, her face softening. "Sure thing."

"Her name is Sarah," he began, pleasured just from saying her name. "And she's one of those prissy, know-it-all females. To avoid getting her drawers tied up in a knot, she needs a sensitive handling."

"No problem."

He rubbed the crick in his neck. "Uh...I hired her on as the new gardener."

"Seb, you want to tell tall tales, go tell 'em to somebody else. No call to bend my ear with 'em. This here is Molly, and so you can stop trying to hoodwink me. That gal ain't no ordinary gardener. She must mean something to you. Otherwise, why have me play nursemaid?"

In his book, a half-truth was better than no truth, so he confided, without going into details, "I treated her mean, and now I need to make it up to her."

Molly smoothed lotion down her throat. "Not like you, treating a woman mean." She opened her black silk wrap, and the gaping edges revealed her womanly voluptuousness as she spread the lotion over the upright slopes of her bare breasts.

"How old is this Sarah?" Molly asked, smoothing lotion over her brownish-red nipples.

"Just turned eighteen."

"Hell! The gal's a baby." Molly swiveled on the boudoir chair to look at him directly. "You only keep company with experienced women."

"I am not keeping company with her!"

"Whatever you say. That goes for anything." Molly let her wrap fall to the back of her boudoir chair. "No need to ask."

"I knew I could count on you. And matter of fact, there is something else. I need you to arrange a house party. To do business in New York, I need to make connections."

"And the right society marriage," Molly added, guessing the underlying reason for the party.

"You know me too damn well," he said wearily. "Here in the East, to get ahead, a man has to hobnob with all the right people and marry up with a well-placed wife."

His thoughts slid away from those vapid society misses he would woo, in favor of the lively and intelligent and plant-loving Sarah. "Can I trust Rattler to provide some muscle for a female while she amuses herself in the flower beds?"

Molly applied lotion to her legs, and her large breasts shifted from side to side. "Why the hell not?"

He darted her a sharp look. "Is he respectful?"

"Seb, the man is a killer for hire. The fastest draw on the trigger I know. Do you expect a gunman to shoot with his pinkie finger waving in the air?"

"Like I said, Mol', I need sensitive. I want the prissy miss protected and watched over, not frightened."

Finished spreading lotion over her supple belly, she walked nude to the armoire. "I think you should let me in on why the gal needs babysitting."

"She might have tried to take her own life." His chin scraped his chest. "She was drugged."

Molly whipped around. "Who done it? Not you—"

Bless Molly and her faith in him! Even when things looked bad, she still gave him the benefit of the doubt. "Len's housekeeper done it."

She reached inside the armoire, pulling out a chemise and corset—in all the years Seb had known her, Molly never had bothered with drawers. "She whored at the club?"

"She was the new gal, and a whole peck jumpy on account of her being a virgin and all."

Molly pulled on the chemise, her full breasts plumping out the neckline. "You bedded an eighteen-year-old virgin?"

"I told you—I done her wrong, Mol."

The redhead snapped the corset around her waist; beneath the whalebone, her bush shone like a tangle of copper wire. "Next time you need a little something, come to me."

"Ain't I here now?"

As he had done so many times before in the past, Seb sidled up behind the madam's hourglass figure and placed a hand on her womanly hip, so different from Sarah's boyishly narrow hips.

"Have at it, sugar," she said, spreading her legs.

A lump formed in Seb's throat. Mol' always did know how to make a lonesome cowpoke feel welcome. "Ain't no one like you, honey."

"Aw, shucks. If I start bawling my eyes out, you git the blame." She braced her arms against the wall. "Do me hard."

"Hard? You sure?"

"No quarter given."

Just like old times, Seb started pulling on Molly's corset lacings.

But gently. "I can still span your waist with my hands. No hard lacing for you."

"You and your sweet talk, Seb Turner." Molly chuckled, then sighed. "Rattler did a fine job protecting me and my girls at the Red Rose Saloon. No one ever got past him. He can look out for that little gal of yours, too."

Seb tied off the corset. "Sarah Winslow will be plumb flummoxed when she meets up with her new helper. Shoot! Imagine that! A lady like her and a Mexican desperado."

Molly did an about-face. Recognition moved across her features. "Ain't that the name of Clearbrook's former owner? And ain't Winslow the lizard-livered scoundrel responsible for killing your ma?"

"Yep to both. Michael Winslow was Sarah's old man."

"Well, hell and tarnation! Revenge must taste real sweet in your mouth."

"Ancient history. Over and done, and best forgot. And do me another favor and say nothing about this to Sarah." Seb dropped a kiss on Molly's cheek. "You can get back to your primping now. Not that you need it," he fired over his shoulder as he walked out the door and headed for the library.

As a lad, his Bowery accomplices had given him a shitload of grief about books. Whoever heard of a thief who loved the printed word? But his mother had taught him young to read, and the habit had stuck—even if the book he had his nose buried in had come to him dishonestly.

In no mood for reading now, Seb slumped into the burgundy leather chair behind the gleaming mahogany desk, where a bottle of celebratory whiskey awaited his enjoyment in the top drawer. Pulling it out of hiding, he poured himself a glass and swallowed it down neat. Gullet burning, he poured himself another. And another after that.

During the past eighteen years, he had often pictured himself here in Michael Winslow's big ol' library. When cold, the thought of avenging his mother's death warmed him. When hungry, getting even filled his gut. When lonely, spite kept him company. When he was all three at once—cold, hungry, and lonely—hatred for one man had kept him going. Unfortunately, hate needs something or someone to fuel it, and a corpse makes for poor fodder. So Seb had substituted the daughter for the deceased Michael Winslow. Owing to his systematic ruination of her, Sarah Winslow had nearly drowned in a muddy river—

Seb flung the empty glass into the fire. The glass shattered below the portrait of some eighteenth-century Winslow, name unknown. But whoever the hombre, for Sam-shootin'-sure, his blood ran blue.

Unlike his own thieving blood-lineage. He had stolen the house and everything in it the same way he had stolen a virgin's innocence.

To hell with gentlemanly niceties!

Seb lifted the bottle of whiskey to his mouth. He was fixing to get himself goddamned good and drunk, drunk as a skunk. Either that, or crawl back to the cottage and get into bed with Michael Winslow's daughter again.

Beautiful Sarah. Stiff-spined Sarah. Passionate Sarah. He wanted her more than he had ever wanted anything, and that included every possession in this big house. How come no portrait of beautiful Sarah graced the library wall?

He would pay to get a likeness of Sarah done. Commission an artist to do it up right. Spare no expense. And when he was an old and bitter geezer, drinking himself to death in this fancy room, he would look up into her painted face and—

Remember her falling into that raging river.

The picture branded his mind. When he'd seen her lying pale and not breathing on that muddy bank, he just knew…he just knew…

Seb swiped a hand over his eyes.

What did he know, anyway? Not a damn thing. He knew shit.

Except—this ain't how he had imagined he would feel. Definitely not how he had planned it. Revenge did not taste sweet—Molly had gotten that all wrong. Truth was, revenge had left a gaping hole inside him.

Sarah could fill it. Her sweetness would fill him right up.

Christ, what a little con artist! The gall of her trying to bribe him with her body! And what did she bribe him for? Diamonds? Rubies? Pearls?

In a pig's ass. She demanded none of the things a woman usually demands from a man for the use of her body. Hell, no! Not Sarah. She put it all on the line for the sake of getting her hands dirty.

A lady working as a gardener made about as much sense as a Bible-toting gunslinger.

The idea sure did tickle his funny-bone, though. Too bad the laugh got stuck in his throat.

The whiskey. And all this thinking. Thinkin' and drinkin'—a fool's combination. Turned a man maudlin, is what they did. Which accounted for his stinging eyeballs. Only a fool bothered with regrets. He would get himself roaring drunk and then get himself good and laid. None of this gentle lovemaking shit, either. All that had gotten him was his gut tied up in knots and his eyes turned all rheumy and his throat so damned tight not even spit would go down. Where was the good in that? Hell, who needed this? Not him!

But he did need Sarah.

Sarah. Sarah. *Sarah...*

He needed Sarah. For all her prim airs, she had driven him wild in that bordello bedchamber. He had a hankering to repeat that night. Do everything they had done together. Only without the drugs. Without the deception. He wanted them to come together as a man and a woman should come together, naked and truthful.

Truthful! What a hoot. Sarah would hate his guts if she learned the truth about him.

After sucking that first bottle of whiskey dry, Seb reached for the next in line.

Chapter Seventeen

Sarah awakened with a start, still on her back on the bed but no longer chained. When had Mr. Turner released her? Sometime late last night? Early this morning? Had he come in during one of her dreams?

She certainly hoped not!

At times, especially during periods of upset, she talked in her sleep.

Or so a governess had told her after throwing a pitcher of cold water into her face to break her of the unladylike behavior.

Last night, one doozy of a dream had made her toss and turn on the tick. No romantic, rose-colored vision this time. No virginal fantasy where the scene fades to waves lapping upon the beach. This dream had featured no-holds-barred copulation. Raw mating, in other words. Grunts and groans and wet secretions, to be precise.

Unable to resist the lusty words whispered in her ear, flooded with desire, her body betraying her, she had rounded her arms about her dream lover's neck and kissed him. Deeply. Tongue to tongue. Her abandonment total. Complete. Instinctual.

Her dream lover had roamed and stroked and coaxed her body, the foreplay making her sopping-wet ready, the gentle poetry of his rough voice touching her heart and breaking through her reticence and taking her self-consciousness along with the protective barrier. In the dark, she had screamed as one climax after another had slammed into her body.

If her dream reflected reality, she had behaved outrageously with Mr. Turner. The morning after, erotic sensations continued to besiege her.

Hotly excited, craving the weight of his body on top of hers, her hand found its way to her loins.

One finger, then another, went up inside the wet folds. Moving, rubbing, stroking. And when that incredible, amazing *something* happened, she thrashed the bedding and screamed and screamed and screamed, and kept screaming, just like in her dream. *Sebastian, yes, Sebastian, yes!*

What kind of lady would do that?

No kind of lady at all.

As luck would have it, her owner was no kind of gentleman.

Self-made, the hard way, he lacked the indulged air of those born and raised to privilege. He was everything she had never known, everything beyond the sphere of her narrow and safe existence—

And his rough physicality set her afire.

Every time he came near, and that was *every* time, her nipples peaked and she went wet between the legs, all because of the illicit danger, the wicked depravity, of him. Mr. Turner was her forbidden fruit, her immoral indulgence, her prohibited pleasure. He made her come alive, and, yes, feel cherished—

A sad commentary, indeed, as he had brought her to Clearbrook to perform the services of a prostitute.

Enjoying the performance of those services was not in her best interests. Rather than reveling in carnal enjoyment, she must concentrate on the hard realities of survival and plan for a future when her owner no longer had any further use for her.

Dragging her overheated body out of bed, Sarah made her way to the trunk. It was the start of a new day, and she needed to get dressed...to find herself. Who was Sarah Winslow now that she was no longer a lady?

Eyes glued to the dressing mirror, she surveyed her face to see if unsanctioned carnality had changed her.

The same face as always stared back at her from the glass. On the exterior, she discerned no outward difference. Though, searching deeper than the superficial, her eyes did look a bit more knowing, her mouth a little more giving, her expression slightly more aware, her attitude more accepting of her own faults and shortcomings.

She had lain with a man without benefit of matrimony, thus violating her own high standards of behavior, and the world had not crumbled. Perfect or not, life went on, and she with it.

As a courtesan, she would make her way in the world. To that end, she would need to arm herself, educate herself, *know* herself.

Sarah's glance fell to her loins, to the black pubic hair that shielded her genitals. What inside her female body sparked a man's desire? What made her hunger? And why should she know less about the inner workings of her body than a man did, than Mr. Turner, did?

Sarah reached for the hand mirror that hung on a nail beside the dressing glass. Raising her leg up onto the trunk, she opened the outer lips of her privates, placing the mirror so she might view within.

There. A man's member went there, inside that passage. That narrow channel provided pleasure...and the creation of new life. Startling, the appearance of her internal body. Wondrous, too.

With a newfound daring, she searched out that small pleasure-giving nub and purposefully appeased her dream-prompted frustration. Again. And in an expert fashion, too, if she did say so herself.

A woman's body, Sarah decided, was truly a magnificent creation. There was nothing shameful or sinful about her reproductive organs, despite what one governess had repeatedly insisted. From here on out, she intended to pleasure herself whenever she damned well felt like it!

Curiosity appeased, she returned the mirror to its nail and rushed into a shirt and breeches, finishing the last button just as the door opened without a warning knock.

"Mighty fine seeing you up and about, Sarah, honey," drawled a deep-bosomed, red-haired woman attired in austere black silk. At her side stood a tall, olive-complexioned man dressed in fringed Western attire. Both stepped inside the cottage.

Experiencing a mild return of her drugged confusion, Sarah looked to the woman first. "Do I know you?"

"Mrs. Smith, housekeeper at Clearbrook. And this here gent is Rattler."

The *gent* doffed his large-brimmed Stetson hat. "How do, ma'am?"

"Very nice to make your acquaintance, Mrs. Smith. And I do very well, thank you, Mr. Rattler, and you?"

"Just plain Rattler, ma'am. And I do me just fine." His dark eyes crinkled. "From what I hear tell, you just got yourself made the new gardener around these parts."

Mrs. Smith interjected, "Rattler and his men will help out with heavy work. He comes in right handy for other things, too."

Housekeeper and gent exchanged a look of fond regard, and then Rattler flashed a brilliant white smile. "Ain't much for flowers and such, ma'am, but I surely am willing to learn."

His lack of horticultural expertise did not surprise her. Clearly her new helper was more accustomed to cattle-drives—or whatever cowpokes did out West—than the arrangement of bedding plants. Nevertheless, Sarah found herself returning his easy smile, instantly liking this man with the musical south-of-the-border accent, who so obviously adored the curvaceous redhead at his side.

Oh, yes. Attraction strummed between Rattler and Mrs. Smith. Sarah felt it. And she always trusted her feelings. And her dreams.

* * *

Over the course of the next several days, whenever Seb rode up the front drive to the house, he would see Sarah off in the distance, dressed in a dead man's worn clothes, working in the gardens. She kept farmer's hours, toiling from dawn to dusk, tilling and weeding and cultivating the land that had once belonged to her family. Laboring in the hot sun, shoulder to shoulder with her motley crew of helpers, Sarah Winslow constantly surprised him.

Tall for a woman, though only a slip of a thing as far as he was concerned, Sarah worked like a man, performed the same backbreaking drudgery. With shorn black hair, slender body encased in trousers and shirt, she could pass for a gangly lad. But Seb had firsthand knowledge of the sweet, feminine curves her clothing hid, and his cock hardened in memory.

No how, no way, did he cotton to Sarah working so hard. Not for one goddamn minute! But the way he saw it, gardening kept her busy. And while Seb took care of business in Manhattan, Rattler, as instructed, kept a close eye on her. No faulting the gunslinger there. Still, Seb wondered who watched Rattler while the desperado watched Sarah.

Seb had himself some real serious concerns about the trustworthiness of that coyote. Sarah and the Mexican often went off alone together. For coffee, for the midday meal, for whatever the hell they did. Those two had gotten a mite too chummy for his tastes. Pathetic to admit, but he resented every minute Rattler spent with Sarah, envied them their uncomplicated camaraderie, their comfortable way of talking and laughing and sharing the day.

Never before prone to jealousy, a fit of dark suspicion dogged Seb now, driving him to obsessive vigilance. Every move Sarah made interested him. When not spying on her, he was remembering how good it had been with her. *Christ*, how he remembered! In bed, she had acted like a wanton, had held nothing back.

Two-edged sword, her lusty nature. On the one hand, Seb had reaped its benefits; on the other hand, lust often led to a roving eye.

Michael Winslow had been a no-good reprobate. And apples never do fall far from the tree. Had the father sown seeds of infidelity and deceit in his daughter?

* * *

Sarah wiped a forearm over her moist brow. Why, oh, why had dear Mr. O'Sullivan worn only heavy work shirts?

To gain relief from the oppressive heat, she opened her collar and rolled up her shirtsleeves, hoping the occasional breeze would cool her bare skin.

Bare arms and open collars—Heavens! Not at all proper.

Neither was copulating with a man for financial gain.

Not that she had done any copulation of late. If not for gardening, she would have no way to earn her keep, never mind paying off her outstanding loan. Apparently, Mr. Turner had lost interest in her already.

Behind her, Rattler cleared his throat. "Miss Sarah?"

She looked up from her thoughts. "Oh! Excuse me! What did you say?"

"I said, your nose is gittin' pink." He took a slow step toward her. "Allow me, ma'am?" He slipped a slouched-crown Stetson, a hat similar to the one he wore, atop her head. "For the sake of your complexion."

"Thank you." Sarah ran a hand along the wide brim. "I shall return it to you at day's end."

"Keep it. The hat is too small for my big ol' head anyway."

"Oh, Rattler." She took his hand. "Your generosity overwhelms me. What a dear man you are!"

"If only Miss Molly thought so, too."

"Miss Molly?"

He sighed. "That woman is the only reason I came back East."

"You are enamored of her! I thought so! And I can tell you miss the West."

"I miss the freedom, ma'am. Closed-in spaces strangulate my breath." He lowered his voice. "Miss Sarah, seeing you and me are amigos and all, I can let you in on my little secret. I aim to return to the land I love. Fixin' to buy me a small spread, a ranch just big enough for a few hundred head of cattle. I mean to bring Molly back with me. That woman is mighty homesick, too." Suddenly, a bashful look crept over his features. "But that day is in the future. Right now, the men need to break for their noonday meal."

Observing his discomfort, she dropped Rattler's hand. "My goodness! So soon? Where do the days go?"

"For me, the hours drag." He shrugged. "We meet under the oak tree, *sí?*"

She knelt. "As soon as I finish shading these tender new transplants before they perish in the heat."

Sarah had only just finished the chore when a soft footstep fell behind her. Thinking Rattler had returned to drag her away for the noontime meal, she looked up to find Mr. Turner watching her.

"Those tall plants are hollyhocks, right?" he asked.

"Yes, the single pink variety. We grew them here in the cottage garden when I was a little girl. I thought to use them as a back border."

"Good choice Are you using sweet scabious and Salvia sclarea?"

She nodded vigorously, her enthusiasm growing. "Variegated apple mint and white antirrhinums, too.

"You must follow the style of Gertrude Jekyll," he said conversationally.

She felt herself blush. "I do, yes. And like her, I much prefer a natural arrangement of plants. Formal bedding arrangements have never appealed to me."

"Nor to me. Have you read Miss Jekyll's contributions to *The Garden?*"

"No, but I long to." While pleased to discuss a subject near and dear to her heart, frankly, his interest took her aback. Since when did rough men like her owner follow horticultural trends? "The articles are difficult to find," she added, "even in New York."

"I had the back editions sent to me from England. I particularly enjoyed her essay in William Robinson's *The English Flower Garden*. If you like, I reckon I can rustle up my copy for you to read."

She clutched her heart. "*Like?* I should *love* it!"

He bowed his head. "Then, allow me to make you a gift of it."

"Quite improper, sir." She stopped, bit her lip. "Hang propriety! Thank you ever so much!"

As she knelt there on the fragrant, just-tilled earth amongst the birds and flying insects, pangs of her old childhood insecurities returned. "I-I shall do my utmost to ensure that these f-front gardens look presentable in time for your soirée."

"I see improvement already. Expect to receive compliments from all my guests, especially when I show them your plans for the conservatory. Will you make some preliminary sketches?"

"Me?" she squeaked, heart pounding. "You wish *me* to do the drawings?"

"You have my complete confidence. So much so, I hereby appoint you overseer of the conservatory construction."

"But the gardens!" she protested. "I have yet to double-dig the beds for planting—"

"Sarah, I told you, no taxing heavy work. That includes double-digging. Exhaustion courts illness. Here on out, occupy your time with less strenuous gardening chores." After a formal bow, she received an even more formal dismissal. "Expect a visit from me at week's end. Until then, I bid you good day."

Slack-jawed and disbelieving, she stared after him.

After handing her the world on a silver platter, he just walked away without a proper show of gratitude from her, as if he felt undeserving of thanks.

Chapter Eighteen

To justify Mr. Turner's faith in her, Sarah worked all Saturday morning sketching plans for the conservatory project, even going so far as to draw up an unsophisticated blueprint. Afterwards, fairly brimming with nervous energy, she decided to do her wash.

Humming under her breath, she dragged the tin tub from the lean-to next to the cottage, filled it to the halfway mark with cold water from the outside pump, and then returned to the cottage to retrieve the large black kettle she had put to boil on the woodstove. After she added steaming hot water to the cold, in went Mr. O'Sullivan's old shirts, two pairs of trousers, hose, and her overly large nightgown. Apart from what she wore on her back, her entire wardrobe now awaited the washboard.

Though a personal maid had never attended her, in its heyday Clearbrook had employed household staff, live-in servants as well as day help. A local washwoman would come in once a week on Monday to see to the laundry. When her father fell ill, she had learned the desperateness of their financial situation; whereupon she had dismissed the staff and assumed all household chores herself, including the laundering, a dreadful, thankless task.

No argument, gardening was hard work, though still a labor of love. But scrubbing clothes amounted to just plain drudgery. Her attitude explained why she had put off the despised chore as long as possible.

Sarah sniffed an underarm. Nose wrinkled, she surveyed her breeches.

Both would benefit from a good soaking. Should she add them to the tub?

She had always covered every inch of skin with high-necked collars and long sleeves and hems that never showed even a glimpse of ankle. Her gowns, made of practical goods like twill and worsted and serge, never clung to her figure and always scratched her skin. With her hair pulled straight back from her forehead, nary a curl allowed to escape and braided into a tight chignon at the back of her skull, she had resembled a middle-aged spinster. Now, of course, her short hair fell free in a wild riot of ringlets that she could, and did, comb with her fingers. Under her loose shirts and tight breeches she wore nothing at all.

Woods abutted the cottage on one side, the river on the other. No one would see her strip off the trousers. The huge shirt would more than adequately cover her—

Oh, bosh! Whyever not?

With a laugh at her adventurousness, she stripped off the mud-caked breeches and dropped them into the tub. Liking the way the sun felt on the bare skin of her legs, liking the way a mild breeze stirred her loose, curly hair, liking the naturalness of going about almost, but not quite, naked outside, Sarah stirred the brew in the tin tub with a sturdy stick. Once wet, she scrubbed each item with a hard lump of yellow soap, her hands flexing up and down the washboard. After rinsing and wringing, she spread the individual pieces out to dry on a rope strung between two saplings. That done, she headed for the vegetable patch.

After weeding the lettuce, she would return to the cottage for the bed linens. They needed a good scrubbing, too.

When it came to eroticism, Seb figured he had done it all or seen it all done. And that meant everything. He'd come of age in the Bowery, where male and female prostitution thrived out in the open, day and night. Add to that his silent partnership in a private club that catered to every taste, perverted and otherwise, and nothing shocked him any more.

That is, until he happened upon Sarah outside, laundering clothes while wearing only a dead geezer's shirt.

Shocked, Seb reined in his black stallion behind a grove of evergreens.

"Shh. A whinny will give me away, boy," he whispered, stroking his mount's neck, his eyes stroking the nubile temptress as she scrubbed away at a washboard.

What was it about Sarah that had him adjusting his seat in the saddle to accommodate a hard-on to end all hard-ons? What was it about her that made his balls hurt like the very devil? Her pert breasts, maybe, that gently bobbed under a dead man's shirt? Or her adorable ass, which almost peeked out at him as she bent over the tub. Dang! Why did the tails on that shirt have to be so goldarn long, anyway?

Just when Seb thought he could stand no more, Sarah left her scrubbing to weed. As she bent over to cultivate the low plants, her rump pointed skyward. *Mercy!* It was either relieve his tension or allow his tension to erupt all on its own—a messy consequence, and one he had not experienced since he was a green lad of thirteen.

Far better to anticipate his man's weakness than to clean up after it, he decided, unbuttoning his breeches, taking out his ten inches of misery, and jerking his fist up and down the rock-hard length.

As Sarah stretched over a row of lettuce seedlings, Seb whipped his silk handkerchief out of his coat pocket.

Any number of whores would perform this service for him. Generous with his purse and, for the most part, circumspect in his requirements, he seldom even had to ask. But not just any woman would do. Only one.

Only Sarah. Only Sarah would do.

His fist worked out a rhythm. Watching Sarah pull weeds, watching her toss weeds. Watching. Watching. Watching the wholesome Sarah perform her wholesome gardening tasks with her butt up in the air, waving it like a red bandana at a lovesick bull. Always watching Sarah.

Almost there…almost…almost…there. Just a few more beats.

When Sarah stood up and wiped her soiled hands on the back of the shirt, unknowingly rucking it up in back and thus exposing the rounded curves of her shapely buttocks, he grunted and came into the waiting handkerchief.

Sarah headed for the little cottage, fine ass wiggling, and Seb cleaned himself off, still watching her.

He had watched Sarah take Rattler's hand, watched his foreman give her a hat, watched them smile at one another. That was his smile she had given away.

Her smile belonged to him. Only to him. 'Bout time she understood *she* belonged only to him, too.

A knock sounded at the cottage door.

"Who is there?" Sarah called.

"Sebastian Turner."

Sarah hesitated; she wore only a shirt. If she answered the door, her visitor would think her a slovenly slattern just rolled out of bed at midday. Surely, she would lose his good opinion then.

She flattened her palm against the oak planks. *Sebastian, stay! Please stay.*

Hang her pride! "Just a moment," she called nonchalantly, as if her heart would still beat if he left.

Her tenderness for the owner of her note left her open to pain. She so looked forward to seeing him, missed him terribly when he failed to walk through the gardens on his way to somewhere else.

She had never clung like a vine to anyone. All too aware of the transitory nature of life, of the fickleness of human nature, from an early age she had understood that people left her with startling rapidity. And it seemed that those she cared about the most left her the swiftest. Her mother. The O'Sullivans. Governesses hung on for a time, but they too left eventually, some with annual regularity. As for her father—he seemed to leave more often than ever he returned.

This attachment for Sebastian was both foolish and foolhardy, and yet she nourished the idea that perhaps this one time, he would be the one to stay.

All gardeners hoped, or why would they bother to plant a seed?

But as a gardener, she based her hope on reality and practicality. Cold weather defeats some perennials. Only the toughest and hardiest of plants will leave dormancy behind and bloom again come spring. The wise gardener uses those as the backbone of the garden and then mulches the plants well against the likelihood of a harsh winter.

In much the same way, Sarah intended to protect her heart. She would avoid the plague of cynicism and retain her essential belief in love...whilst doing her utmost to assure her own survival. The key was to remain hopeful, despite the odds, and tough regardless of what happened!

"Be right with you," she called through the door and looked around frantically for something, anything, to cover her naked legs.

The bed linens!

With the top sheet wrapped around her waist, she rushed to open the door. "Please come in."

Sebastian grinned at her. "Another bedding ensemble, I presume?"

She could not avoid the comparison. In his dark coat and trousers, her surprise visitor looked the epitome of a well-to-do gentleman; in her makeshift apparel, she looked the epitome of a down-on-her-fortune strumpet.

Sarah shuffled the linen higher, aware, so very aware as she tightened the makeshift skirt at the waist, how her breasts had peaked under the severely tailored shirt. Would he notice their excited state now that she had loosened the voluminous shirt?

"As it so happens, today is my washday," she gaily confided, allowing none of her embarrassment to show. "To have done with it, I decided to launder everything in one fell swoop. Apart from what you see, everything went into the tub."

He lifted and examined her red-roughened hand. "I employ a washwoman. Use her. Mrs. Smith can advise you of her schedule. I will not countenance your getting chilblains."

"In the summer?" She tsked at his needless concern, then told him the heart of her concern—not needless at all. "A servant does not make use of the household staff, sir."

"You are not my servant!"

Her chin dipped. "And neither am I a proper part of your household. Holding the position of gardener on your staff allows me to maintain the illusion of respectability."

He raked a tanned hand through his neatly groomed dark hair. "I admire your abilities, Sarah, but there are easier ways for a beautiful woman to make her way in the world."

She knew what he alluded to—he had finally come to collect what she owed. His less-than-direct approach affronted her intelligence whilst part of her dearly wished to believe his outrageous compliment.

She had received so few compliments, and none of them as extravagant as his praise. Difficult not to preen...

Her susceptibility to him must remain her secret. In toughness lay the key to survival!

She laughed. "Indeed, I am not beautiful. No reason for you to call me so."

He slid his palm up her arm to her shoulder. "Sarah—"

The warmth of his hand heated her through the shirt. His closeness caused her breasts to swell. Her nipples jutted at his rough voice—

A voice, she now realized, that also contained a soft note.

Was nothing ever clear-cut in life? Black and white? Must everything be open to interpretation? Subject to ambiguousness?

She had always thought of herself as a straight and narrow sort of person. Focused. Entirely moralistic. Now look at her! A wreck of indecisiveness, seeing more than one side to every issue.

Mr. Turner. He had opened her eyes to more than one viewpoint. Painful, to say the least, to let go of her self-satisfied superiority. Oh, not toward people—she had never behaved snobbishly toward people—at least not knowingly. But she pled guilty to snobbishness regarding societal mores. She had always firmly ascribed to the notion that there was a right way and a wrong way of doing things. And yes, she supposed she had always considered her way correct. But people who lived in glass houses should not take up stone-throwing as a hobby.

She had gone to bed with a man, without the benefit of marriage, and she craved doing so again—and not out of any sense of debt. Her note only served as an excuse to assuage her conscience, and a welcome excuse at that, as the obligation relieved her from all responsibility in terms of owning her own sensuality.

A mature woman accepts the responsibility for her own desires, and she was determined to do so, but how would she steel herself against the terrible emotional ambivalence she felt toward this man? And how would she ever take him into her body, give and accept physical intimacy, and yet keep her feelings apart from it?

She would start by schooling herself against any outward sign of vulnerability. She would hide, as she had always hidden, her true feelings, her true motivations…messy emotions. She would stitch her façade in place with the tiniest of stitches so that the seam would go undetected. Sentimentality would only hurt both of them in the end.

"I took you for an honest man," she began. "And we have an honest agreement. There is no reason at all for you to expend any unnecessary time on seducing me, no reason to call me beautiful. I owe you a large sum, and I am prepared to honor my debt. Now, would you like me to remove my bed linen skirt and my...er, that is to say...Mr. O'Sullivan's shirt?"

"Another time, perhaps," he said stiffly. "Today, I am here to go over the plans for the conservatory with you."

At his rejection, she flushed with embarrassment. See! He felt nothing of what she felt! Not the horrible lust, not the uncomfortable frustration when that horrible lust went unsatisfied. She had all she could do not to drag him to the bed and have her way with him.

God help her, but her nipples hurt so! The place between her legs wept. And her heart? He seared her heart. So many conflicting emotions warred within her, whilst he appeared not at all overwhelmed or conflicted or swept away. Unlike her, he suffered no sense of urgency; she served only as a take-it-or-leave-it convenience to him.

Today, he had decided to eschew her. Again!

"The plans for the conservatory. But of course," she said, straining the words out between clenched teeth. "Please take a seat at the table, sir, so that we might begin."

* * *

Sarah stretched. Ah, morning! Her favorite time of day. When the sun first came up and the day spread out before her like an empty garden bed waiting for plants, the possibilities seemed endless.

Especially so this morning. In less than a quarter-hour's time, she had an appointment to see Sebastian, up at the house, in her official capacity as his estate gardener!

After selling off Clearbrook, she had never thought to set foot inside the house again. And so, with some trepidation, even misgiving, she stood in the servants' entrance below stairs, waiting to see him.

Wishing to look nice for this, her very first business meeting, she had used a flatiron to press out the wrinkles from her shirt and breeches. She had also trimmed her hair to even out the raggedy ends.

No matter how long she dawdled over her toilette, the looking-glass told her the truth. With all the gardening, her body had grown increasingly muscled. Legs. Arms. Back. Even her bottom. Her small breasts looked smaller. Her hips had narrowed. The little feminine appeal she had once possessed had disappeared.

The appealingly feminine Molly Smith entered the servants' kitchen, the severity of the housekeeper's black gown only highlighting her voluptuousness. "Sarah, honey! How nice to see you," she drawled, just like Sebastian—when he forgot to pay attention to his speech.

"I have an appointment with Mr. Turner. To discuss the new conservatory." She stressed the last, so as not to give the wrong idea about the purpose of her visit. Household staff gossiped...

The housekeeper led the way up the front stairs to the library. When Sarah's father had not been in residence, which was to say all of the time, she would often visit the books, curling up in a big leather chair after making her selection from the shelves.

The big leather chair still claimed the same spot. In fact, the room looked exactly the same now as during her tenancy. The same paintings of long-forgotten Winslow ancestors hung on the walls; the same furnishings adorned the interior—Jacobean chairs, marble-topped tables, fiddle-back maple desk, glazed light fixtures, imported Chinese carpet—Mr. Turner had returned all to their rightful places. How odd, to purchase all the auctioned furnishings intact, rather than decorate in a style and taste of his own.

Mrs. Smith swept back into the room. "Sorry, honey. Seb left unexpectedly for the city and is not expected back until the early part of next week. You will speak with the architect, Mr. Connors, who is due to arrive shortly."

So silly to feel abandoned! And yet, inside her neatly pressed shirt, her shoulders slumped.

* * *

The heel of her boot pressed to the shovel, Sarah double-dug manure into a too-long-neglected flowerbed.

"Thinkin' 'bout askin' Molly to marry me," Rattler threw out for discussion.

"Do it," she promptly replied. "You two belong together. More importantly, you love her."

"And that's a fact." Rattler tilted his Stetson back on his forehead, his rangy body relaxed over the spade fork. "If she agrees, we'll leave right soon."

Letting her shovel drop to the ground, Sarah wrapped both arms around her friend. "I am so, *so* very happy for you and so, *so* very sad for me. But I understand why you need to leave."

"No offence, but hospitality out East is dern scarce. My aim is to git the Sam Hill of New York. Molly is lookin' peaked. Not that she complains none—that woman never complains 'bout nothin'." Rattler's chest puffed out. "I bought that spread I was tellin' you about. So, why wait? This is no place for us, and nothin' is keepin' us here."

"How incredibly romantic!"

"Somethin' told me you would say that when I 'fessed up the news. Now, no tellin' the boss. Not just yet. Molly will break the news to Seb. Those two were real close once."

"Mr. Turner and Mrs. Smith?" Amazed at the disclosure, Sarah stepped back from Rattler.

"Long time ago. But Molly's still got some lingerin' feelin's. Startin' a family should help her git over 'em. Mol's always had a hankerin' for babies. Givin' her a ranch-full would make me right happy."

"You have my word. The boss will hear none of this from me." She poked Rattler in the chest. "After you pop the question, mosey on over and tell me how it went, hear?"

He hooted good-naturedly at her drawl. "Regardless of the day or hour, I promise to fill you in on all those pesky details you ladies are so fond of knowin'. 'Tweren't for you, no tellin' if I ever would have worked up the gumption to phrase the question."

Leaning down and in, he kissed her cheek. "Reckon we should get back to work makin' this here garden purdy for the boss's fancy shindig."

Chapter Nineteen

Sarah dug her heels into the branch. Her chin shelved in her hand, she sighed at the romance of it all.

My, my ,my. What a perfectly splendid evening for a garden party! Or "fancy shindig," as Rattler liked to call the festivities. After a day of off-again, on-again showers, the night had turned out warm and French-lilac-scented.

She pinched her nostrils together. Unfortunately, the perfume of the late-blooming purple blossoms always made her nose itchy. Not a tragedy, to be sure—

Unless one is precariously dangling from an apple tree and a sneeze might send one plummeting.

Sarah gazed down from her lofty perch. The ground did seem awfully far away. Perhaps she should climb down—

Itchy nose be damned! The apple tree afforded the best possible view inside the ballroom. Not while an outside chance of catching a glimpse of Mr. Turner remained would she descend. Regardless of a propensity for sneezing, she would stay, huddled on her hopefully sturdy apple branch, her lamentably bony knees bent to her pathetically flat chest, her sunburned nose poking out from between the leaves, sniffing due to the wine-colored blossoms on the lilac bush below.

Whilst swallowing a dry, scratchy tickle in her throat, the realization suddenly struck her that, perhaps, even an outside chance of catching a glimpse of her owner would prove overly optimistic.

Through the open windows, she *heard* the dull sound of a slight wooden tap, but could not actually *see* the conductor cue the orchestra with his baton. Nor could she see anyone else.

Perhaps if she roosted higher up in the tree—a few feet should do it—she might then see the dancers, one dashing dancer in particular.

Casting caution to the winds, Sarah shimmied higher, one hand over the other, drawing herself upwards in pursuit of a better peek, tree branches cracking under her weight as she went.

Wretched clumsiness made a spectator out of her, but watching others glide gracefully across the floor filled her with delight. To her recollection, her father had never employed the ballroom at Clearbrook for its intended purpose. Mr. Turner had poured a fortune into renovation work on the dilapidated estate.

Immodest to boast, but the gardens had never looked better. And the conservatory! When finished, the glass walls would shine like a multi-faceted jewel. Mr. Turner had given her carte blanche on its design...and a full purse to order whatever plants she liked. Heady experience, that.

Armed with Mr. Turner's faith in her, she had gone full out, sending for orchids of many different varieties, as well as many other exotics, all the way from the jungles of South America. She could hardly wait to give him the grand tour!

If ever he conceded her the opportunity.

He spent most of his time in Manhattan. When he did come home—seldom, and never spending the night—he purposefully avoided her.

On the higher branch, chin cupped in hand once more, Sarah settled in for a nice long snoop. Perhaps she would steal that glance of her patron after all, laughing and dancing and having a grand time with his guests, not thinking about her at all. The swine!

And surer than sin, a smiling Mr. Turner appeared on the dance floor, twirling Miss Eleanor Cabot in his arms.

They made for a handsome couple. Eleanor as fair as Mr. Turner was dark, as curvy as he was muscular. No doubt about it, her erstwhile friend plumped out in all the right places; eating chocolate bonbons whilst gossiping adding immeasurably to both to her popularity and her round derrière.

Sour grapes?

Indeed. Pampered and elegant and shapely, with her mass of golden hair regally swept atop her head and decorated with sparkling amethysts, Eleanor peeved her no end.

Sarah twirled the ends of her short black hair between two grubby fingers. No wonder a self-satisfied grin split Mr. Turner's face. Big jugs, big bottom, and big blond hair—Eleanor was a man's dream.

Always a glutton for punishment, Sarah pressed her nose to the window to get a better look at the dancing couple—

And sneezed.

Clearbrook's grand ballroom swelled with overdressed society guests, and the banquet tables groaned under their burden of rich food. Thankfully, the parquet floor carried the weight of all the full-blown pretension without collapsing.

Seb covered his mouth to prevent his yawn from escaping.

After hours of mingling with his guests—mingling consisting of bowing and nodding and smiling, as well as the all-important back clapping, palm pressing, and conceit stroking—he had all he could do to stay awake.

Tight-assed Easterners knew shit about having themselves a good time. They talked and talked, and said nothing. Conversations centered on the weather, fashions, money, and each other—not necessarily in that order. If an endless round of these affairs was all he had to look forward to, then he had nothing much to look forward to.

When the orchestra broke for an intermission, Seb loosened his tie and headed for the veranda. Maybe smoking a cheroot outside would keep him awake—

Mrs. Vandermire caught him on the way out the door. "There you are, Mr. Turner! May I present my youngest child, Penelope?" The marriage-minded mama gave her pinched-face daughter an unsubtle push forward.

Blue lips stretched into a thin smile, the whey-faced gal bobbed a pretty curtsey at him.

Seb bowed in return. "How do you do, Miss Vandermire?"

Since he had thrown the party to scout the market for a lady-bride, holding up his end of the deal, he struck up a conversation. "Are you having an enjoyable time this evening, Miss Vandermire?"

Pale Penelope shivered her one-word reply. "Yes."

If the little virgin trembled at a question, what the Christ would she do when she got an eyeful of his cock?

Taking pity on her, Seb crossed Miss Vandermire off his bridal-candidate list.

"Well—uh—if you will excuse me?" Turning on his heel, Seb got the hell out of there before timid Penelope wet her drawers, and not in the way he preferred.

Within inches of his escape, the orchestra filed back in for their next set.

Shit! No time for that sneaked cheroot out on the veranda now.

Doing his duty to his future progeny, Seb went in search of his next waltz partner.

After an exchange of introductory bobbing up and down, Miss Eleanor Cabot asked, "Do you believe rain is at all likely tonight?"

Seb swallowed another yawn. "The sky looks clear to me."

"You ease my mind. Mr. Worth created this gown, you know, and comparatively speaking, its expense far exceeds that which the other ladies wear. Even a few drops of moisture would spoil the kick flounce—"

Achoo!

Seb only heard one sneeze. At first. And then, from out of nowhere, they attacked, one loud expulsion ripping after another, so many *achoos* that they interrupted Miss Cabot's fashion narrative.

Looking for an excuse, *any* excuse, Seb broke off the dance. "Sounds like a wild animal out there. Excuse me while I go investigate."

"Really, Mr. Turner! It never is! I spied a scruffy lad there earlier."

"Scruffy lad?"

She nodded. "Most likely an orphan from town—the ugly shirt gave his affiliation away. He peeped in at us through the open window while we danced. That is the miscreant sneezing now."

Ugly shirt...?

The description fit Sarah.

"All the same, Miss Cabot," he began, "for your protection, I must take a look. On the way to your carriage, a fox might very well accost you. Or a..."

Seb did some fast thinking. "Or a...skunk," he improvised. "Think of what an odiferous encounter with a skunk might do to your gown."

Though she cringed at the prospect of a sprayed Worth, Miss Cabot nevertheless continued to cling to his arm. Unable to extricate himself, Seb dragged Eleanor after him, ball and chain—

Until a loud *crack* outside set his heart to thumping.

Cutting loose from the shackle, he raced for the door.

Sarah! Had something happened to Sarah?

Sprawled on the ground, wiping her runny nose on her sleeve—the shirt needed a good scrubbing anyway—Sarah looked up into the dark eyes of Mr. Turner.

Regardless of his formal attire, he knelt in the dirt beside her. "Do you hurt anywhere?"

A suitable answer had just sprung to mind—a reply that would encompass both her loins and her heart—when Miss Eleanor Cabot rounded the corner and screeched for all to hear, "Euuwwe! *Dis*-gusting! The peeping Tom is blowing his nose on his shirt!"

"I am not *blowing!*" Sarah corrected from her prone position. "I merely dabbed at the secretions."

With a loud sniff, she inhaled said secretions.

"Lilacs," she croaked somewhat nasally, although drawing herself upright had cleared her sinuses considerably. "I dearly love the blossoms, but do naught but sneeze whenever they are nearby."

A pristine square of smoky blue silk floated into her lap.

"Blow," the handkerchief's owner said.

"Oh, so unseemly! I could *not* possibly."

"Force yourself."

Sebastian's acerbic tone prompted her to blow with gusto.

Unfortunately, not quite loud enough to drown out Eleanor's plaintive squeal. "Sarah Winslow! Is that really *you?*"

"None other." Sarah stuffed the soiled hanky into the back pocket of her filthy trousers. "Mr. Turner, I shall return your handkerchief after giving it a good washing." She scowled up at him.

The worst cutthroat in all the parish had caught her at her unladylike worst. By the morrow, everyone from far and wide would know how far and wide she had fallen, and not just from the apple tree.

"But Sarah, dear, whatever possessed you to climb a tree and peer in a window at us?"

Eleanor turned the golden halo of her head to Sebastian, who answered without pause, "Sarah is my gardener. I asked her to inspect all trees and bushes for blight. Tonight was the lilac's turn."

"The apple tree," Sarah corrected.

He raised a devilishly dark brow. "Pardon?"

"I was ensconced in the apple tree, not the lilac bush. I fell into the latter on my descent."

Sebastian's dark brown eyes danced. "Ah, I see. The latter. I gather the latter required a hard pruning?"

She replied evenly, "Lots of dead wood on the estate."

And one facile liar. Sebastian, just like the boys in her charge at the orphanage, could tell untruths without blinking an eye—a talent of a desperately hurting heart.

The owner of the hurting heart gave a jaunty bow. "Well, thank you for taking care of the problem."

"Inspecting trees in the dark? And where, pray tell, is your pruning device?" Eleanor asked, belaboring a point that served no purpose save one.

"I dropped it," Sarah said, refusing to own her former friend's attempt at humiliation.

"Too humorous, really," Eleanor continued. "Imagine you, Sarah, dear, the gardener, when you once served as the lady of this very estate." She looked down her nose at Sarah on the ground. "Well, I must say the occupation suits. Is that your Eau de Manure I detect?"

"Sir, I am so deeply sorry for the inconvenience I have caused you this evening, taking you away from your guests, causing a scene," Sarah said, 'fessing up to her misdeeds. "In truth, the music drew me and I did look in the window at your party. But only for a few minutes." She crossed her fingers behind her back.

"Allow me to help you up." Her owner extended her his large hand.

She shook her head. "Nothing of the sort. You look so nice. Dashing, really. And look at me—filthy. You mustn't touch me."

"Sarah," he said sternly, "You will stop this silliness at once and give me your hand."

No choice but to do so, she grabbed his palm, but only for as long as it took to stumble to her feet. "Thank you."

"Any the worse for wear?" he inquired, as though falling from the limb of an apple tree whilst in the act of spying was a perfectly natural occurrence.

She brushed herself off. "It was a relatively soft landing, all things considered."

"Glad to hear it. To avoid further accidents, come watch the dancing from the safety of the ballroom's ground level."

"Mr. Turner! Whatever are you thinking? A gardener joining the guests?" Eleanor shook her blond head. "Inappropriate, to say the very least."

For some odd reason, her owner looked up at the sky. "Storm clouds moving in. Allow me to escort you back inside, Miss Cabot, before your kick flounce gets drenched in the rain."

Chapter Twenty

After giving Miss Cabot over to the care and protection of her doting mama, Seb headed for the door once more. "If you need me, Mol', look in the gardens."

His housekeeper glanced up from replenishing the hors d'oeuvres. "Hold on one cotton-picking minute! You just got back in!"

Seb stopped midstride. "So?"

Molly's hands went to her rounded hips. "What will your guests think if you go hightailing back out again after just gettin' back in?"

"What do I care what my guests think? Sarah is outside, upset. I belong there, not here."

"What happened?"

Seb grinned in memory. "Miss Cabot found my adorable gardener flat on her cute ass, wiping snot with her shirtsleeve after a sneezing fit sent her falling out of an apple tree where she had decided to play voyeur."

The former madam of a Western bawdyhouse whooped out a belly laugh. "You know somethin', Seb? I like that gal."

"Me, too," he admitted, though uneasily.

"Say what you will about the spineless snake who sired her, Sarah's got gumption. But that Cabot woman! Jumping-jacks! What kennel raised her?"

Mol' plunked a teeny-tiny sandwich on a plate. "Bitch," she said under her breath, but not so low under her breath that Seb had to strain his ears to hear. "Rattler thinks highly of Sarah, too. And his word is solid gold. Knowing one of your uppity guests hurt Sarah's feelings makes me see red. Punch red."

His housekeeper poured a glass of red punch to the rim. "Me being upset and all, no telling where this here drink ends up."

Molly always did have a temper to match her fiery hair, and Seb knew enough not to stand in her way when a bee flew up her petticoats. "Have to, honey, and with my blessings. Aim for the kick flounce, and tell Miss Cabot to send the bill for a new Worth creation directly to me."

Seb found Sarah outside arranging a bouquet of cut flowers.

His big hands burrowed deep into his pockets. Arranging flowers for her childhood home had to cost her a heap of pride, and his admiration for Sarah Winslow soared. "Looks right nice."

"Thank you," she said solemnly.

"A mite stifling inside." At Sarah's confused blink, he added, "I needed a breath of fresh air. Out West, folks really know how to shake loose and have a good time. The whole town turns out for a social event, no invite needed. Down to the schoolmarm, everyone kicks up their heels, hootin' and hollerin' and raisin' hell."

Seb ran a finger around inside his tight, starched collar. "A mite confining here in the East. The clothes. The overheated drawing rooms. The stuffy manners. Hard to get used to all the bowing and scraping a man has to do to get ahead."

Sarah stared at him in a concentrating way. "Rattler tells me stories about the West. He misses the wide-open spaces."

"The land can be rough and uncivilized, too."

"And you love it."

"I guess."

She sighed. "The West sounds like a good place for new beginnings."

"I never thought about it that way, but you have a point. The West is the last place in this country a man can make something of himself, on his own merits."

"Someday, I should like to go there and see those wide-open spaces for myself."

"Empty land that stretches as far as the eye can see. And the cleanest, freshest, sweetest air to breathe. Here in New York, ain't no escaping the stink of the tanneries. No seeing the sky for the tenements."

"My goodness! You hate it here! Whyever did you come back East?"

"Some loose ends in my life needed tying up." He looked away.

"Ah, someone done you wrong and you needed to *git* even," she drawled.

"Yeah. Something like that."

"Tell me, did you accomplish what you set out to do?"

Sweat broke out on his forehead. "Matter of fact, I did. The score is settled."

"And yet—you seem unhappy. Sir, revenge has a way of turning around and biting the avenger on the backside."

Seb loosened his starched collar. It felt like the hangman had just knotted a noose around his Adam's apple and pulled the cord. "And I suppose you speak from personal experience?"

"I lived quietly here on this estate. Certainly, I never attended a party as lavish as the one you host here this evening. But I am acquainted with all of your guests, having attended church socials and charity teas with many of them. Some, I even considered my friends. Yet, when my father fell into disgrace, I never heard from them again. When he sickened and died, not one offered their respects. I passed my childhood in seclusion, yet never did I feel as alone as during that year of solitary mourning. I have experienced moments of anger. Self-pitying moments when I have wished to scream and shout and rail against my fate, to retaliate in kind."

"What prevented you?"

"My temper tantrum would have served no useful purpose." She tilted her head. "And there are compensations in a loss of respectability. For the first time, I am free of societal restrictions. Living out West must feel much the same."

It did. Exactly. Funny, how she understood.

When the orchestra struck up another number, Seb gave a formal bow. "Would you do me the honor of this dance?"

Sarah swallowed repeatedly, and the long column of her throat, exposed in the open collar of the huge shirt, tightened. "Even after years of dance instruction, I am only passable at the waltz," she confided. "Compare me to a stiff board, and I would come out the loser. I have it on good authority that my social accomplishments are just about nil."

Who had told her so? Who had stolen her self-confidence?

Her father, Seb decided, answering his own unspoken question. Michael Winslow, an all-around swine.

"Dancing is a lot like lovemaking," he said conspiratorially. "Practice makes perfect."

"I fear you are a bit of a rogue, sir."

"You see right through me, Miss Sarah." He held out his hands.

Pleating her rough twill trousers with her fingers, as she would a fine silk ball gown, she executed an elegant curtsey. "I have forewarned you, sir. Do not blame me for stomping all over your shiny shoes." She walked into his arms.

He laced her callused fingers with his slick thief's hands. "These here shiny shoes pinch my toes. As soon as everyone leaves, my boots get pulled back on."

Sarah felt so damn good in his arms. So right. She matched him in every way that counted. In that gaudy bedchamber on Park Avenue, their man-woman passion had smoldered. He had to have her in his life. Naturally, marriage was out of the question, but an arrangement based on mutual attraction and reciprocated benefit would serve them both equally. He would act as Sarah's protector, she his mistress. The relationship would satisfy his needs and award her financial independence, a fair and square deal.

Now to convince her of the same.

As they waltzed in time to the music drifting out the open window, Seb breathed in the clean soap smell of Sarah's hair. No cloying perfume for the lady in his arms. Her womanly scent served as her only fragrance—

And it was all the fragrance she could afford. Guilt. Guilt Guilt.

Because of him, Sarah did without a bottle of scent. She only needed a protector because he had destroyed her chance of making an advantageous marriage. By orchestrating her father's financial downfall, which, in turn, had ruined the Winslow name, he had forced her to sell everything to pay off some of her father's debts. The loan Len had extended to cover the rest of the debt had come with strings attached. When she'd been given the opportunity to do the work she loved, to design gardens, he'd made sure she lost those opportunities, thereby eliminating her one avenue for respectable employment. After duping her, he had taken the drugged virgin's maidenhead. He might just as well have pushed her from that bridge—

He had come damnably close to losing Sarah in that river. That she'd survived the fall and the rushing current seemed nothing short of a miracle, almost as though the grace of a Higher Authority had interceded and saved her and given him a second chance.

Seb shook his head. Grace? Second chances? Divine intervention?

Bullshit! Seb's faith in the power of good had died with his mother. And the Bowery had taught him that second chances and miracles only existed in the Bible.

And yet he wanted to believe.

Seb looked down into Sarah's face. He could not lose her! She looked rosy-cheeked and healthy, but he knew firsthand that life is damnably fragile, that outward appearances mean nothing at all. Despite an impression of stamina, Sarah was too thin. Her hideous dead-man's shirt hung on her slender frame; her trousers revealed the narrow hips and coltishly long legs of a female who had yet to reach full maturity.

Barely a woman, certainly not a light-skirt, and he had used her like a whore. He had stolen much from Sarah—her home, her virginity, a carefree youth—and now he sought more.

"Lilacs," he said, recanting his earlier observation that Sarah wore no perfume. "You smell of lilacs."

She giggled. "From the bush next to the apple tree. A sprig broke off when I landed. Regardless that lilacs make me sneeze, I placed the blossom in my back pocket. Too lovely to discard!"

Out of the blue, she started to cry those silent tears of hers. "Climbing trees! Peeping in windows! Blowing my nose on my shirtsleeve! Whatever must you think of me?"

He lifted her into his arms. "Scream, Sarah. Let it out. No need to shut it all inside like this."

She obstinately shook her head. "Put me down! Granted, I behaved like an infant, but I am not a child."

Ignoring her ladylike protests, Seb carried Sarah to a nearby bench. Taking a seat, he lowered her onto his legs.

She cuddled in his lap. With a sigh, he stroked her shorn hair, savoring the texture of black silk gliding through his fingers. He had never known someone so in need of comforting and who fought that comfort so much.

After a while, he lifted her pointed chin up onto the crook of a finger. "This is about more than wiping sno—er…boogers on your sleeve in front of Miss Cabot. Tell me what caused your upset."

"Far too scandalous," she demurred.

"I can handle scandal."

She sniffed. "No, I really think I should go. Right now." She pulled away.

His arms clamped around her waist, holding her tight. "Too late to return to the cottage alone." He showed her his timepiece. "See? Almost midnight. You, my little tree climber, need an escort home. That responsibility falls to me. But first, tell me what has you all bothered."

As she fought the disclosure, her face took on a vast range of nuances, her expression changing from resistance to capitulation to wistfulness. "Sometimes…I think I have spent a lifetime wearing a mask. The only time I have shown my true face is with you." That said, Sarah jumped down from his lap and ran off into the night.

Seb let her go. Unlike her brave confession, the darkness that had always surrounded him swallowed up his baring of the soul. "Me, too, Sarah," he confessed. "Me too."

Chapter Twenty-One

After another week-long business trip to the city, Seb galloped up the tree-lined lane to Clearbrook, anxious to see Sarah again. Unfortunately, upon spying an all-too-familiar buckboard tied to the hitching post at the mansion's front door, he knew he would need to delay his visit to the gardener's cottage.

Miss Eleanor Cabot had stopped by for another impromptu visit.

The lady had a yen for matrimony, and she had targeted his pocketbook. As it turned out, the Cabot wealth was more about appearance than substance.

Seb played along. Why the hell not? He needed a blue-blooded wife to beget a legitimate blue-blooded heir, and the shallow Miss Cabot was no worse than any other shallow miss he had met; all set their bonnets on finding a rich husband. Letting her do the romancing freed him to pursue Sarah.

And the building of his financial dynasty. Gossip had already linked the Cabot name with his. Formerly closed doors had started to swing wide. Marrying into an old, established New York family made for a sound business plan.

Too bad Miss Cabot left him cold.

In her company, nothing went on below his belt. No activity whatsoever. None. Not a twitch. Not a tickle. Which made her fussy insistence on a chaperone during their carriage rides out to the countryside such a damned hoot. No need a'tall for that watchful lady's maid. He never tried to steal so much as a kiss when Miss Cabot sent her maid scurrying away on some trumped up excuse or other—

Which boded ill for his future progeny. Christ! He hoped the woman proved as fertile as she did silly! Seb doubted he would make many repeat performances in the marital bed.

Upon entering the house, a froth of pink taffeta and rose lace jumped him. "There you are, Mr. Turner!" Miss Cabot gushed. "After a trip to the seamstress, I just happened to find myself in the neighborhood, and I thought, rather impulsively, why not stop in for a chat?"

Seb inclined his head. "Always a pleasure to see you again, Miss Cabot, regardless of the circumstances."

"I know this is terribly forward of me, since I am here without my maid and we shall be *completely on our own*, but might we take a stroll through the gardens?"

Seb sighed. Looked like he was about to get himself compromised.

He presented Miss Cabot with his arm. "You can trust me with your reputation," he replied, knowing the truth of that statement only too well.

Miss Cabot tilted her round chin to the sky. "I do hope the rain holds off…"

While his pursuer spoke at great lengths about the possibility of imminent precipitation and what that possibility might do to her damned kick flounce, Seb searched for a figure wearing a beat-up Stetson amongst the flowerbeds.

Sarah. Their attraction, mutual and powerful, included a mountain of guilt on both sides. Sweet Sarah felt guilty for lusting after him; he felt guilty for everything he had done. And so he stayed away.

Damn! Continue that meek and mild thinking, and he could forget all about doing business in this cutthroat town.

And still Seb surveyed the raised beds for Sarah.

Miss Cabot came to a stop in the middle of their slow-as-molasses promenade. "My word!" She fanned her gloved hand before her face. "I do believe I feel faint! The heat. The sun." Taking his elbow, she dragged him under the leafy cover of an old chestnut.

The tree had nothing on her overused ploy.

Seb recognized a matrimonial ambush when he saw one, and this old chestnut had molded with age.

Sun? Thunderclouds threatened overhead. For once, the fashion-conscious lady had a cause for concern over her kick flounce. Her gown was in for a soaking.

So was he.

"Anything I can do?" he asked the conniving Miss Cabot.

Lace-covered fingers fluttered to her throat, clutched at her windpipe. "Suffocating," she gasped.

The way he saw it, he had two choices—watch her complexion turn a self-inflicted blue, or fall into her trap.

Getting it over with, he reached for her collar. "If you will allow me?"

At her gleeful nod, he proceeded to undo the lady's buttons.

"Sebastian! Sebastian! Sebastian!" she screamed, and yanked his head onto her heaving bosom.

From his perspective, Eleanor could breathe pretty damn good.

Unlike himself. Smothered in cleavage, he started gasping for air.

With a backward stumble, Seb narrowly escaped her bounty. Only to have his stones grabbed and squeezed and his sleeping cock groped as the lady bent her knees.

"Miss Cabot." He pulled her up from her descent to the ground. "I mean to say—Eleanor...I respect you far too much to ask this of you."

Seeing that he had not dissuaded the lady—Lord! The misguided woman was still attacking his buttons—he hastily added, "And, alas, I am celibate."

"Cel-cel-celibate?"

He batted his lashes. "I am saving myself for the wedding night."

"As, of course, am I." She put her pink taffeta bodice to rights. "All this heat brought on a faint. Thank you for keeping me on my feet."

"My pleasure," he said dryly. "Perhaps a tall lemonade up at the house will cool you off?"

Either that, or dunk Eleanor in the rain barrel. The lady was hornier than a she-goat in springtime.

Forty-five *long* minutes later, his virtue still intact, Seb had arrived at his gardener's door. Sarah, in all her radiant beauty, looked up at him with a question in her eyes.

What to tell her? How to explain his unexpected visit?

For the first time in his life, glibness failed him. Mouth agape, he could only stare at the young woman he had rushed to see.

Sarah finally drew him inside.

"Oh, sorry!" She dropped her hold on him. "I rarely receive visitors, you see. Actually, I *never* receive visitors. Apart from you, of course. My unseemly behavior has nothing to do with you personally, I assure you."

She stepped back. "How did you find the city?"

He found the city dull. But why talk about Manhattan, about long, boring meetings, about meaningless business deals, when he could listen to Sarah's gardening stories?

To ensure a full recovery from her fall into the river, he had allowed Sarah to till the soil, figuring fresh air and sunshine and an occupied mind would aid in her recuperation. Now that her health had improved, it was high time he disabused her of the silly notion that she had to work for her keep or pay off her debt. He had brought Sarah back with him to his estate to act as her benefactor, not her damned employer! In exchange for warming his bed, he would make her a generous allowance, buy her haute couture clothing, expensive jewelry—treat her like a pampered pet on a satin pillow, not an overworked servant. And a male servant, at that.

Though, he had to admit, she looked damn good in men's trousers.

She had filled out some. Her breeches now fit like a second skin, the twill fabric threadbare in the most interesting places.

Sarah smiled. "I just put the kettle on to boil. Will you join me for a cup of tea?" At his nod, she turned toward the stove. "Have you seen the conservatory yet?"

"Not yet." He had only wanted to see Sarah. "I thought maybe you would show me around."

"Of course," she said serenely. Then clapped her hands together. "Oh, bosh dignity! Nothing would please me more than to give you the grand tour."

Nothing pleased him more than seeing her lively grin and bouncing eyes. To ensure that those eyes kept their sparkle and that full mouth kept its saucy grin, she had to quit working so hard. He would not have her overburdened. Miss Sarah Winslow acted too responsibly already, as he heard told a child born of irresponsible parents often did.

He had also heard in the village tavern all about how Sarah had cared for her dying father. No household help. Just a young girl managing everything on her own. Seems like he had falsely condemned Michael Winslow's daughter as a spoiled miss—

"Sir, wait 'til you see the interior of the conservatory! The light is spectacular. And the plants! Quite exceptional. I cannot wait to start an orchid propagation program. It would mean my spending more time in the conservatory. But I view that as time well spent." Suddenly shy, she looked up at him through the cover of her lashes. "In my pursuit of orchid hybridization, I promise not to neglect the gardens."

What about him? Hours spent with her plants meant she would neglect him. "Speaking of flowers…while in the city, I found the copy of Robinson's latest work, *The English Flower Garden*."

"You never did!"

Grinning, he brought the brown paper-wrapped package out from under his coat. "Sure did. See?"

Her arms went behind her back.

He chuckled. "Take the gift, Sarah."

She launched herself at him. Started raining kisses all over his face. Artless, unsophisticated, innocent kisses. On his nose. On his cheekbone. On his jaw. Everywhere.

But on his mouth.

Once a thief, always a thief.

Angling his jaw, he stole a kiss away. When his mouth opened, her tongue plunged inside. Wildly inside. Nothing-held-back inside. She tasted his tongue, sucked on his tongue. Her arms wound around his neck, and her breasts—*Mercy!* Firm and round and high, they pressed against his chest. Straining. Rubbing. Groaning open-mouthed, she moved her hardened nipples back and forth against him.

"Please?" she moaned into his ear.

Breathing hard, Seb did the unthinkable.

He fell back.

Sarah fell back, too. "What in Heaven's name is wrong with me?"

"Nothing," he ground out. "Absolutely nothing is wrong with you."

"Oh, but indeed there is! I just threw myself at you!"

"Only to show your appreciation for the book."

"By forcing my tongue into your mouth? By rubbing my bosom against you? A thank-you would have sufficed." Sarah shook her head back and forth. "What kind of wanton woman am I?"

The best kind. The kind who acts on genuine feelings.

Seb touched a strand of curly black hair. "Your honesty is charming, Sarah. Never apologize for it. Now, tell me what you need. And please, hang politeness. I know you need something from me."

She looked away. Gulped. "I ache so. All the time."

"Where?"

"My nipples. Between my legs. The torment is excruciating. I lie awake at night thinking of you." She licked her lips. "I need for you to take the ache away. Please take the ache away." She covered her mouth. "Oh, Heavens! Why did I say that? I should never have said any of that! Shocking, really, how I blather on. Disregard everything I just uttered. Could we possibly pretend everything I just did and said never happened?"

"I ain't one for beating around the bush—so, here goes: Hell no, woman, we cannot pretend! Not about nothin'. But rest easy, you cannot say or do anything that will offend me. Say whatever you please, whatever is on your mind." He palmed a dainty breast, and her eyes drifted closed. "You have nothing on beneath this shirt?"

"Yes, sir." She shook her head ruefully. "I mean, no, sir."

She wore no chemise. No corset. No petticoat. Under that damn ugly shirt, she was all naked, hurting woman.

Seb smoothed a careful finger around the periphery of her nipple, circling the jutting tip, alarmingly distended in arousal. He thumbed the tight point, and her jaw went slack and her mouth gaped, erotic little noises escaping. Back-of-her-throat kind of noises. Woman-in-heat kind of noises.

"My shirt," she whispered, his for the taking. "I would like to open it."

"Go right ahead."

She stumbled over the buttons. "My fingers are too clumsy."

Gently pushing her hands away, he worked the buttons for her, parting the edges of the shirt. Not touching her, just looking at her bright pink nipples.

"Please, sir, would you possibly do what you did before? But not on top of the shirt this time." She gulped. "On bare skin?"

"If it would please you. I only want to please you, Sarah."

"Actually, it is I who wishes to please you, sir. I am still under the obligation to repay my debt, and I doubt very much that gardening alone will accomplish that goal. I shall more quickly dispose of my indebtedness, will I not, if I also act as your whore?"

"Courtesan," he corrected as she had corrected him that first night. "And I never asked you to repay me." He played with her pretty pink nipples, and she clung to him, both arms wrapped around his neck.

"I shall repay you, every penny."

"When would you like to begin?" he asked icily, not liking the direction of this discussion.

"Now," she moaned.

"You understand I cannot offer you marriage?"

"I saw you dancing with all the ladies the other night. I know you need a respectable wife, and I know I am no longer respectable. Not after my sojourn in a house of ill-repute. I am soiled, irredeemably besmirched."

A sojourn in a house of ill-repute he had arranged, the necessity for which he had manipulated. He had destroyed her reputation, made her an outcast. By his hand alone, she had lost her respectability. So while her honest display of passion nearly cut him in two, his reciprocal honesty would cut her from him, a circumstance he would not allow.

"As a wealthy man, I can afford to see to your support. I am prepared to take care of you. Financially. You will never want for anything again." He could not make a decent woman of her, but he would do the right thing by her monetarily.

He gave her distended nipple a pull. "You liked it hard," he explained.

She blinked. "I did?"

"Uh-huh."

"I have dreamt of you. Of this. Of you doing this to me. Of us doing it together." Her voice dropped to a hush. "I shall die if I cannot have my way with you."

He increased the pressure of his fingers. "Just tell me what you want."

"Where to begin? I wish for so many things, so many touches. Your hand on my belly, I should think, to start."

"Like so?" he inquired politely.

"No. Lower. Go lower."

"Undo your trousers," he ordered, expediency edging out politeness.

When she did, his fingers extended under the loosened waistband. Moving lower, his fingertips spanned her pubic bone, wove into the fleece. "So soft," he crooned as he petted her, the luxuriance of her woman's pelt putting him in mind of midnight velvet.

Her thighs fell open, no coyness. In bed, Sarah had behaved honestly, no stilted manners getting in the way; in bed, she had clawed him like a she-cat, an alternately purring and hissing pussy. He wanted her to claw and hiss and purr again.

His palm slipped south. "Steady, little one," he said, supporting her with an arm around her back.

"Lower," she ordered. "Touch me lower. Between the legs, lower."

He rubbed the heel of his hand into the cleft. "Wet," he said triumphantly.

No dissembling for Sarah. "Yes," she promptly replied.

He nodded at the dead man's trousers. "Take 'em off."

With a wiggle of her slim hips, the breeches slid down her legs.

Breasts heaving, pelvis tilting, she made her need clear as day.

Still, he insisted, "Tell me!"

"Why?" She panted. "Why must I say it?"

Because he carried gruesome pictures of Sarah in his head, horrifying images of her nearly drowning in dark waters. Sarah trapped beneath rotting debris. Sarah not breathing on the riverbank. No matter how hard he tried to push them aside, those pictures stayed stuck in his mind, incised with a dull knife.

He reckoned he deserved those scenes, but he wanted no repeats. "Spell it out, or this goes no further."

When she remained obstinately silent, he took a deep breath. Flagging control restored, he dropped his hand from the center of her body.

Sarah was capable of red-hot passion, but this was not something he intended to do *to* her. He would not propel her along to satisfaction on the strength of his own excitement; she would go to that place with him, hand in hand, or they would both stay put.

"Sarah, if you would like to show me around the conservatory tomorrow, I am free in the late afternoon. Shall we say three o'clock?"

Without waiting for an answer, Seb got himself the hell out of there.

Chapter Twenty-Two

Seb checked his watch. Almost time.

And still no sign of Sarah.

Sweat beaded his brow. By raising the stakes, had he overplayed his hand? Demanded more than she could give? Had he gambled the house and lost?

Just when he considered folding, Sarah arrived at the service entrance to the conservatory.

He entered the glassed interior, eyes fixed straight ahead, uppermost in his mind the draw he had used to get her here.

The plants. Sarah took pride in the indoor green world she had created, and rightly so. She had worked hard and accomplished much. He admired her ambition, if not the hard, back-breaking work that her labor involved.

Stealing a sneak preview of the vaulted green space would disappoint her, so Seb's sights stayed true, his gaze locked only on Sarah.

The lady stared at her feet.

He let go a sigh. When they came together, he wanted her chin raised, merriment dancing in her eyes, her body proud and naked, joint travelers along the road to passion. All his life he had settled for less, and he refused to settle for less now. He wanted her to want this as much as he!

Seb opened the door and let Sarah in. Casually. The hallway floor carried traces of scuffmarks, put there from his frantic back and forth pacing, and he had thought about nothing but their explosive kiss, had checked his timepiece at every pass of the minute hand, willing the hours to pass until he saw her again, but showing his hand now might scare her off. No pressure. No obligation. No heavy-handedness. Her decision all the way whether or not they did this.

"Please come in," he said evenly, and then just about took the damn door off its hinges in his haste to get her inside.

She looked up at him shyly. "Thank you, sir."

That blasted *sir* again.

He could have corrected her. "About time you called me Sebastian," he might have said with a wink and a smile. But secretly, he needed the distancing of that word. That word reminded him that, though he would lay a fortune at her feet, their association had to remain strictly business. No emotional entanglement, no possibility of a future.

Without delay, Sarah launched right into the tour. "I had the workmen apply a whitewash glaze to the uppermost portion of glass," she lectured, leading him around the glass-domed interior. "Partial shading prevents the plants from overheating. Ceiling windows and vents also help." A wistful look fell over her solemn features. "I should love one of those new electrical generators installed. Fans will greatly improve ventilation."

"Then, by all means, do it."

His private tour came to an abrupt stop. "Really?"

"Yep."

As a smiling Sarah pointed out the various plants, the names all given in Latin, he thought about kneading both cheeks of her bottom. Round and soft, yet with a firm underlay of muscle, her ass would make a hot little handful.

He stopped in front of an exotic plant with fleshy pink petals, reminiscent of female genitalia. "Tell me about this one."

While she did, he pictured his hand moving from her backside to her front, smoothing over her belly, dipping to her pelt. Always caressing. Sarah had real silky curls, and in his imaginings, the lower his hand sank, the damper those sweet curls got, until he circled the very wet petals of her pink flesh.

The botanical lecture stalled. Sarah's eyes fluttered to his. "Oh, my. All this talk of plant reproduction has made me—"

He bore down on her. "Has made you what?"

"Hot," she said, looking so wanton, he could easily have taken the little spitfire there, against the planting box. "I consent."

"To what?"

"To everything."

"Get specific."

"Sir, I am hiring on for the courtesan position at the Clearbrook Corral," she drawled.

"The position is yours," he managed to say.

One obstacle down, one more to go.

Though all this starting and stopping gave a whole new meaning to the word torture, the same old worm twisted inside Seb's head. Her father, Michael Winslow, had been a lying, cheating, promiscuous devil. Sarah had to understand, he would not put up with the same from her. No stepping out on him, no sneaking around behind his back, no double-dealing, no two-timing. To keep things fair and square, he had to set down ground rules—

"Fair warning," he growled. "I expect exclusivity. No other men."

"Men!" she cried, aghast. "I would never—"

He held up his hand. "I need your word."

"I am not dishonorable."

No, but maybe her hot nature precluded fidelity.

He reached for her little tittie and squeezed.

When she whimpered out a "Please," he forgot all about collecting her word, saying instead, "Tell me what you need."

"My breasts. Keep touching my breasts."

"On top of the shirt?"

"Bare skin." She trembled.

Her shivering made him want to wrench that ugly shirt out of the way with his teeth and go at her until they both moaned simultaneously.

He gritted his teeth against the urge. "Anything else you need me to do?"

"Suckle my nipples."

"Suck 'em soft or suck 'em hard?"

She bit her lip. "Until my hide is raw."

Rawhide.

He went harder than hard at the image. The gal had the makings of a first-class courtesan. "The shirt has to go."

Torn between desire and convention, she wavered. "But, sir, this is a glass conservatory. Anyone walking outside will see us."

"Do you care what people think, Sarah?"

"Not at all." She dropped the ugly shirt to the floor.

"Now the trousers."

A frayed rope held them up. She was slender, the waist loose; a wiggle would dispatch them.

She shimmied her hips, sashaying her way out of the breeches.

"Step clear," he said.

He waited until she kicked free, before saying, "Open your legs."

She widened her thighs outward, but arrowed her eyes downward.

"No. Look at me, Sarah, not the floor."

Obediently, her eyes flew to his face.

He told her of his appreciation. "Your body rivals your face in beauty."

A confused expression clouded her features. "I am passable at best."

"You are the rarest of flowers. By far the most exotic blossom in this conservatory."

She expelled an "oh" on a breathless whoosh.

"No more ugly breeches and shirts for you. Now on, you wear only the finest of gowns."

"But when I garden—"

"You are not a common laborer, and I will not have you working your fingers to the bone on this estate! No more digging in the dirt."

Her eyes, formerly unfocussed in passion, sharpened. Her chin took on a stubborn jut. "I am a landscape gardener! Digging in the dirt is what I do."

Obedience and willfulness. The conflicting sides of her personality translated mighty fine in bed. The clash of their personalities, their verbal sparring, heated his blood to a boil.

He enjoyed her tempestuousness far too much to put her in a muzzle—

Plus, if she spoke her mind, he would know her mind—no better way to keep her out of harm's way than to understand how she thought.

As to this current bone of contention—he would make her a concession, give her a small victory in favor of winning her total confidence. Only then would he know how far he could trust her.

Her convenient lack of agreement to faithfulness pestered him like a gnat. His convenient dropping of the issue bothered the hell out of him, too. Why had he let the subject drop so easily, without pressing her for her word?

Because he knew Sarah's word would amount to shit?

"Very well," he offered conciliatorily. "You need not burn the clothes. And you may continue to garden, but only as a pastime, and not so long each day that you tire yourself."

"Tell me why you feel as you do!"

He would know how she thought—reciprocation was not in his best interests. And full disclosure would sure as hell lose him the advantage.

"Sarah, why not accept what I can give you? Why not allow me to make life easier for you?"

"Because I have learned the hard way to protect myself, as any woman who finds herself in this situation must. An easy life now means greater difficulties later. Allow myself to become dependent upon you now, either emotionally or financially, and I will never enjoy self-reliance and independence in the future."

"You will never want for anything in the future," he roared.

"I shall want for respectability."

He shook his head. "Marriage is out of the question."

"I, more than most, understand the kind of lady you need to take to wife, and I realize I am not that lady, that I shall never again be that lady. Circumstances beyond my control destroyed my good name. And then afterwards, after my father's death, I...I..."

She looked at him bleakly. "I sold myself into prostitution. I accept what I have become." She laughed dismally. "To survive in desperate times, a person must do what a person must do. I make no apologies for choosing food over starvation—"

"I hardly think less of you for choosing to live. In fact, your good health makes me ridiculously happy—"

"Let me finish! I accept the responsibility of what I have become, but I shan't allow you or any man to keep me locked up like a bird in a gilded cage. I shall continue to work as your gardener, and then when our arrangement is through, you can honestly give me a good reference."

"Sarah, a reference? Why? I have told you several times already, I plan on settling a fortune on you."

"A principle is at stake here! Even whores must keep to their ethics."

She stood naked against a wall of glass and fought for her dignity. He had never met a woman quite like her. Never knew a woman he liked more, respected more, admired more. Even her prissiness appealed to him. But one way or the other, through fair means or foul, he would win this contest of wills. Sarah was healthy and happy and brimming with life, and he intended she stay that way. It was his *charge* to keep her that way. He would not see her sicken from overwork.

Pure pleasure to take care of her. Buy her nice things. Treat her like a lady. If not for his interference, she would have lived the life of a society debutante—

Hard as a stick of the dynamite he had once used for blowing up mountains, and feeling just as volatile as the nitroglycerin inside, Seb was on a short fuse, and Sarah was all he needed for detonation. When she squared her shoulders, her heaving breasts seemed to point right at him, and his blasting cap sizzled, ready to go off, ready to explode. And there she stood, talking principles and ethics. What did he care for either?

"Sir, it is not your money I desire, but my restored pride. And you. I desire you. My carnal feelings for you shame me, but I cannot deny them. My body yearns for your body," she said woefully. "I believe in love, sir, and yet I lust for you. All I think about is having you between my legs. But I cannot stay on here after you marry. The position of other woman is not for me."

Her legs widened as she took her principled stance. "I shan't dishonor sacred vows. So, upon your wedding, I shall seek a position elsewhere. Furthermore, do not expect me to sleep with you in the house of my childhood."

The explosion came swiftly. "We damn well are sleeping together—"

"You may share my bed at the cottage, but this conservatory is as far as I go into your house, into your private life. I consent to be your mistress, your whore, your kept woman, your courtesan because I cannot stem my yearning for you, but I must keep something back for myself."

Seb took a step forward. Then another. Until his much larger body effectively walled her in. Dipping his mouth to hers, he whispered suggestively, "Someday, you will sleep in my bed up at the house, Sarah, because you will not be able to help yourself."

She shook her head. "No."

"Yes, Sarah."

Her hand went to his lips. "Oh, your mouth draws me so."

And the argument was done. Over. Finished. Above all else, he wanted her to want him. And she did. Stubborn miss! Let her keep her useless principles and empty ethics. He dealt in expediencies, not lofty ideals.

Once exploded, his anger quickly dissipated. Intangibles were important to the high-principled Sarah, and so he would relent. Again.

Before he had chance to tell her so, she raised her lips to his. "A kiss to seal the agreement, sir."

Chapter Twenty-Three

Would Mr. Turner take her on her terms?

If he did, would he kiss her first, or bypass that romantic gesture in favor of a quick and practical consummation of their business deal?

She had laid herself bare to him, emotionally as well as physically, openly admitting, without any attempt at self-protective subterfuge, her aching need for him. In her desire for this one man, she had gone against every tenet of social conduct. Willingly, knowingly, joyfully, she had cast aside convention and agreed to *openly* become his mistress.

But to maintain her self-respect, she would continue to garden and she would not sleep in the house of her childhood.

Would he accept the terms? Or try to bend her to his will?

He could bend her so easily, take her dignity, make her grovel. And she would do it. She desired him enough to forsake all her romantic notions about love. But must she give up everything? Could she not keep something of herself, for herself? One small corner of her dream?

"You strike a hard bargain," he said, one breath removed from her mouth.

Oh, how she craved that sensuous mouth, those irresistibly masculine lips; his closeness was as compelling as any aphrodisiac. If she but raised her chin a notch, pleasure would be hers.

But she held steady. "A kiss, sir, to seal the contract."

"I accept your conditions. But only because I know you will soon change your mind."

"I shan't change my mind. Not about my conditions and not about my need to have you inside me."

He bent his head to hers and captured her lips, each one separately, before sucking on her entire mouth like a succulent whole fruit. He toured her body with his hands, slowly, as they had just a few scant minutes before toured the conservatory. Against a wall of glass, she floated on the drugged cloud of Sebastian's soft kisses, even as she surrendered to her own carnality.

Sebastian's mouth *finally* opened over a nipple and pulled on the elongated flesh. Sensation, deep and dark and wicked sensation, coursed languidly through her, washing slowly over her from the tips of her nipples to her belly to her loins. The air, heavy and humid, laden with the aroma of exotic flowers, rife with forbidden expectancy, weighted each of their breaths. And the sun! Milky from the whitewash applied to the uppermost panes, the opaque light saturated the conservatory, pouring through the large facets of glass, warming her naked backside.

Hullo, decadence!

She went up on her toes. "Yes, yes, yes," she said, hurrying through the introductions.

Holding onto Sebastian's wide shoulders, giving herself over to him…yet keeping back that one small corner of herself in abeyance.

She had to. How would she go on without him otherwise?

Self-preservation was not selfish; self-preservation was the way to survive. She would have Mr. Turner and she would enjoy him, too, and when it was over, she would let him go to his society bride while she walked away whole.

Premature to worry about that now. It was too soon to think of leaving him. For right now, he was hers. All hers.

She opened to him. Her tongue matching the fury of his, entwining with his, her arms winding around his neck, her fingers in his hair pulling him close against the glass wall. Putting up no fight, he went along with her. Until panting, he broke them apart.

"Tell me," he rasped.

She knew, she knew, she knew what he wanted, and this time she refused to hesitate. "Come into me."

"I need to ready you."

Ready? She was long past ready! Her legs felt like insubstantial blades of grass, unable to hold her upright.

Drugged on Sebastian, she slid down the sun-warmed glass wall.

He caught her before she fell and pinned her against the glass wall, still mouthing her flesh.

Seconds passed.

Too long. Much too long. Every moment without him seemed an eternity.

He stroked over her breasts, down her belly, between her legs. "Please," she begged again. Shamelessly. Uncontrollably. Melodramatically. "Please, sir. I will die without you."

"Not because of me! Never because of me."

"Yes, because of you," she said, and reached between their bodies. Boldly, she opened the placket on his trousers, took him out, her fingers barely closing around the tremendous width of his shaft.

He was hard, so very hard, and at the same time, flower-petal soft. But the length! Good Heavens! The extension was prohibitive. Combined with the width, she would have thought his make impossible to accommodate.

Save, she had accommodated him once already.

Though a more complete remembrance of the occasion would have helped her, still with instinctual confidence, she brought him to her gate—

"Miss Eleanor Cabot, here to see you," Mrs. Smith called through the open conservatory door. "Shall I send her in?"

Sebastian's eyes never left Sarah's face. "Have her wait, Mrs. Smith."

Standing naked against a glass wall where anyone might see, two ladies just outside the door awaiting permission to enter, and Sarah felt disinclined to care. If every resident of New York state watched and waited, she would still have to have Sebastian.

Licking her lips, she moved him into her. Just the bulbous head—

"No."

"No?" she wailed.

Removing her grip, he put himself away.

How could he forsake her?

But wait. He had not completely abandoned her. His thumb massaged the top of her opening, his fingers moving in and out of her sluicing wet vagina, faster and faster.

"Oh, yes," she murmured, writhing against the warm glass. "Mmm, oh, yes. *Lovely.*"

Allowing him all rights to her body, uncaring who might see, who might hear—far past those petty concerns now—shaking and shuddering, she felt her orgasm pulse but seconds away.

"Scream," he ordered.

"Bloody hell!" she rasped, and grabbed great bunches of his black hair in her fists. No pomade, just clean and sweet-smelling curls. "You are a tyrant."

He chuckled. "You enjoy my tyranny. You crave dominance."

She did. And she enjoyed games, too. Like taking her pleasure naked against a glass conservatory wall, knowing just that outside the door a grand society lady waited for admittance.

Her muscles tightened, strained. Her hands clutched at his hair, her fingers clawing his scalp, her thighs going taut.

"Scream," he whispered, blowing the single-word command into her ear.

The tension building inside her was just too much to contain. Scream she did, and in blessed release, the terrible knot inside her breaking, shattering as she came.

She sagged against the glass, replete, limp with fulfillment.

As she was too weak to dress herself, Mr. Turner gathered up her shirt and trousers and did the task for her—after licking his fingers, the same digits he had only just used to stroke between her legs.

A naughty sight, and the finest tribute she could ever have imagined.

After making her presentable, he took her mouth, and she actually tasted herself dripping on his tongue.

"Delicious," he crowed—the arrogant cock!—before calling, "Mrs. Smith, you may show my guest in now."

Had Eleanor Cabot heard her climactic scream? Did she suspect what had just transpired while she awaited admittance at the threshold?

"There you are, Mr. Turner!" her former chum enthused, giving no indication that she had heard anything amiss. "How fortuitous to find you at home! And alone, too."

Standing as she was, directly in Eleanor's sight, Sarah took this remark none too kindly.

Her owner bowed at the waist. "Fortuitous when certain persons find one at home; a colossal misfortune when others do."

Eleanor giggled. "Oh, Mr. Turner, you flatterer, you!"

After replaying Sebastian's words in her mind, Sarah found no specific flattery in the remark. In her opinion, Eleanor had heard flattery where none existed.

Sour grapes again?

Perhaps. And what she would give to throw a bunch at the cow!

Her patron continued. "Sarah has just given me a tour of the conservatory. She designed the entire structure. Her talent is remarkable."

"Yes. Remarkable." Eleanor sneered at a spot somewhere above Sarah's head.

Whilst the man who had championed her talent smiled directly into her eyes. "And to think, Miss Cabot, you once had the privilege of calling Sarah your friend. I declare, every utterance that falls from her lips is a pearl. I suggest you hang onto her every word. Someday your former friend will be famous."

"Or infamous," Eleanor said under her breath.

"Pardon?" he rejoined.

Eleanor fingered her bonnet. "Mr. Turner, I am here to invite you to an impromptu soirée this evening at our home. I know the invitation is horribly last minute, but do say you can make it! Mother and Father have invited associates of some influence, and I am told they are most anxious to meet you."

Busying herself with the orchids, Sarah heard her owner say, "How can I possibly refuse?"

Easily. Sarah snorted to herself as she walked away.

Eleanor had set her cap for Mr. Turner, a pursuit made necessary because of the Cabots' diminished coffers. As to the afore-named—he was an ambitious man of less than impeccable breeding—the Cabot influence could help him rise above the obstacle of his birth and advance his career.

How foolish to hold on to her girlish dream! Only an exceptional man would thumb his nose at society and marry purely for love, Sarah mused, letting herself out the servants' backdoor.

Chapter Twenty-Four

With Eleanor dripping like spun sugar upon his arm, Seb worked the Cabot's shabby drawing room, identifying easy marks the same as he had in the back alleys of the Bowery. Laughing and joking, scoring all the right moves, at the end of the evening he knew squeezing a wedding band on Eleanor's finger would guarantee his entrée into New York society.

And not for the life of him could he bring himself to give a shit.

Everything but the memory of Sarah's flushed face as she climaxed had faded in importance. He continued to charm the drawers off all the ladies and impress all the gents, but the grift had lost its shine.

The fine, upstanding folks he cozied up to as an adult would have spat on him as a lad. And hoodwinking them into believing he was something he was not had lost its appeal.

Why should he have to convince these stuffed shirts of his worth? Why should he have to work a con game to get them to accept him?

He had put the squalid tenements far behind him, along with the pervasive and nauseating stink of the tanneries and the rotting smell of cabbage soup. With the sweat of his brow and the gift of his crafty intelligence, he had made something of himself, proved his worth, built himself a fortune out West.

He missed making deals with a handshake. Missed having his word serve as his bond. Missed having folks respect him for his abilities, not for his connections. He missed the basic honesty of the place he had called home for the last eighteen years.

Strange to compare such a soft female to such a hard place, but Sarah reminded him of the West. Her uncompromising integrity brought to mind the frontier. He had always admired integrity...

As a lad, he had fleeced fat purses with his tricky fingers. He had the knack for stealing, and so he had done it. To survive. Just as Sarah now struggled to survive. What if, like him, she also ended up hating herself?

In the conservatory today, Sarah had brought him to her moist opening. One push, and he would have slid inside her wet sheath. The lady who had attached herself to his wealth, leech to flesh, had impeded that push.

He put up with her manipulations until the grandfather clock bonged twelve times, and then disengaged himself from her bloodsucking and galloped back to Clearbrook.

To Sarah.

After seeing to his mount, he made his way through the woods. Crossing the bridge over the river, he let himself into the cottage.

Darkness greeted him, save for the ambers glowing red in the hearth. By that spare illumination, he discerned a slight form in the bed.

Stripping off his evening clothes as he went, Seb climbed naked into bed with her just as he had done after her near drowning to warm her.

This time, he was the one who shook with the cold; he was the one nearly drowning.

Sarah, warm and toasty, slept peacefully on.

Kneeling on the tick, he rolled down the bedding. Starting at her feet, he kissed each toe before licking the high arch. Raising her nightgown, he mouthed her leg up to the thigh, kissing the sweet cleft at her body's center. He split her, his tongue piercing the mark and lapping her juices—

And sweet Sarah sighed.

Encouraged, he straddled her, a leg on either side of her hips, his arms bracketing her upper body, his manhood clubbing the air.

"Sarah," he whispered softly, so as not to jar her awake.

She moaned sweetly in reply.

Though his aim had been to awaken her gradually, her body boneless with sleep, her core wet with erotic dreams of him, his cock lanced.

"Let me inside, Sarah," he enticed, and found himself similarly enticed just with speaking her name.

When she raised her hips, he nudged the opening. Not entering. Not penetrating. Savoring her. Sarah felt so damned good.

"I want you," he told her, openly admitting to that one truth, the only complete truth he had ever told her. "I want you so bad."

"Then you must have me," she answered. "But would you kiss me first?"

"Romantic miss." As a man, genitals were his first consideration, but to please her, he slid his lips over hers, worshiping her mouth until he forgot he was trying to please her, not himself.

And then he did something completely unplanned—he rolled onto his back and spread himself for her taking.

His gift to Sarah.

And his penance for taking advantage of her drugged state before.

"Do with me as you will," he said gallantly, shifting the reins from his hand to hers.

She sat up, rubbed her eyes, stared at his bucking bronco. "Oh, my. Difficult to imagine all *that* fitting inside me."

He rubbed her shoulder reassuringly. "Go on. You can do it."

"I feel so silly, but you see, most of the details of losing my virginity are missing from my memory, and you look so big. Huge, really—"

"Not so huge." He tugged on her nightgown. "Take this thing off."

He helped her, and then his untamed Sarah, his ladylike Sarah, rose over him, her thighs clamped on either side of his hips—sweet imprisonment—hovering above his weeping cock.

When she teased him, he could have squalled like a baby, but he forced himself to lie there and not take, not surge or spike or do any of those things his man's body cried out for him to do.

She started to come down, started to lower. Too soon!

He reached between her legs to start the stroke that would turn damp to wet.

Obstinate miss, she pushed his hand away.

"Wait," he whispered. "You need—"

"You," she finished for him, and sank down onto his throbbing flesh. "I cannot be without you another minute." She sighed.

What could he say to the starry-eyed miss?

Not a damn thing. She had to learn certain *hard* realities firsthand. She would soon find out, and all on her own, that romance has no place under the bed linens. In bed, foreplay beat the hell out of any sonnet.

"Have mercy," he croaked as he shot up inside her, filling her. Too soon.

"Oh!" she cried, at a fit more an uncomfortable rub than a slippery glide.

Her hands tightened on his shoulders. "I think I may have acted precipitously. I think, perhaps, I have changed my mind. I appear not at all suited for this activity." She lifted up.

"Stay, Sarah." No favor allowing her to give in to fear now.

Miss Sarah Winslow had been raised a proper lady, groomed to make some proper gentleman a proper lady wife. Proper ladies reclined on their backs, nightgown pushed aside only enough to allow for a respectable intercourse. Proper ladies granted connubial rights only to their proper, gentlemanly husbands.

He was no proper gentleman. Nor was he her wedded spouse.

And here he was, getting in her deep.

"I feel so clumsy," she murmured low and self-conscious.

"You are the most graceful female I have ever seen or held in my arms."

She slid back down on top of him again, sheathing his cock…but with a hell of a lot less eagerness than before. "I am?"

"Absolutely."

Inch by torturous inch, she accepted him into her body. "I absolutely am!" she said at the last gulp.

But her wince stung him, even in the dark. And the dark did nothing to disguise her tensed muscles.

Arching up off the bed, he kissed her tight lips. "Next time, when I tell you to wait, listen to me. In carpentry as well as in fornication, a little grease makes the screwing easier."

"How very prosaic," she snipped.

He playfully smacked her ass. Everyone copes with fear differently. Sarah hid her fear behind snobbishness.

"Cad," she grumbled, rubbing her posterior.

Smiling at her orneriness, he began to apply some much-needed grease. First, with words. Then with touch.

"You done good, Sarah. Real good. Some females never manage to take all of me in this position."

She sniffed. "I did good?"

He felt her muscles relax. "Whoa, yeah, gal." He smiled as her honey started to flow around his cock. "Mighty good."

Words first, then came action.

He felt around to where her pubic lips had stretched to accommodate him, and massaged the opening, kneaded her belly, fondled her pretty little titties, soothed her into letting go. Then, unable to remain passive a breath longer, quickly flexed his hips, sending himself higher. He shot home, making the deepest penetration allowed a man inside a woman's body.

Her bottom rocking, her internal muscles pulsating around his shaft, tightening, then releasing, Sarah squeezed his ten inches.

"Easy, gal," he warned, smoothing a palm over her pumping buttocks, cupping her bottom cheeks. "Easy."

Disregarding the caution, she rode him hard, bouncing up and down, no self-consciousness. In animal sync, they both quickly approached orgasm. No longer able to place her needs ahead of his own—he was only a man, after all, not a saint—he drove faster, the wet sound of his flesh mating with her flesh reverberating in the cottage, drowned out only by their mutual cries of release.

Chapter Twenty-Five

Mr. Turner awakened her with his mouth, a warm kiss applied to the nape that her short hair left uncovered. A fine start to a day, Sarah thought and rolled to face her lover. "Good morning, sir."

He stroked her bare shoulder. "Are you all right?"

She smiled. "Never have I felt more alive."

"Last night...was I too...hard...on you?"

"Can a man ever be too hard?" Her eyes dropped. The jaunty angle of his penis tented the sheet. "I mean, is it possible?"

Beneath the linen, she captured his hardness in her hand. His hot, pulsating hardness. He sucked in his breath when she tried to span him.

And failed. His dimensions far surpassed the span of her fingers. "Curious thing, your size, sir. No complaint, mind you. I certainly enjoyed the internal friction. And the tensility—quite remarkable. But you are awfully—I believe the expression is *well-hung*."

"Whew, Lordy! No how, no way, did you pick that up in any goldarn anatomy book!" He whistled through his teeth. "Sometimes—in fact, pretty nearly all the time—you amaze me. But keep doing that with your hand." He chuckled and then took another deep inhale. "And to answer your question—that kind of hardness is not the kind of hardness I meant. Nothing much frightens me any more, but I do fear hurting you, Sarah. With my size. With my force. You," he said, touching the tip of her nose, "are a fragile little miss."

She laughed full out. "I never am! You must have me mistaken for some other bed companion. I am not *fragile* in any respect. My constitution is embarrassingly hale and hearty. Not a day of sickness have I known, not even in childhood."

She rushed out the rest of the words. "And about last night…I feared I would fail, that I would not perform correctly. I do so wish to excel at *something*."

"You excelled plenty last night."

"So gratifying to hear. La! You may just turn my head with your effusiveness. Not that I was hinting for a compliment, you understand—"

"You want the truth?"

"Always."

"You make one mighty fine courtesan."

"Oh, my! Could you possibly include that in a letter of reference? 'Miss Sarah Winslow, a mighty fine courtesan—'"

"But, next time, let me work it."

She drew back. "Pardon? Work *it?*"

"Your passion bud," he explained. "Between your legs. Where I touched you in the conservatory. You know, your clit at the top of your pussy."

"Oh! Clit, as in clitoris. The small, elongated erectile organ at the anterior part of the vulva, homologous with the penis. Of course! So nice to have familiarity with commonly used colloquialisms for genitalia and their associated activities. Rather endearing, really, to have pet names for parts of the anatomy. Like pussy."

She tilted her jaw to his mouth. "Kiss me? And not like a hothouse flower, either."

His kiss, still dismally restrained, left her more frustrated. So, she forced the issue, leaning into his mouth, her leg tossed up over his hip, aligning her pelvis to his admirable erection.

They had made love twice last night, both occasions with her on top. Only fair, she decided, to give him a turn at domination.

Fair! What a jest. She yearned to have all his power, all his force unleashed upon her, even if she had to command dominance of him.

Breaking the gentle kiss, she fell back, bringing him over her as she slid assertively into submissiveness.

"Sarah, we did it twice last night. Your pussy has got to be sore."

"Tell me, did my *pussy* concern you this much the first time?"

Like a seaside cottage readied for the approach of a hurricane, his face shuttered down. "Yes. And no. The first time, you just about blew my control to kingdom-come. I ain't chancing that again. No how, no way."

"That's too dang blasted bad, cowpoke. Cuz I reckon I ain't taking no for an answer." She bit his earlobe. "Make me scream, sir. Any how, any way."

"Gluttonous miss!" he said but, giving in to her demands, moved over her. Though ever so carefully, his weight suspended on his arms, gazing down into her eyes, as if she were the most precious and delicate of celestial beings. He sought her body's opening reverently, solemnly entering as one might enter a house of worship.

She combated the urge to give him a good, brisk shake.

Sebastian's vision of her far underestimated the reality of her. All day long, she double-dug manure into the earth, and she had the lean-muscled body to prove it. Though she possessed the strength of an ox and the endurance of a stubborn pack mule, he insisted upon treating her like a puny weakling. Whence had his misguided perception of her sprung?

His mother, she decided. There must have been only the two of them, for he never spoke of a father, and so the task of nursing had fallen to him, a young boy. When, despite his best efforts, his mother had failed to recover, her death must have devastated him. Defeated him. Filled him with rage at the unfairness of it all. Made him feel...well...impotent.

She, too, had experienced early loss. But Mr. Turner's grief differed from hers; his was mixed with another emotion, a corrosive sort of pain. And guilt. Why? What had happened to the boy to cause such pain and guilt?

Her investigation into his past would need to wait for another time; a different sort of investigation had moved front and foremost in her thoughts now.

Reclining on her back, experimentally, she brought her limbs up around his waist, clenched her thighs, her ankles crossed at the base of his spine. Because of the change in her positioning, his breach deepened. The pulse of him, there at her womb, felt ever so life-affirming.

She tightened her muscles. Then relaxed them. Tightened, then relaxed. Until he shuddered and shook and forgot caution. Only then did he move harder, driving up into her with a force that left her breath ragged and her body sweaty.

The climax, messy and noisy, left her limp as a rag.

She adored it. All of it. The sounds, the smells, the disorganized chaos. Most of all, she enjoyed the replete feeling afterwards.

Highly satisfied with how events had played out, sleep claimed her with her owner still lodged inside her.

"Do you plan on staying abed all day, young lady?"

A palm smacked her bare bottom, a sharp slap that let Sarah know she had Sebastian's full attention. As a child, she had usually escaped notice altogether unless she misbehaved, and then that notice had always taken a physically punitive form. At times, she had deliberately provoked a whipping or belting or caning, some sort of corporal discipline, as a way to acknowledge her own existence, to assure herself she had not faded away. Pain was preferable to invisibility.

Sarah rubbed her smarting buttock, the physical attention making her feel, if not exactly loved, at least visible.

She smiled into her pillow. "So long as you are in bed with me, sir, I can think of no better way of passing the day."

"Aw, shucks, ma'am, you just 'bout make me want to puff out my chest," he drawled, sounding for all the world like a bumbling and indolent cowpoke.

He constantly poked fun at himself in this manner. A self-made man, a busy entrepreneur, far from lazy or faltering, Mr. Turner wasted not a moment on his climb to the top.

A point well proven less than a moment later.

"Up you go," he said, hurrying her along. "I have an appointment at the house in five minutes."

"I suppose I should thank you for squeezing me in between engagements." Lifting up on an elbow, she turned to him. "I suppose I should feel honored you visited me at all last night, especially after the impromptu visit you received from your Miss Cabot in the conservatory. How is dear Eleanor, anyway?"

"Fine," he said, voice clipped.

"Do you intend to wed the lady?"

He ran a finger down her spine and said, "More than likely."

"I would wish her well the next I see her, but as she was the first in the parish to snub me after my father's passing, I cannot bring myself to play the hypocrite."

"Sarah, the marriage will amount to a business association, nothing more."

The tickling finger hovered at the small of her back before moving lower. She raised her hips for him.

"You tempt me," he growled.

"As you have that appointment to keep, I shall remove temptation." She wiggled to a cross-legged seat amongst the wildly disarrayed bedding.

His gaze darted between her legs, just as she intended it should. "Remove temptation—in that pose? You look like a hot little piece of tail ready to—" The sentence came to an abrupt halt. Mr. Turner wore a look of horror.

Her owner's speech pattern was polite, but rough. Rarely was he crude—at least not in her company. He slipped at times, but for the most part, he spoke with a stiff exactness, his manner of speaking always correct— save for the occasional Western phraseology, the colorful regionalism of which she found very romantic. But this morning and a few times prior to this morning, too, his speech had relaxed. Most curious.

Exciting, too. Goodness, everything about him excited her!

"Pardon me, Sarah," he said bashfully. "I can offer no excuse, except to say my appetite for you makes me forget my manners at times."

How easily she could fall head over heels in love with this complicated and complex man, to the exclusion of everything else, including her own best interests, including her own survival. She would need to summon up every ounce of her waning willpower to resist losing herself completely to him.

She began immediately to hike her defenses. "I believe you mentioned an appointment in five minutes' time?" she asked sweetly and hopped from the bed. "You may be willing to keep *your* appointment waiting, but I told Rattler I would join him for coffee this morning, and I plan to arrive for *my* appointment on time." A deliberate nettle, using Rattler as her barb. She would not play second-fiddle to Eleanor, of all people!

Rising too, her owner pulled on his trousers and drew on his shirt, the formal attire he had arrived in the night before, now hopelessly wrinkled. "You ain't seeing Rattler today."

She tossed her head. "I certainly shall see Rattler today. There is work to do!"

"Open your legs," said the man she had succeeded to provoke.

No longer invisible, Sarah widened her thighs.

He stalked to her, claiming that moist space that seemed made just for him.

"You are *not* seeing Rattler today," he seethed. "Today, you will not leave this cottage. You belong to me, Sarah. *This* belongs to me," he said, spanning her pussy with his large fingers. "Understood?"

"Yes, sir."

She understood, but comprehension differs from obeying.

Though his punitive attention had buoyed her spirits, no directive ever given would make her forsake her duties or surrender a true friend. Mr. Turner would need to learn and adapt to the strength of her mettle. He would need to *understand* she had dreams too.

And ambitions!

Chapter Twenty-Six

On a flap of scarlet skirts, Michelle Beauvais entered the gardener's cottage. One look at Sarah, and she threw a Frenchie fit.

"Seb—you never told me the gowns I made were for *her!*" Her large leather satchel hit the floor, and her carmine-painted fingernails clawed the air.

Yes, sirree—the tempestuous Chelle was just scratching for a fight.

A plump bunch of sun-ripened grapes nestled in Seb's lap, harvested that very morning from the newly repaired arbor. To give Chelle a little breathing space, Seb popped the succulent fruit in his mouth, savoring the warm juice as it trickled down his throat. Though the fruit tasted sweet, Sarah's lips tasted sweeter.

Seb picked the stem clean with his teeth and then got to work nipping the female tantrum in the bud. "Chelle, I asked you to make the gowns for Sarah because I knew you were a right fine seamstress."

"But theez situation eez eemposseeble!" Chelle said with her Frenchie twang. "When you gave me the measurements, you did not tell me to design outfits for a whore!"

He cut her complaints off at the pass. "Sarah is a high-class courtesan, not a whore. Huge difference."

"Outfits!" Sarah exclaimed. "Sir, you told me *one* dress, and that is all I agreed to accept."

"When you gave me a bunch of gifts, I never once protested. I just accepted them in the spirit in which they were intended and said my heartfelt thanks, all mannerly-like."

"Pardon?" Sarah tilted her head in a concentrative sort of way. "I never gave you a gift, never mind a bunch of gifts."

"You surely did. You gave me grapes. And the bunch tasted delicious. The least you can do is allow me to show my appreciation in return. Rejecting my present would make me feel right poorly."

"Do not think to bamboozle me, sir! I am not as gullible as all that!" She pointed a work-worn finger at him.

A red-nailed finger followed suit. "You should have told me theeze gowns were intended for *her!*"

Before he lost an eyeball to all the finger-pointing, Seb vacated his seat. He wedged himself between the two discontented females.

Not exactly a first for him. No brag to say he had found himself in the middle between two women before, and they always came away smiling. This circumstance presented a challenge—though a surmountable one, if delicately handled.

"Sarah," he began, "did you know Chelle is a talented modiste who learned her skills in Paris?"

"Why, no—"

"Chelle," he cut in, turning on the charm as he unruffled some Frenchie feathers. "What *fabulous* fashions have you brought with you today?"

"You told me theeze ensembles were meant for a young girl. Your *ward*, you said."

"Well...well...now, hold on here one goldarn second. Sarah is young. And she certainly is female. And...uh...in a manner of speaking, she is my ward," he said, placating the females into a corner.

Sarah came out shooting. "I certainly am not your ward. I am nothing of the kind, and you know it."

Time to surrender.

Seb held up his hands. "Gals, can we maybe bury the hatchet and get down to work here?"

Both females shot him looks that said that hatchet was getting buried deep in his back. Having none of his white-flag-waving, they ganged up on him.

"Who asked for new outfits?" Sarah grumbled.

"Theeze outfits are childish gowns. Smocking and checked dimity. Not at all sophisticated."

No choice left him, Seb struck a compromise.

His gaze went first to Sarah. "Please do me the honor of accepting the gifts."

Seb then looked to the pouting Chelle. "Unsophisticated gowns are exactly what I had in mind. Sarah is only eighteen. Too young to dress her like a Bowery floozy or a honky-tonk madam."

Like a gunslinger looking to protect his rear, he hightailed it back to his chair against the wall and rewarmed the seat. No way could the females ambush him there. "Show me what you brought, Chelle."

Frenchie opened the leather garment case. "You said from the skin out, so we start with the undergarments, made in a very fine lawn material. Had I known theeze were meant for your whore, *naturellement*, I would have made the chemises and drawers in silk."

Seb nodded. "Try 'em on, Sarah."

"Here?" his prim mistress squeaked.

"Here." Clean out of compromise, he folded his arms over his chest.

"But, sir, I wear nothing underneath my trousers and shirt."

"*Alors!*" Chelle rolled her eyes. "I have already seen you naked. When you took the Spanish fly, you paraded all over the house wearing naught but love bites."

Sarah gasped. "I did?" Big cornflower-blue eyes widened on him. "Sir?"

Now Chelle had gone and done it, gotten Sarah all upset. "Aphrodisiacs tend to bring out the exhibitionism in a person. And you were *not* nekkid—you had on a sheet."

"A sheet," she glumly repeated, her expression reflecting crestfallen remembrance. "I wore it toga-style."

"And you looked right purty in it, too. Now, get this here show on the road." Like a sultan with a harem, he clapped his hands. "Strip!"

Straightaway, Chelle went for her buttons and bows.

"Not you, honey," he told Frenchie. "Sarah."

His bashful mistress turned a bright shade of head-to-toe pink as she dropped the ugly shirt and pants to the floor. Bare and beautiful, she took center stage in the gardener's cottage.

While he ogled Sarah, Chelle corralled her. Tapping her Frenchie chin with a red-painted fingertip, the dressmaker then brought that same fiery talon to within an inch of Sarah's tittie, which had gone pointy with excitement. All the attention had roused Sarah's hot nature.

"The bosom eez quite nice. Small, of course, but the conical shape is unusual. The *petit* size will show to best advantage if I place a dart high on the bodice. Like so—"

Chelle moved a sight closer and drew a line high on Sarah's chest. Afterwards, she cupped those petite mounds underneath. "No need to lift theez, as they are already quite high. But a corset will define the waist."

Seb resettled in his seat, all fired up at the gal-on-gal action.

"No corset," he rasped and made a discreet adjustment to his inseam. "Sarah's figure is trim and shapely already without the addition of lacing."

"If you say so, Seb. And I suppose you are correct. The waist eez tiny. Even my hands can span it." She did just that.

But when Chelle's seamstress measuring drifted lower, Sarah spoke up.

"Mademoiselle, I believe you are under the mistaken impression that I am a Sapphic." She let go a sigh. "Though the vagina is a wondrous creation, beautiful, mysterious, and provocative, I favor the more prosaic services and utilitarian function of the male penis."

Seb coughed. "I can vouch for that."

Chelle turned to him. "But, Seb, she eez yet young. How can one know for sure to which gender she is disposed?"

"Take my word for it, honey. Sarah is disposed to cock."

"*Alors!* There eez only one way to know for *certainement.* Perhaps after the fitting, we can put her preference to the test. A *ménage à trois,* hmm?"

Two frisky fillies seeing to the needs of one randy man and playing with each other, too—nothing to think on there! He had plenty enough stamina to go around, and guaranteed both females would come away happy. High time he introduced his high-thinking mistress to some lowbrow ideas. Threesomes were bawdy and dirty, and flew smack-dab in the face of straight-laced society. After putting up with snooty Easterners for a sight too long, he reckoned shaking loose behind closed doors sounded just about right—

"How about it, Sarah?" he asked.

"Whatever you say, sir. I am at your command."

Was that condescension in her tone? Was she playing snob to his back-alley tastes?

Seb narrowed his eyes. "Give me a preview, Chelle. Show me what you have in mind."

"But, of course." Chelle kissed Sarah's cheek, then took her lips.

And Seb squirmed in his chair.

Double-edged sword was a man's imagination. Introducing Sarah to the wilder side of carnal pleasure had him all hot and bothered. But—to put the fantasy into practice meant sharing her passion, a move that squeezed at his gut. No doubt about it, Michael Winslow's daughter had a hold on him.

Spots of red appeared before Seb's eyes.

Dammit! He would not let that devil control him from beyond the grave through his daughter. He called the shots here! Sarah Winslow did *not* have a hold on him—

"Open your legs, Sarah," he coolly instructed his mistress when Chelle finally let her come up for air.

Lips swollen, blue eyes dazed, Sarah obediently split her thighs.

Chelle dove her red-tipped fingers inside Sarah's pussy and did what fingers inside pussies normally do.

Sarah shook and writhed and trembled, involuntary kinds of moves she did before coming—

For him. Always before for him.

That one thought alone should have been enough to make him call Chelle's seduction to a halt, but the devil in the shape of Michael Winslow was riding Seb's tail, and so he allowed the sham of foreplay to continue.

Until Sarah's glazed-over eyes made contact with his.

When he saw despair lurking within their blue depths, he called it off. "Go try on the clothes behind the curtain, Sarah, and then come on out and give me a show."

A threesome ain't fun unless all participants are willing. Sarah's hot nature might have been willing, but her mind had shut down.

For the rest of the fitting, Frenchie behaved like a consummate professional as Sarah tried on all the new duds—lawn chemises and drawers, and umpteen gowns, too. In a yellow dimity, she looked as pretty as a picture.

"She stays in that one," he told Chelle and, real quick-like, ushered the dressmaker out the door.

Stealing back into his chair, Seb beckoned his mistress with a crooked finger.

Sarah came to a shy stand between his spread knees. "Thank you, sir," she said prettily, like a well-mannered little girl, "for all the new gowns and underpinnings."

"The thanks are all mine." His Adam's apple jerked up, then down. "You look real demure in that gown, just like a yella flower. A daffodil," he drawled.

"Never have I owned so many new ensembles at one time." On a cloud of yellow dimity, she dropped a chaste kiss on his cheekbone.

Chaste had its place, but spice was nice, too.

He slanted his jaw, taking Sarah's mouth in a kiss that was anything but chaste, tongue down her throat, his big hands roaming. She was only eighteen, and a sheltered young miss, but he had a terrible yen to do naughty things to her.

At his directive, Sarah had foregone a corset, and womanly points jabbed his palms through the yellow dimity, thankfully contradicting the cradle-robbing image he suddenly had of himself.

Still, he had a hankering to play a game of lecher and ward. Would she join in?

He separated his lips from hers, surveyed her schoolgirl-tight bodice. "Your nipples are quite large, miss. They must hurt," he said sympathetically.

She looked up into his eyes, paused for a moment, and then nodded. "Oh, they do, sir. They do. Dreadfully so. I believe I may have started to grow on top. My breasts, I mean." She giggled self-consciously, as a schoolgirl would.

"No need to needlessly suffer when I can make you more comfortable." He got to work on her back fastenings.

When the gown was a puff of yellow around her trim waist, he examined her bosom, the tips distended to the length of his thumbs under the lawn of her chemise. "Any better?"

"A bit, sir." She worried her bottom lip, her chin tilted down, her gaze following.

"Only a bit?"

"Yes, sir. Of late, I have gone without a chemise. And this one feels rather...well...confining."

"Confining. I see. You could dispense with it, I suppose."

"I could?" she said uncertainly. "I should dearly love to. Only..."

"Only what?" he coaxed.

"Would removing my undergarment constitute the proper thing to do?"

"As your...er...guardian, I really should examine this new growth spurt you mentioned, if only to give the seamstress your new measurements."

"If you tell me to do so, sir, then of course, I shan't disobey." Grinning from ear to ear, his mischievous mistress sent the straps of her chemise down her shapely arms. "I shall do everything you tell me to do," she purred, and wiggled her shoulders so that her chemise drifted around her waist and her now bared roundness shifted and bounced.

"Such pretty titties," he said in rapture, his dirty talk hopefully disguising his absorbing delight. "Shall I touch them?"

"Oh, yes. Please do. A hard pinch, please."

He did. He pinched the tip, and the pleasure of it had him grinding his teeth together.

"Shall I suck them?" he strained though his tensed lips.

"Oh, yes, sir. Please do."

He lowered his head, his clenched jaw barely cranking open wide enough to take the huge, blood-suffused paps in.

He clamped down, his teeth scraping the sensitive skin of the areola, and she reached for the hair atop his head and yanked, the action feeling like she had pulled a fistful of strands out by the root.

"Ah!" they gasped together, his utterance almost lost because of the nipple in his mouth.

"The other one, too," she cried.

He popped the engorged tittie from between his tight lips. "Shame on you!" he reprimanded. "You are not to behave so brazenly."

She fluttered her lashes. "Did I do something wrong, sir? I meant only to show you my growth pattern—"

"Perhaps I misunderstood your motives," he conceded. "And they are extraordinarily large. Your titties have graduated to tits."

She pouted. "I told you so, sir."

"Do not talk back to me, Sarah," he warned.

"Sorry," she said, not at all contritely. Her eyes dancing in merriment, she stuck out her tongue.

"That does it, young lady! Your insolence must end. Over my knee you go."

Faster than a tail-shake, she rounded her tail over his lap.

After tossing the childish yellow puff of skirts and white lawn petticoats over her dark head, his hand came down five times on her rump.

"Oh, God, please, sir," she cried at the end. The game was over, and the little girl had fled, a needy woman taking her place.

Her new drawers came with a slit crotch for necessary trips; his palm slid easily inside.

After watching that female-on-female kiss, he was all reared up and ready to go.

He rubbed his fingers into Sarah's cleft, and she moaned. "Mmm."

"You are not to come just yet," he said soft and low. "Wait 'til I get it up inside you."

She bit into his leg. "I shan't come if you also agree."

"You just bit off more than you can chew. I can go for hours without popping my cork."

"Oh, really?" the saucy wench said. "Shall we see who can outlast the other?"

"You, little lady, are on," he growled.

Seb drew his hurting mistress up and over his lap, leaving her coltish legs to dangle one on either side of his bent knees. Like that of a salon fancy-woman, her bottom, soft and giving, commenced to bumping and grinding.

"Lift up!" he cried hoarsely.

As soon as she had complied, he ripped his trousers apart and got himself out. Two hands at her waist, he lifted her up on top of him and drove into her clasp.

He exploded before the first completed stroke.

"Sorry," he apologized, his forehead to hers, as humbled as a man could get. He had not pleased Sarah.

He pulled back a little, gazed up sorrowfully into her eyes.

She greeted him with a sunny, self-satisfied grin. "You know, sir, you really should refrain from gambling. At least with me. With me, your face is akin to an open book, and my reading comprehension is really quite excellent. I knew from the outset you would never make it."

Laughing, she kissed his mouth.

Sarah took the sting right out of losing.

As long as he never lost her.

Chapter Twenty-Seven

Sarah craned her neck upwards to the purple beech. "Master William," she scolded. "You will remove yourself from that branch at once! Do you wish to fall and break your neck?"

"No, ma'am, Miss Sarah. If'n my neck broke, my head just might roll away." Cheeky Billy Breen grinned, a crooked smile that displayed a missing front tooth.

Oh, to climb onto that branch beside him and tweak his freckled nose! How to play the strict disciplinarian in light of such joyful boyishness? How to lecture on the hazards of tree climbing after her own recent spill from a rotted apple tree?

After extending Billy a helping hand to safety, she ruffled his already mussed hair. "Next time, confine your climbing to smaller trees. Personally, I recommend fruit trees, where a fall to the ground is less likely to break any bones." One last ruffle of his cowlick, and she clapped her hands together, much as Mr. Turner had done to her but a few days before. "Dinner is ready. Go wash up."

"Will you read to us tonight at bedtime, Miss Sarah?"

"I always do, do I not?"

"Yep, but I just like to make sure."

And that uncertainty summarized the whole sad story of these children. The world of an orphan was never sure, never certain. After the loss of both parents, a child lost all sense of security—

With another huge grin, the recently orphaned William Breen scampered away to the run-down building next to the village workhouse. Billy's smile attested to a child's unique ability to live only in the moment. Later on tonight, though, when the lonely darkness closed in, the little lost boy would sob into his pillow. All the new orphans did. And that was why, regardless of Sebastian's latest dictate about not leaving the cottage, she would be there for Billy, to hold him in her arms, to tell him and the other children stories, to try her best to fill that motherless void they all, including herself, had in common. She would need to sneak past whichever lackey her owner had assigned guard duty over her to accomplish this end, but to her mind, that was but a small inconvenience when considering the rewards.

Seb paced the floor of gardener's cottage. Where the hell had Sarah gone?

After a swift conclusion of his appointment in Manhattan, the hastiness done with an eye toward spending the remainder of the day in bed with his mistress, he had discovered her nowhere to be found.

Had Sarah gone off someplace alone? Or was she off on a tryst, a secret rendezvous, with a secret lover? Like her guard, Rattler, who had also gone conveniently missing?

That she might be in the company of that desperado fueled Seb's rage.

The alternative struck terror in his heart.

The image of Sarah's white body trapped submerged beneath the muddy waters of the river would not give him peace. That picture would cut into his thoughts when he least expected to find it there, always with a horrific rendering.

Which explained why, if given a choice, he would rather think she had gone off someplace safe with Rattler than dwell on the possibility of her having gone off someplace unsafe alone.

Still, safety was a relative term.

Goldarnit! His thoughts kept going 'round and 'round inside his head without a solution.

A black mood descended over him, its darkness competing with the moonless night. Never before had he suffered a woman's absence. When a female went from him to another man—sometimes in the course of the same evening—he let the bed-hopping go with a shrug. Jealousy was a moot point since he always kept his attentions confined to working gals. Now jealousy had him by the balls.

Prove me wrong, Sarah!

But, as the hour grew long in the tooth, Sarah's ability to remain faithful seemed less and less likely.

That Michael Winslow's daughter might have played him for a fool ate at Seb—

Unless, something had happened to her and she was out there right now, somewhere in the dark, all alone.

Inactivity sent him climbing the walls. He had to do something. Anything! If only to put a lid on the cauldron of his imaginings.

Seb raced outside, his destination the river. Knowing the action made no sense, he found himself pulling off his boots on the bank, preparing to dive into the water to search the bottom. Before he scrambled down the slope, he saw her. Sarah. Hurrying along the dirt path to the cottage.

He shot after her, barefoot, hardly breathing, his skin too tight for his frame. "Where have you been?"

"Gathering wildflower seeds. Native plants grow in purple and yellow drifts further down along the river. So pretty in the spring," she said nonchalantly. "I thought to grow some closer to the house."

"Gathering seeds—in the pitch dark?"

"Hardly pitch." She clucked her tongue. "The sun only just went down, sir. It took me a while to walk back."

Anger rose to the forefront, beating down his awful sense of panic. "I told you not to leave the cottage."

"I took that to mean I might not leave the grounds."

To hide their twitching, he folded his arms over his chest. "Where are these seeds you say you gathered?"

"Seeds?" Her brow furrowed. "Oh! Yes, the seeds. They—uh—are drying on a rock in the woods."

He read the lie in her expression. "Return to the cottage. Now! Immediately!" Steam had to be shooting out his ears. Did she notice? Hell, no! Not Sarah. His bare feet held her attention.

"But where are your boots?" she asked, her glance lowered. "Have you just returned from fishing? The night-crawlers at the river's edge make most excellent bait."

"Dang my boots! And dang the dang night-crawlers, too. You are not to go near the river ever again. Do you hear me?"

"Of course I hear you. Who cannot hear you? Your shout would carry to the town center, where orphan children sleep in their narrow cots. I certainly hope you have not awakened them. As to your boots—tooled leather uppers are quite costly." She lectured like a schoolmarm. "Carelessness is on the same footing with wastefulness. You really should take better care of your wardrobe."

The gall of her! Sermonizing him after he had just caught her in a lie!

He stomped after her into the cottage and slammed the door shut. Rocking back and forth on his bootless feet, he gave her a second chance to take back her untruth. "Were you alone?"

She cast him a wide-eyed innocent look. "Alone? Alone when, sir?"

"When-you-were-out-on-your-walk-collecting-seeds!"

"Certainly, I was alone, sir."

"Where is Rattler?"

"Rattler? Why ask *me?* The man works for *you!*" She shook her head. "I do not see how your foreman is relevant to this discussion. Besides, wherever he is, he is more than likely handling your business in an expert fashion."

Sarah sprang right quick to the defense of that hombre. Now *there* was loyalty. Her devotion to that gunslinger made Seb mad enough to spit bullets. What had that low-down coyote done to earn her trust? The desperado made his way in life as a paid killer, and yet Sarah stuck up for him—

Because they were lovers?

Accusation tightened his vocal cords to a harsh whip. "I 'spect you were steppin' out with my foreman today."

When she opened her mouth to answer, he cut her off at the pass. "No more lies!" Then, temper flaring, added, "And once and for all, get out of those dead-man's clothes."

In a garden gazebo, an idealistic young lady had spoken of her belief in love, and now that same young lady had acted like a cheap whore. How had he believed, even for a magical evening, that Michael Winslow's daughter had the capacity for fidelity?

But what stuck in his craw the worst was not that he had fallen for her lies and deception, not that she had made a fool of him, but that he was still not safe from her. No amount of distance would keep him safe from her. If he stood at one end of the earth, and she stood at the polar opposite, he would still feel Sarah's pull. He had always felt her pull. Even as an infant, she had drawn him to her.

She had dropped her trousers. The pants hobbled her at the ankles, tying her up like a heifer awaiting the branding iron.

Taking out his knife, he moved in on her.

"Please, no!" she cried, fear threading her voice.

What the hell did she take him for? Did she really believe he would take the blade to her flesh? He would sooner slash his own throat than hurt her—

But how would she know that about him? And why would she trust him?

He had never allowed her to see inside his mind, to know what made him tick; he had withheld all but the sketchiest information about his background from her.

And why?

So she would never find out that he had hurt her.

And he had hurt her. Not a clean cut made with a blade, but a cut all the same. He had severed her from her old way of life, from opportunities rightfully hers. She would be a fool to trust him!

And because of her blood connection to Michael Winslow, he would be a fool to trust her. Where did that leave them?

Right where there were now—a woman cowering in fear from a man with a knife, neither trusting the other not to inflict hurt.

"I only meant to free you from this damned tangle." Boots first. Then breeches. Straightening her out, he attacked the homely shirt, slicing the threads holding the buttons in place, popping them off one after another until none remained.

Every time he clapped his eyes on that ugly shirt, it reminded him of all the ugly things he had done to Sarah.

He threw the rag on the floor. "I told you to stay put in the cottage."

"Continue ripping my clothes to shreds, and I shall have no choice left me." Her eyes twinkled. "Unless, of course, I adopt jungle ways and start going about stark naked. Not that I should mind. Nudity is vastly liberating, as well as providing a certain male personage with fantasy material by which to self-indulge."

"Vixen! You saw me that day."

"Which day is that?"

"The day you washed clothes wearing nothing but a dead man's shirt."

"I never did. But I did discover your rolled-up handkerchief today on my way back through the woods. After its libidinous usage, you must have dropped it. I merely put two plus two together. You, yourself, have just confirmed the sum."

"You grifted me!" How did she do it? Every time they went toe to toe, he came out the loser. This time, she had caught him in the middle of a male frailty. Humiliating to have her see him in that weak, all-too-human light.

She grinned. "I really think you should spank me. How else will I ever learn my place?"

"Your *place!*" he grunted. "I could whup your bottom until it glowed bright red and I doubt you would learn that lesson."

"Bright red?" Her eyes went wide, as if he had just offered her a treat.

Defeated, he yelled, "Strumpet! Get on the bed."

Making a beeline for the four-poster, Sarah flopped down on her belly.

He had his male weaknesses; she had some female ones. But unlike him, she had no qualms about bringing them to his attention.

Bemused, he followed her to the bed.

She panted over her shoulder at him. "I never thought you would harm me. Not really. But I did experience a moment of doubt, a small twinge of misgiving. I should never have assigned that sort of violence to you. You are not a violent man."

"Oh, but I am. And you, Sarah, require violence to derive the most pleasure." His palm came down hard on her buttocks.

She yelped in pleasure. "The need shames me—"

"No call for it to." His past had shaped his present; made sense that Sarah would have things in her past, too, that had shaped her.

"Today—did you worry for me?" She purred, raising her bottom for more.

Instead of another spank, he bit into her ass.

Females thought spreading their legs left them wide open for a male. That sort of vulnerability had no comparison to when a man left his emotions wide open for a woman. To protect himself from hurt, he had been less than truthful with Sarah; he would be painfully truthful now.

"Hell, yeah, I worried over you!"

That admitted, he proceeded to kiss away the hurt he had just inflicted.

The rest of the hurt would take a lot more than kisses to heal.

Chapter Twenty-Eight

No use dissembling, Sarah thought, as the evening gave way to the dawn of a new day. She loved her owner without pretense, beyond reason. And because she loved him, a pure, indestructible love, she arranged herself on her back on the bed for the fourth occasion that night.

But not without qualms.

Though he had physically pleasured her, he had left her emotionally unsatisfied. As a result, a festering hurt, a bubbling discontent, brought on by what she considered a certain typically male disregard for feminine feelings when it came to coitus, would not permit a full response to his foreplay. She desired him, oh, yes, she did, but it was a brooding desire, for whilst she always came apart at the end, he stayed all of one piece.

His stroking stopped. "Well?"

"Well, what?" she snipped.

"When are you gonna tell me?"

"Tell you what?" she grumbled.

"What I did!" he exploded, withdrawing from her body. "And do not say 'nothing,' when I know something is wrong."

"No one likes to be made to feel anonymous," she said heatedly.

"Anonymous!" he shouted, as though *he* were the aggrieved party, not she. "Never once have I lost sight of who you are!"

"Well, perhaps you would prefer not having the reminder."

"What are you talking about?" he asked, voice edgy.

"Darkness has surrounded us all night. You never once thought to light a lamp to dispel the anonymity. Visual contact with your face would have been ever so appreciated, if only to reassure myself an actual man is attached to the reproductive organ diddling me."

"Diddling you!" he repeated, and she heard, rather than saw, his jaw drop. "What the hell kind of a thing is that for a lady to say?"

She bit her tongue at Sebastian's slip in speech. In truth, she was no longer a lady. Through his inclusion in her life, she had risen to something so much better, so much more real, than that trite and pretentious societal status. She had become a woman.

A woman in love.

That love gave her strength and patience. She would need both to reach the orphaned child trapped in Mr. Turner's angry man's body.

Though the understanding hurt, she knew why he refused her his face—far easier to take her as a whore, to trust only in the physical, than to believe in the possibility of something deeper.

At any rate, she had to reconcile herself to the reality of her situation with him. Because of some terrible trauma in his background, Mr. Turner might never summon up enough courage to take the leap into faith that was love. He could only handle what he could see, smell, taste, hear, and touch.

A pity, Sarah mused, for solid proof is often illusion, and only the intangibles in life are real.

"You want light?" he asked querulously.

The shift on the mattress told her Mr. Turner had left the bed.

"There," he said, drawing back the single curtain beside the four-poster.

As the light she had requested slowly crept into the window, her owner reclaimed his position in bed. In a golden morning glow, he knelt before her open legs. With strength born of love, she patiently reached up and smoothed the thick black hair away from troubled dark eyes. "You know what I think?"

"No, I do not. I never do."

She sensed him skulking away from the discussion, hunkering down inside the protective fortress he'd built around himself. Though exasperated, she maintained her calm composure. "I think, sir, you keep some deep, dark, hidden secrets."

"And I think you, miss, are given to flights of fancy."

"If, someday, you would like to talk, I should like to listen."

"No, thank you."

"Sir, you can trust me. I vow never to give the real you away."

He looked up at her, and something resembling hope flickered across the set of his dark features.

A rap at the door shattered the possibility of that hope coming to fruition.

"If we stay very, very quiet," he said with a forced chuckle, "maybe whoever is out there will give up and go away. Or maybe," he said, leering at her, "we can stay real quiet and sneak in a quick one?" He made a grab for her.

She swatted at his hands. "Do you even know how to do *quick?*" she asked under her breath. "Because I seem to recall nothing but hour-long sessions."

"I know just as much about being quick as you know about being quiet," he whispered in return. "And I regard your hour-long-session remark as a compliment to my manly stamina." He sniffed pompously.

His officiousness sent her hurdling into a gale of the giggles.

"See?" he rejoined, "You have not the least notion of proper bedchamber etiquette. Did none of those scandalous books you read on copulation relate that laughter deflates a man?"

Sarah eased herself away from an all-too-distinctive prod. Despite Sebastian's advisement, he had not at all deflated. On the contrary, his shaft had lengthened and hardened.

She licked her lips in greed.

But, alas, concern for propriety had returned, and with it, decorum. Restraint replaced spontaneity. "That door is not at all thick. Whoever is out there can probably hear our every hushed word."

Bristling, she hopped from the feather mattress to search under the bed. "Where have my boots gone?"

"How should I know?" Sebastian's voice contained a lad's mischievous rumble as he moved in behind her.

Before she knew what he was about, he had picked her up off the floor, hoisted her legs right out from under her, and held her up in the air whilst swiveling her about to face him. Pressed to his groin, her legs split asunder on either side of his hips, she dissolved in laughter, through which she sputtered, "Sir, you cannot actually think to do *it* like this?"

"Oh, but I do," he gamely replied. "And I intend to fill you to the brim."

With that insufferable boast, Mr. Turner began to do just that, as their visitor cooled his or her heels outside.

While his bashful mistress dressed behind the curtain, Seb sat at the edge of the bed and pulled on his breeches, finishing up on his shirt buttons as he flung open the cottage door.

"Ah, Miss Cabot!" At the threshold, he combed his fingers through his short hair. "What a surprise."

With an ungracious snort, Eleanor elbowed her way past him into the cottage. "Have you forgotten our morning appointment, Mr. Turner?"

"Unlikely event," he dryly replied, "with you here to remind me."

Ignoring the sarcasm—unkind, but to the point—he had directed at her, Eleanor kept right on rolling. "There is much I wish to relate about the charity event Mama and Papa are hosting."

He tucked in his shirttails. "Charity event?"

"Yes. To be held next week. Surely I told you? The proceeds go to support the local orphanage. Anyone who is anyone will put in an appearance. The invitation list includes people of some influence. It might serve your interests to meet these guests, Mr. Turner."

After taking a nosy look around the single room, she spun to face him. "Will you be able to attend?"

"You may count on me to support the charity, Miss Cabot. But I need to beg off attending. I have plans for all of next week."

The young lady very much involved in those plans stepped out from behind the privacy curtain, wearing, as always, the usual abominable outfit that hid her unusually sensual nature. The night before, Sarah's sensual nature had whipped him into a feverish frenzy. He looked forward to more of the same today...

As soon as he rid himself of Miss Cabot, who even now plucked at the strings of her reticule, an irritating habit of hers that appeared whenever she failed to get her own way.

Disposing of her could take hours. First, he would need to endure a damnably long ride in a closed carriage discussing the weather and Parisian fashions and the latest society gossip. As no one was spared Miss Cabot's blistering tongue, Seb's skull pounded in anticipation of her endless droning. More talk of kick flounces. More gloomy forecasts of rain. More cattiness.

Duty to future progeny would carry a man only so far. The prospect of playing hooky in the here and now with the delightful Sarah had him wracking his head for excuses to cry off from his obligation.

"Well, I never!" Eleanor turned to him, but pointed to Sarah's unshod insteps. "Her feet are bare. Why are her feet bare, Mr. Turner?"

Better to suck on her pretty toes, Seb thought.

Regardless of the space that separated them, regardless of the third party present in the room, his carnal tension clamored for release. Luckily, he had some small experience in these matters, and so he managed to camouflage his longing.

Just. Barely.

Not nearly as practiced as he, Sarah flushed. As though she could read his thoughts, her blush suffused her pale skin under the collar of the hideous shirt. The heat of that flush would spread from her breasts to her belly. Then, pearled honey would flow, sweet and bountiful, from the delightful notch between her shapely thighs.

His salivating glands demanded the immediate discharge of Miss Cabot.

Eleanor stamped her foot on the wide pine flooring. "Mr. Turner! I have asked why your gardener's feet are bare!"

"Because she has yet to don her hose and boots," he replied, taking a wild stab at a passable answer to a ridiculous question.

Eleanor cast her eyes in speculation upon his shirt, the same shirt he had worn the day before—coincidentally, at her house. Only yesterday, his linen had been neatly pressed, and today the cloth looked like a sex-rumpled bed.

Her narrowing gaze spoke volumes. Eleanor was on to him.

Seb gave no alibi, offered no excuses, submitted no apology. Too late for those maneuvers. Time to pay the piper. But how to spare Sarah embarrassment while simultaneously appeasing Eleanor's affronted pride?

A quandary. But not the first tight spot he had ever escaped. As it so happened, he did his best maneuvering when cornered.

He reconsidered that last thought and decided he could dance 'til the fiddler ran out of tunes, and his fancy footwork would just dig him deeper into a hole.

Eleanor now shredded the drawstring on her reticule.

Though no authority on the subject, it seemed to Seb that society had at its foundation certain unexpressed rules of conduct—ignoring the obvious being one of the more important dictates.

Providing he gave in to her demands, Miss Cabot would overlook a few of his more glaring manly transgressions. She would pretend Sarah's bare feet signified nothing, while he would pretend innocence of any and all hanky-panky regarding those lovely bare feet, and they would all go on merrily, much as before.

Anxious to get that merriment under way, Seb set up the swindle. "Who will do the floral arrangements at the charity event, Miss Cabot?"

Eleanor pursed her lips. "Who said anything about flowers?"

"But, of course, you must have vases of floral arrangements for the tables." He rolled his eyes. "Dear me! So déclassé not to go the extra length for a soirée. You know, I received absolutely *scads* of congratulatory praise for the bouquets Sarah designed for the party I gave here." He made a swishy motion with his hand and sniffed. "I tell you, my head is still positively *swollen* from the lavish compliments. Most especially from Miss Cynthia Hornsworth. She utterly *adored* the blossoms."

Miss Cabot's thin mouth grew thinner. "Cynthia?"

"She is a dear friend of yours, is she not?"

Not. Cynthia Hornsworth rivaled Miss Cabot on the social scene.

Seb laughed up his wrinkled sleeve—nothing wrong with a little healthy competition.

"Yes, Cynthia is a dear friend. As is Sarah." Eleanor turned to his mistress and offered a tight smile. "Dear, so fortunate to find you at—er—home. I have a favor to ask."

"A favor?" Sarah asked suspiciously.

Eleanor stopped her reticule-plucking to rearrange her kick flounce, a yard width of nonsensical ruffles that must have taken an army of bespectacled seamstresses to stitch.

"Yes, dear, a favor. Although all the ladies of the parish will pitch in for next week's charity affair, we are still short of hands. We must dig deeper for help. To the bottom of the barrel, to be sure. With that in mind, I wonder if you might come and help out? With Mr. Turner's permission, of course."

Eleanor looked to him. "Sarah may do the flower arranging." Her thin smile grew tighter and tighter, until her lips stretched to a grimace. "Is that acceptable to you, Mr. Turner? She is *your* servant."

"Sarah is the resident gardener at Clearbrook. A professional artiste, not a servant, and as such, the decision is entirely up to her."

Seb thought this reply downright magnanimous, considering society events always ran late and hence Sarah's agreement would cut into their private time together. And did he complain? Hell, no! He stood there, manfully suffering in silence.

"I should be delighted to help out with the bouquets," Sarah said. "The orphanage needs all the financial support it can get."

Sarah's agreement left Seb with two choices: stay home alone, or go to the charity event in the hopes of seeing Sarah there.

Easy decision.

"I will personally escort Miss Winslow there and back," Seb offered.

"And stay?" Miss Cabot bribed.

Seb conceded to the con. "And stay."

While Eleanor preened into a nearby mirror, he sent a beaming grin to Sarah.

But his mistress turned her head away, refusing to meet his gaze.

Chapter Twenty-Nine

On the day of the charity event, Sarah alighted not from the leather comfort of Mr. Turner's sumptuous carriage, but from the bumping and jarring of the Cabot's feed wagon.

Emergency business in Manhattan had called Mr. Turner away at the last possible moment, and with him went her manner of transport.

Like a sheep going to market, the wagon driver herded her through the servants' entrance, where Eleanor met her with an ill-disguised sneer. "Sarah, regardless of what Mr. Turner allows you to get away with at Clearbrook, in this house, we require servants to wear suitable livery."

Sarah surveyed her gardening attire. Assuming she would spend her time outside cutting flowers for arrangements, Sarah had worn a shirt and trousers. "What would you suggest I do, Miss Cabot?"

"Downstairs in the kitchen cloakroom, you will find appropriate apparel—gray serge gown, white apron. Undergarments," she added pointedly.

Sarah nodded. "Yes, ma'am."

"As Cook is one girl short tonight, you will do scullery duty in the kitchen."

"But what of the floral arrangements?"

"You are not to question my orders." Eleanor sniffed. "Mr. Turner would expect his servant to do as told. Do not force me to give him a bad report about you."

"Yes, ma'am." Honest work was honest work. If washing dishes would help the orphans, Sarah would be the best lower maid Cook had ever supervised in the kitchen. And if Eleanor thought to humiliate her, she would need to try a great deal harder.

"I cannot expose my female staff to you," Eleanor said, trying a great deal harder. "Who knows what prostitute diseases you carry." She shuddered theatrically. "I shall order everything you wear burned as soon as you are done."

She looked Sarah up and down. "Built like a lad, dressed as a lad, you will change like a lad in the barn with our male staff. Just mind you keep your hands to yourself. Here, we do not tolerate promiscuity. Is that understood?"

Promiscuity!

Sarah opened her mouth to defend herself, only to close her lips again. Where was the argument?

She was a whore, a prostitute who had come to love her owner—was there anything more pathetic?

Yes, that Eleanor had succeeded in humiliating her.

Dejected, and, yes, gloomy too, Sarah retrieved the servant's attire from a cubby in the cloakroom, then walked to the barn, where she searched out some private space in which to change.

In an empty stall, way in the back, she listlessly removed her gardening clothing, hanging shirt and trousers neatly on a nail—melancholia did not excuse slovenliness. Naked, she shook the folds from the plain gray servant's gown.

The brittle crunch of footsteps in the hay warned that someone approached.

Borrowed garment clutched to her breasts, Sarah called, "Who is there?"

Silence answered her.

"Anyone there?" she called again.

Only her imagination, Sarah concluded upon again receiving no response.

Nevertheless, she scrambled into the servant's garb and raced for the main house.

Sarah had washed, dried, and put away the dishes. After sweeping the kitchen floor, she scrubbed the oilcloth on hands and knees, then scoured the stove and all cooking surfaces, using a bucket, a brush, and caustic lye soap.

As she stretched her cramped back, Cook turned to her. "Miss Cabot wants you above stairs."

What did the shrew want now?

Only one way to find out.

Sarah rolled her water-splashed sleeves back down to cover her wrists; then trudged up the two flights to face her childhood friend.

She dropped a curtsey. "Yes, ma'am?"

Eleanor tapped her toe. "As it turns out, my service wagon is not available this evening—a broken wheel or some such foolishness—so I must rescind my offer of transportation back to Clearbrook. You will pass the night here instead."

Sarah had only just barely digested the meat of this bad news, when Eleanor heaped her plate again.

"For decency's sake, I cannot force a maid to share a bed with you in the servants' quarters, so you will retire in the stable with the horses. Here." Eleanor shoved a blanket at her.

Bitch.

"Yes, ma'am." Before giving in to the irresistible urge to throw her erstwhile friend to the floor, pounce on her buxomness, rip out her golden blond hair, and pummel her perfectly white complexion, Sarah headed for the door.

"Just who do you think you are?" Eleanor shouted at her back.

Fists clenched, Sarah turned.

She would *not* knock the bitch's teeth down her throat. She would *not!*

"Ma'am?" Sarah gritted out.

"You are a scullery maid in this house, not a guest. Return below, and use the servant's entrance."

"But this door is less than a foot away."

"Do not think to get uppity with me, Sarah Winslow. You are to keep a civil tongue in your head when speaking to your betters. Insolent baggage!" Eleanor raged, her face reddening in her fury. "How long do you think Mr. Turner will keep a lowly prostitute under his roof? Not long," she said, answering her own question. "Then, you will end up walking the streets."

The vitriolic nature of Eleanor's outburst took Sarah aback. Though, once again, how futile to argue the truth! For, with no money, no family, no prospects, no place to go, she most likely would end up on the streets.

The last of Sarah's pride died. Without another word, she slumped back down the stairs and out the servants' door to the stable. The dim light of a single lantern guiding her, she made her way to the stall where she had changed earlier in the day.

Silly to give in to useless emotion. Useless to cry. Really, she should be grateful to Eleanor! Employment as a garden designer was a foolish, romantic dream! A young girl's innocent dream. Yes, she loved Sebastian, heart and soul, but there would come a day when he would no longer require her services. Through marriage or through fickleness, he would cast her out, and she would end up on her own.

A wise woman planned! She must take what resources she had—her body, her youth, her intellect—and use them to the best advantage.

Whilst undoing the buttons on her borrowed servant's gown, Sarah mulled those plans.

An abbreviated contemplation, the planning of her future ending when someone blew out the single lantern, grabbed her from behind, and threw her to the hay.

Chapter Thirty

"Sebastian Turner, here to escort Miss Sarah Winslow home," he announced to the Cabot parlor maid, who had answered his summons at the front door.

At the conclusion of his business appointment in the city, Seb had beaten a hasty return to the gardener's cottage, only to find that Sarah had yet to return from that day's charity event. Too impatient to await her delivery in the Cabot carriage, as previously arranged, he'd jumped back into the saddle to fetch his mistress back to Clearbrook himself.

The high-pitched shrill jarred his bones. "Mr. Turner!"

Eleanor. The very person he wished most to avoid.

Elbowing the parlor maid aside, she beamed up at him. "Please, do come in."

After pissing the day away, Seb had determined he would salvage the evening. For that to happen, he needed his mistress. Everything else was optional, including Eleanor's belief in his excuse. "Though I should dearly love to stay and visit with you, Miss Cabot, unfortunately the day was long and tedious, and I require my bed." He looked beyond Eleanor's blond crest of curls, searching for a dark head. "Where is my gardener?"

Eleanor's thin lips snapped like a pair of tight suspenders. "That harlot! However do you tolerate her immoral behavior?"

"Immoral behavior? Sarah?"

"None other. As you know, today's event was a charitable fund drive. As those poor, unfortunate orphans are in desperate need of new housing, preferably in another parish, I worked my fingers to the bone to raise sufficient moneys for them to move, as did all the other ladies present, whilst *that one* lazed about making eyes at the stable lads."

Seb admitted to concerns over Sarah's familiarity with Rattler. But lazy? If anything, she worked too dang hard.

"The last I saw her, your...*gardener*...was headed for the stables. Again. That is where the males congregate, if you understand my meaning."

Only a fool would not.

Seb bowed low over the lady's hand. "Please accept my humble apologies for disturbing you, Miss Cabot." Turning on his heel, he left for the stables, a portable lantern taken from Eleanor's front post to guide him.

Following a thrashing sound, Seb made his way inside the dark outbuilding, finding his mistress in the last stall, rolling in the hay with a hired hand.

A well-placed kick sent the stable boy crawling for the door.

Seb let the youthful barn rat go. He had more important concerns than a lad who could not keep his breeches closed.

He turned to his faithless mistress, disheveled and splayed in the hay, her front-buttoned gown undone to the waist. "You will not say a word until we have arrived back at Clearbrook."

Sarah reached a hand to him. "But, sir, the situations differs from what it appears."

He looked away from her face, from the lying lips that still carried the evidence of her deceit in their swollen fullness. "I warn you, not one word."

Helping her up from the hay, he escorted her from the stables to his waiting horse. A lift placed her onto the saddle, and he swung up behind her. While she straightened her clothing and picked the straw from her hair, he reached around her and took up the reins.

She never cried, not even in the extremity of passion, but her lack of tears now infuriated him. Had she spilled some crocodile tears, begged with studied artifice for mercy, he might have relented, softened a bit. As it was, he felt as hard as stone as he kneed his mount to a gallop.

At the cottage, he jumped to the ground, sweeping the cheating little baggage down after him.

She squared her shoulders. "I have done naught wrong." Her chin jutted at him under the moon, and God help him, but he wanted to hang everything, including his pride, and take her right then and there!

Grabbing a handful of her gown, bunching the cheap gray stuff at the shoulder, he pushed her ahead of him through the door.

Inside the single room, he asked straightaway, "Why the hell are you wearing a servant's gown?"

"Cook was short of help. A servant's gown is required in the kitchen."

"I may not have been raised a gentleman, but I know damn well where livery is required!" He paced the cottage floor. "I never agreed to have you work as a scullery maid, Sarah. It was never my intent to publicly embarrass you in the house of a friend. I sent you there to do what you enjoy doing— namely, arranging flowers!"

"Working in the kitchen served a good cause. The village orphanage is always short on funds—"

"I have taken care of their financial situation."

"You have? Thank you, sir! Your generosity was most kind."

He brushed her gratitude aside. "I was orphaned myself at an early age."

"Your dear mother—once again, please accept my sorrow for your early loss. An orphan's fate is a cruel one. I admire you for rising above your early sad start in life."

Seb stopped his pacing and stalked to his cheating mistress. "I seek neither your admiration nor your sympathy."

"What do you seek from me?" she asked, looking up at him, searching his face.

How strange they shared the same dark hair, Seb thought, crushing her black curls between the fingers of both hands. How strange that they had spent their early years in the same house, calling the same man "Father."

As he slanted his jaw to her, Seb rejoiced that they shared not one vein of blood. For not even a blood bond would have kept him from her. Nothing would have kept him from Sarah. Not incest. Not treachery. Not a lifetime of lies.

"You," he said, speaking low against her black curls. "I seek you. And it maddens me that other men seek you out the same. You give off the scent of animal receptiveness. In the stable, the scent of eagerness wafted from you, competing only with the aroma of mares waiting to be put to stud. I own you, eager Sarah. I bought and paid for you, and I do not share what is mine."

"I am eager, sir. Very eager. But my eagerness is only for you."

Her black curls sifted through his fingers. "I wish I could believe you."

Sick at heart, he lifted the servant's gown and borrowed petticoat to her waist.

"W-what do you think to do?" she said sharply, too sharply for innocence, and tried to yank away from his grasp.

He held tighter to her arm. "Open your legs!"

Her chin trembling, she split her thighs.

Through the slit in her drawers, he investigated her passage, a one-finger penetration that was neither gentle, nor rough, but only expedient and thorough, and then brought the digit to his nose.

He sniffed the slick of wetness.

"Wh-what purpose does this s-serve?"

"My purpose is the determination of another man's leavings." He inhaled deeply again, let the breath out.

Recognizing only the scent of Sarah, he brought his fingertip to his mouth.

No come could he discern on his palate; he tasted only her honey upon his tongue.

Her let her skirts and petticoat drop. And still his jealousy continued to boil. "So, he never put it to you, eh?"

"No. You arrived in time. Y-you saved me."

"Saved you? Do you think me a fool? Eleanor said you flirted mercilessly all day, with any male who would look in your direction."

"Untrue, sir. I never did. That man came upon me whilst I disrobed in the stable. He tried to r-rape me"

"*Now* you cry rape. Why not before, first thing?"

"In your anger, would you have believed me? I was attacked!"

He let that assertion go in favor of feeding his jealousy.

"Why disrobe in the stable?" he demanded to know.

"Your fiancée directed me there to change."

"Miss Cabot is not yet my fiancée," he muttered, pondering Sarah's words.

Who to believe? The opportunistic Eleanor—a born manipulator? Or the carnal Sarah—the daughter of a known philanderer?

Thus far, Sarah had asked nothing of him. Neither jewel, nor coin. She had accepted new gowns only under duress. Forthright and hardworking, she performed the most backbreaking jobs, even after he had told her to quit—

But she enjoyed cock a little too much, more than a lady-born ever would. And she disappeared from Clearbrook for a half a day at a time. Where did she go during those missing hours? Did she tryst with someone in the village?

She looked so guileless. And beautiful. How could a young lady who had spoken of love so eloquently be guilty of lying, of betrayal?

It felt as though he had awakened from a sound sleep to the twist of a knife in his gut to find Sarah held the handle. And while expecting the cut, he had not expected the hurt.

She rocked back and forth, her arms clamped around her waist; all color had drained from her face. "I should not have gone to the stables. I should have trusted you would come to collect me at the main house. I should have awaited your arrival at the end of the drive. My lack of faith in you has caused this rift between us. How may I make amends?"

"I am sure a woman like you will think of something." He raised a brow.

She nodded. "I see." Unfolding her arms, she began unbuttoning her servant's gown.

Seb let her.

Wanting her out of that servant's gown, wanting to see how far she would go in the name of deception, he stood there mutely while she stripped to the skin.

The elongated red tips of her small breasts pointing to her guilt, her belly so white above the bush of black curls, the pubic hair so shockingly earthy in such a prissy miss, she sank to her knees and reached for the front of his trousers.

Seb let her.

She kissed him first, a treacherous kiss for all that its hesitancy connoted an undeserved innocence. Perhaps Sarah had never sucked a man off before, but hers was a skill lying in wait, an accomplishment she was born to perform and perfect on those who would come after him.

Her tongue encircled the head, slithered about like a snake at the apple, catching the droplets—jealousy in pre-come form—that dripped off the blunt end.

In his besotted weakness for her, he groaned.

Taking this for encouragement, not for the despair that it was, she parted her lying lips, placed him in her mouth, and took him down her long white throat, proceeding to make *amends* the way harlots always do for paying gentlemen. Only this paying customer was no gentleman, and he had ten inches of pent-up rage to accommodate.

Holding her in place, fingers digging into her skull, Seb gave Sarah no mercy. No reprieve, either, as he thrust and thrust again.

Whores should expect hard use. If she hurt, well, so did he! She had no cause for complaint.

With a grunt, he exploded against the back of her throat, which most certainly must have shown bruising with all his driving in and out, the hot stream filling her mouth. Only when her throat convulsed as she swallowed did he release her from his hold.

Sarah drooped to the floor, her red lips come-coated and swollen. "I did naught to incite that man in the stable. I swear it."

After his having pronounced her guilty until proven innocent, the facility of her performance did nothing to convince him otherwise.

He put himself away. "Whores routinely suck cock. Money for services. This, I understand and respect. But you only did what you did to dispel my suspicions. I thought you more honorable than that, Sarah."

"Honor!" she scoffed. "I have no honor, not when it comes to you. Dispelling your suspicions was not the reason I welcomed you."

Seb refused to listen to any more of her lies. "From this point forward, you are not to step foot outside this cottage."

The order flung over his shoulder, he slammed out the door.

Chapter Thirty-One

The next morning, Sarah awakened alone in her bed, resolved to leave Clearbrook sooner rather than later. Bitterness slowly consumed the man she loved; staying would only hasten the process. She saw the same sad result at the children's home. Those boys and girls needed so desperately to fit in somewhere, a place where they belonged, and yet in their anger over their loss, in their fear of losing a special someone again, they often pushed away those very ones who would love them.

Mr. Turner was coming to care for her, and in his fear, in his anger, he was pushing her away. He would rather substitute a place in society for a place in her heart. He must have been hurt very badly as a child.

All the night before, she had slept in fits and starts. And this time, not because carnal dreams kept her awake. Her sleep was disturbed for wanting to hold him in her arms. The solid, real, imperfect man. He needed the comfort she could give him.

She could use some comfort, too—or was that just too damn much to expect from the high-handed, arrogant, self-serving ass?

A knock at the door.

Heedless of her nightgown, Sarah flew out of bed to answer the summons. Perhaps, that was the high-handed, arrogant, self-serving ass now—

But no. Rattler stood at her threshold, hat in hand. "I asked Molly to marry up with me, and she agreed. We leave today. I came by to say *adios.*"

"Congratulations!" Drawing her friend close, she gave him an affectionate hug, right there at the threshold. Then, slipping free of his arms, took Rattler's hand, leading him into the little cottage.

When Mr. Turner and Eleanor went off on their morning carriage rides, she would sneak off to share a cup of coffee with Rattler. Those few stolen minutes of companionship caused her endless guilt, but she refused to give them up. Real friendship was precious, and she treasured the bond she had formed with Rattler, more than she treasured an arbitrary obedience to her owner.

Disinclined to give in to her owner's authoritarian dictates, Sarah put the coffee pot on the stove.

Rattler shook his head. "I surely would like to stay and sit a spell, but Molly's waiting for me in town at the train station."

"How exciting! Talk fast. Tell me everything."

Rattler held up a finger. "One catch."

Sarah bent to stoke the fire in the stove's potbelly. "Yes?"

"No tellin' Seb about Molly and me gittin' hitched. Leastwise, not right away. She told him she was goin' back out West to start up—er—a gamblin' establishment. And that was all she told him. I would appreciate if you kept the real reason for her leavin' under your hat. Seb's opinion of me ain't too high."

"Not a word will I say. Promise," she said, spinning to face him.

Unbeknown to her, her twirling had fanned the stove flame. A spark raced up the back hem of her voluminous nightgown.

As swift to strike as his name implied, Rattler stomped on the trailing hem, tearing the flaming cloth away and tossing it into the open door of the potbelly stove, where it would burn safely to ashes.

Afterwards, he brought her into his arms. Patting her down with his palms, he asked, "Are you all right, Miss Sarah?"

"Yes. Thanks to you." In the aftermath of terror, and still in the throes of sadness over losing her best friend, she clung to Rattler.

An affectionate embrace Mr. Turner intercepted upon bursting through the cottage door, a murderous expression twisting his face.

He flew at Rattler, landed him a terrible blow. For all his wiry toughness and despite his desperado reputation, Rattler quickly proved no match for her crazed owner.

Punches flying, the two men rolled on the floor, her friend getting the worst of it.

As she would in a brawl at the orphanage, Sarah threw herself bodily into the fracas. Two arms wrapped around his neck, she melded her body to Mr. Turner's. "You are to let him go." Her voice remained quiet but firm. "Your rage is not with Rattler, but with me."

"Get off me," her lover snarled, trying to shake her free.

"Never."

As a measure of her love, she cuffed him, the open slap sounding bright and oddly feminine after the thrown punches between the two males. "This is between us. You will release Rattler immediately!"

His hands fell from Rattler's throat.

"Go!" she told her friend.

Bleeding, one eye shut, Rattler shook his head. "No. Not when Seb is all fired up to do murder." He went for the gun at his hip.

"You are to put that *thing* away, Rattler. No one is getting murdered here today. I am perfectly fine here. Now go."

When the hurting Rattler stumbled reluctantly from the cottage, she returned her full attentions to her owner. "You are not to go after him."

"I saw you with him." Her owner tried to pry free of her restraining arms.

She held on to him fast. "You saw wrong."

"Before the door even closed, you two were going at it." Breathing hard, on the slippery edge of control, inches from snapping, he tried to stand.

Her defense came to an abrupt end. In a black and furious place, the man who had once championed her would refuse to believe any explanation she might offer. For now, she would accept the crazed accusations. Denying nothing, she would take the full blunt of his wrath onto herself.

With her refusal to give him up, years of self-discipline fell away. This thing between them was raw, primitive, uncivilized...messy. To reach him, she would need to mirror those same emotions, which meant surrendering herself. No corner of her dreams could she withhold.

Seb jumped to his feet, and she hung on to his arm; he hauled her up after him. Horse's hooves pounded outside the door, signaling Rattler's departure, and she allowed her arms to hang limply at her sides.

She bowed her head submissively. "I shall do whatever it is you want me to do, if you would just let Rattler leave unharmed, if you do not go after him. I cannot bear to stand by and see either of you do murder."

"Your wet pussy in exchange for your lover's life?"

His uncultured voice sent a shiver through her, and she feverishly licked her lips. "Yes"

"At last! A confession of guilt!"

"Yes, I have been unfaithful—"

"I warn you, Sarah, I will not be made a fool—"

"If you would please allow me to finish, sir." After a moment's hesitation, she proceeded. "I have been unfaithful to you, but only at night, and only in my romantic dreams. I cannot help my dreams, sir! In the light of day, the reality is, you paid for me," she said meekly, a part of her wanting to submit, wanting to let go of all prudery, all her polite manners, all societal strictures, and just be the woman he needed her to be. "Why not make use of me?"

"Damn you for the liar you are, Sarah Winslow. How many lovers have you had since me? Are there enough hours in the day to fit them all in?"

She slid down his body. Still hanging on to him, one arm wound around his, her hand locked to his wrist. Only when he grasped her gold wristband in return did she finally relinquish her hold.

"Come with me."

Some self-protective instinct still remained. "Where?"

"Up to the house. Now on, you sleep in my bed."

Clutching at straws, she delayed a return to the house she loathed. "I am not properly attired."

He laughed. "You ain't the first female ever to cross the lawns at Clearbrook not *properly attired.*"

"Indeed, I know I am not. On the rare occasion my father took up residence here, he invariably arrived with painted ladies in tow. He would often take his prostitutes strolling naked outside. When I was a little girl, I would watch them cavort on the front green. My loss of innocence."

"Everyone loses their innocence eventually."

"How old were you when you lost yours?" she asked, both stalling for time and honestly wishing to learn all she could about this enigmatic man.

The fight seemed to drain out him. "Twelve."

"So young. Was the whore very beautiful?"

"I lost my innocence through an act of supreme callousness, not through whoring."

Never before had Mr. Turner spoken of his past, and his despairing tone struck her heart. He sounded so tormented! "What was this act of callousness?"

"When my mother took ill, I went to her former lover. She had been this man's mistress for many years, and still loved him. I thought if he visited her, she would rally against the consumption that stole her life. I made the mistake of telling her of my mission, and when I returned alone to our squalid tenement room, she knew once and for all that he had abandoned us. She died within the week."

Her eyes swam with tears for the warm and caring boy Mr. Turner had once been. "Such a tragedy."

"I should never have told her! I blame myself for that. Everything else, I lay at the feet of the swine she loved. No money for a proper burial, she was thrown into a pauper's grave. The swine never so much as sent a funeral bouquet."

"But why?"

"Why, what?" he said, tersely.

"Why would your mother's lover not go see her?"

"The turd had just recently married. A society lady. She had just presented him with a child. A daughter. A pretty little thing. And so he had no further use for my mother or me."

He narrowed his eyes at her, dark eyes that held no hope at all. "You know—you were right about something. Your attire is all wrong for what I have planned for you. Take off that nightgown."

Too shocked to protest, too mournful to speak, much too concerned for this man to push him any further, to probe any more into his unhappy past, she removed her covering.

"Be right back," he said with an evil grin, then stepped outside.

"To ensure you stay put," he said upon his return, holding something up for her to see. "This here is an authentic rawhide lasso, the kind cowpokes use out West."

Smiling grimly, he encircled her waist with the narrow strip of leather. "Otherwise, who knows, you might run off to your lover as soon as my back is turned."

He cinched her tight, tighter than any corset, and in instinctive compensation to that tight fit, she brought her ribcage up high and thrust out her breasts in a vulgar parody of the current hourglass whim of ladies' fashion design. Only, she was naked, shamefully naked.

Oh, God, no! How could this be happening?

As a result of her shameful excitement, her nipples lengthened and she went damp between her legs.

No! Not damp. Wet! She was wet between the legs, shamefully wet.

Her face must have reflected her humiliation, and most probably the cause, for he fisted the free end of the lasso and gave it a shake, as one would with a cow one intended to brand. "You know what I want to see."

She did! Oh, God! She did know.

"Go to the floor," he said. "You can show me it there."

Like candlewax, she melted into a pool of shame at his feet, into a closed-kneed squat that told him nothing.

He shook the rawhide lasso again. "Open it."

So shameful, this stimulating effect he had on her, and in that shameful stimulation, she inched her knees apart.

"Wider," he instructed.

Moving her bottom back to her heels, she stretched her knees a bit more.

He shook his head. "Miss Winslow, you can do better than that."

She did do better! Spreading herself wide, she placed her shameful wetness on lewd display.

"Is all that honey for Rattler?"

"For you, sir. I am wet for you."

"We shall soon see about that. For now, jerk me off. Use your hand."

Anger acts on people in powerful ways, and her owner was hard as flint when she freed him from his trousers and took him into her steely palm. Sparks flew as she struck the beat that would bring him surcease, but before he reached climax, he pulled away.

"Stay," he grunted and exploded, the ejaculate tagging her naked belly, seminal fluid rolling like a strand of pearls into her black pubic hair.

He looked at her glistening curls for a long moment, and then taking up the rawhide lasso, led her naked, like the lowliest of semen-sticky prostitutes, the kind her father used to flaunt, across the grand expanse of plush green lawns and into her ancestral home.

As it turned out, she received a reprieve from total humiliation. The halls and rooms were empty, as the servants, all transplants from the West, had returned to their former lives with Mrs. Smith and Rattler.

Upstairs, inside the master bedchamber, work-roughened hands smoothed over her body. Callused fingers stroked her sticky pubic curls and spread her thighs. She made no comment, no complaint, no outraged protest when he breached her in a hard and relentless manner he had never used before with her. Rather, she opened her legs wider for the cruel invasion.

"If my demands prove too much, say my name."

Dazed, she could only stare at him.

"Say my first name, say Sebastian, and everything stops," he said, repeating the odd instruction. "My name will keep you safe. Do you understand?"

"Yes," she replied, not understanding at all.

He brought her to the bed. The four massive mahogany posts dominated the entire master chamber as he now thought to entirely dominate her.

He would not succeed. Not entirely.

Her love for him would bring him to his knees. Eventually.

A long way away from that eventuality, she mused as he spread her on her back crosswise on the tick, her bottom situated at the edge, limbs dangling to the floor. He tied her there, the rawhide lasso holding her in place.

"Open," he said curtly, naughty banter a thing of the past.

Like a well-trained sycophant, she separated her thighs.

Standing to one side, he rubbed the heel of his hand into her slippery cleft, sending first one finger, then two, then three up inside her, moving there, massaging deep within her.

The fit discomfited her. He had such large hands, powerful hands, thick fingers. A laborer's hands, a laborer's fingers. She rocked her head back and forth on the coverlet as those big, thick fingers spread her wide.

The accommodation burned.

And her breasts peaked from the pain.

He knew it.

Knew she had fallen victim to pained excitement. Knew she was aroused. Knew she was his whore. But what he refused to see was that she would be his whore for love, for no other reason.

He withdrew the fingers lodged inside her. "Draw up your legs. Open it up all the way."

She pulled her legs up off the floor. Bent them to her belly. Opened her thighs wide. Spread herself open all the way, every demand setting her afire.

He knew it.

He knew she burned for him.

"Your cunt belongs to me. Say it!"

"My cunt belongs to you," she repeated the word, guttural in sound, precise in description, honest in their very bluntness. "You own my cunt," she said, as though calling the term into usage at high tea.

"So beautiful," he continued. "Say it! Say, 'I am beautiful.' Repeat it."

Much harder to accept those words, and so much more difficult to parrot the sentiment. She had never felt beautiful.

Until that very instant.

Spread naked before the man she loved, she felt confident, desirable...*beautiful* for the very first time.

But why make her a gift of those feelings when he doubted her character? What was going on inside his mind?

"I am beautiful," she whispered.

As she sprawled wide open on the coverlet, he left her.

But not for long, only as long as it took him to drag an embossed green satin chair to the bed. She recognized the chair as one that had held a position of distinction in the master bedchamber since she was a little girl.

"Prop your feet up on the back," he told her.

Raising her heels onto the high back of the hunter-green chair should have been a graceless maneuver. It was not. Like a dancer, she stretched each limb up in the air, flexed each toe, and brought each foot down on top. That accomplished, without being told to do so, she opened her knees for him again, exposing herself for him again, opening herself up to him again. Far too late for modesty now. He owned her body as he owned her heart.

He took a jar from his pocket. A lubricant, she discovered when he greased his hand with the stuff. Three oiled fingers pushed up inside her and soon became four. The digits spread apart.

She bit her lip. Clawed the coverlet beside her raised bottom. The burning had worsened.

"You are made small," he said, and she felt his fingers close tight, the width narrowing at her cleft. "Bearing down when you feel my knuckles go in will make the fisting go easier for you."

How slowly he worked his hand up inside her. How carefully she felt his hand twist inside her, felt his wrist rotate.

She bore down as he did the unthinkable.

"Look," he demanded when he was done.

Panting as a woman does in labor, she looked up over her belly to see that his hand had disappeared inside her, her black pubic hair ringing his wide wrist, an erotic halo.

Helpless not to, she started to moan. Full out. No holding back. No trying to prettify the primal quality of this act, no trying to couch it in civilized terms. There was nothing refined about accommodating a man's fist.

Belonging to him this way was barbaric and bestial and savage. And she thought, *Sebastian, Sebastian, Sebastian.*

But she refused to speak his name aloud. Refused to end it, whatever this unholy thing was between them. She trusted this deeply conflicted man, trusted that the warm and caring boy was still imprisoned somewhere inside him. Enraged as he was, troubled of mind and soul and heart as he was, she trusted him not to hurt her—

More than she wanted him to.

"How great is the pressure?" he asked.

"Tremendous," she weakly replied between animalistic pants, her peaked breasts rising and falling.

Reaching up his free hand, he massaged her aching breasts, deftly ministering to the hard nipples. "Is the pain good or bad?"

"Good," she whispered from a throat gone dry, the single word forced through grimacing lips. So difficult to admit that she loved the pain of it, that the pain of it made her feel alive, that it had always been that way for her.

"I want this, Sarah."

"I know."

"I need to have this from you."

"I know."

"The next man you go to, gentleman or otherwise, will want the same. Better I do it to you first. Get you used to it," he said and then started to move his hand inside her, a determined anvil hammering into up her narrow passage. "I can stretch you, without tearing you. And Sarah—your next patron will want it done hard. I do you no favor holding back."

Hurt, hurt, hurt. It hurt so good.

The pain made her feel alive. Made her know he could see her, that she had not suddenly become invisible. And regardless that he said he would pass her over into another patron's hands, she knew in her heart he would not. He would not abandon her, as everyone else had abandoned her.

He did her hard, as he said he would, but she felt no fear. The man who owned her was not brutal by nature; he was a wounded bird, a proud dark hawk with a damaged wing, who needed her love.

Her eyes fully open, she gave herself over to him, submitting to his will, trusting him completely, as her body writhed and shook, then arched like a bow off the bed, as far as the restraint tied around her waist would allow, the tendons in her thighs tightening as her vagina spasmed around his fist.

She cried as she came. Cried and wept as she had never cried and wept before.

For both of them.

Chapter Thirty-Two

When her owner next rejoined her in the bedchamber, he took her harshly, a merciless intercourse done without preamble. Her body heaving and shaking, he brought her a profound release.

And still he kept at her, laying siege to her body.

She climaxed once. Again. Until the orgasms slammed into her, one atop the other, and she was mindlessly sobbing.

He came on a grunt and then collapsed fully on top of her, no consideration for his weight, which was sizeable. He then peeled his sweaty body off hers and left her alone on the bed. No cuddling. No post-coital chatter. No afterglow whatsoever.

Well, Sarah had had quite enough of his highhandedness!

Her independent streak rising to the occasion, she shouted after him, "Come back here and kiss me. Do not dare to leave me like this!"

The door slammed on his way out.

Sad to say, his dominance left her more excited than before.

The hours dragged until her owner next returned. At least it felt like hours, though of course she possessed absolutely no certainty as to the passage of time. She might have slept, but then again, perhaps not. She floated on a timeless sea of carnality, sliding in and out of awareness at the opening of the bedchamber door, her only timepiece her owner's comings and goings.

Intercourse, then rest. Intercourse, then rest. He would join her during the day or during the night, have his way with her, and then abruptly leave. In her mind, she ticked off this stalemate between them in terms of penetrations, each differing in some shape or form or manner from the ones preceding and following.

"If this continues, I fear my pubic hair will become quite as stiff as an old man's beard," she complained after one lengthy session. She had a leg wrapped around his hip, her arms languidly around his neck; the fingers of one hand intentionally mussed his absurdly short hair. They were both naked and sweaty, and still lodged to the absolute hilt inside her, her owner seemed unwilling to leave his firm entrenchment.

As an indicator of his resolve to stay the course, he started to move again, ever so slowly, an easy slip and slide due to the volley of semen he had discharged inside her.

"Pardon?" he said, polite but vague, a man obviously on a mission. "What is as stiff as an old man's beard?"

Bluntness was her ally. "I need to bathe."

He pumped his hips, just once, and lazily—a man on a mission, but in no particular hurry to reach his destination, both of them well aware this siege was far from over.

Nose nuzzled into the hollow of her raised arm—the wretch—he took a sniff. "You smell de-lightful," he drawled.

"I smell of come," she said, taking bluntness to the extreme.

"I like you sticky." His nose moved around her jaw and down her throat. "Your scent is a constant reminder of how we have passed the time."

"Fucking," she supplied, filling in the blank.

His hips stopped flexing. His nose stopped sniffing. Indolence at an end, her patron took surprisingly swift leave of her, another shot of semen rolling down her thigh in the wake of his abrupt withdrawal.

"I wish you would refrain from calling it that," he said, looking down and away, anywhere but directly at her.

She propped herself up on an elbow. "What do you suggest I call what we do?"

Turned away, he moved to the edge of the bed. And said nothing.

"Fornication?" she suggested. "Rutting?" she called at his back as he retreated.

Making love? she said to herself as he departed the room.

He came back within the hour—or at least she *suspected* his return was within the hour—and played yet another game of bondage with her. A strenuous workout, to be sure! She must have dozed then, and deeply, too, for she missed the rattle the door made upon opening and closing. When she fluttered her lids to a scattered wakefulness, he was busy tickling her bare feet. He had a *thing* for her toes.

He also had a thing about feeding her. "Wake up, sleepyhead. Time for a late breakfast."

She sat up amidst the sex-rumpled linens and ran her hands clumsily through her bed-tousled hair, quickly giving up all attempts at looking presentable when he uncovered the tray he had carried into the chamber and held a steaming cup to her lips.

"Sweet tea and toast with marmalade," he said as she sipped from the cup in his hand.

He replaced the china and held out a dainty triangle of bread. She had only enough time to note that he had sliced the crust away before he said, "I want you to finish all of this. Baby birds eat more than you." He forced the pointed end at her lips.

"Well, I am not a baby bird, and I can feed myself," she said between chews. "That is, if you would only release me." She held up her conjoined wrists—a gold chain attached from bracelet to bracelet made doing anything for herself utterly impossible.

"I enjoy taking care of you," he said and left her wrists linked. "Now, eat every bite."

When she had finished *eating every bite*, he inquired, "Need to stretch for a spell?" At her nod, he lent her a hand to rise.

Sebastian had bathed and shaved and changed, and looked scrumptiously rakish in a white shirt, sans cravat, and informally tailored trousers. She was naked and sticky and felt like a trollop.

"Stretching feels lovely," she said, her linked hands reaching to the ceiling, conscious of hot, dark eyes perusing her with her every extension of cramped muscles.

Not only had he chained her wrists in gold, he had also anchored the rawhide lasso to the bedpost. She had just enough play to make her way to the raised rosebud chamber pot situated in a far corner—not precisely a queenly throne, but close.

When seated, her gaze strayed longingly to the separate little room off the bedchamber that held a large, claw-footed cast-iron tub and a newly installed WC, which he forbade her to use.

He enjoyed watching her pee, a fetish she simply could not understand, but humored.

His eyes between her legs, he said, "A bath awaits, milady."

"Oh, really?" Finished making water, she pattered over to the bathing room—also accessible—to take a peek.

Heavenly scented steam swirled above the white porcelain. "May I make use of it now?"

"I would never tease you with the opportunity of a hot tub and then rescind the suggestion. Here, let me help you in, darlin'."

Tease? Perhaps not the hot bath, but that endearment was most definitely a tease. By no stretch of the imagination was she his *darlin'*.

Yet.

Someday, yes, but that day had not arrived. They still had a rocky road ahead of them.

Living in the moment, she rushed joyfully to the porcelain tub.

"Hair first," he told her once he had undone her leather tether and she had submerged.

"You cannot be serious!" Was this rugged man actually proposing to perform the services of a lady's maid? "You intend to wash my hair?"

"Why not? I enjoy taking care of you."

Far be it for her to explain that patrons did not normally wait upon their mistresses, that it was generally speaking the other way 'round. She happily submitted to his shampooing, feeling quite like a pampered lady of leisure.

After soaping her hair, he rinsed the abbreviated strands until they squeaked, then proceeded to bathe the rest of her, his soapy hands sliding over and under and in between.

For a rough-and-tumble man, he owned a gentle touch. With his white shirtsleeves rolled up to the elbow, he saw to her every nook and cranny, paying particular attention to her breasts, which he heaped with bubbles and sculpted to mountain peaks. As he built her bosom outrageously high, her thoughts went to Eleanor's proportions, far more womanly than her own meager offerings.

"Dissatisfied, are you?" she quipped.

With two scoops of water, he showered the bubbles away. "Not about these."

She refused to let that enigmatic answer stand. "Then about what?"

"This and that."

"And here I had the distinct impression you had achieved everything you sought. Or will, after wedding Eleanor Cabot."

Refusing to elaborate further, he played with her nipples, his thumbs stroking the glistening wet tips back and forth until her back arched and her limited endowments poked his palms. Wanting him desperately, she allowed her bent-up legs to fall open. When her knees pressed the sides of the tub, his hand went where she needed.

"Such pretty curls," he said wolfishly, combing his fingers through. "Not like an old man's beard at all."

She waited for his fingers to find her, as they always had done before, only realizing her waiting was in vain when he stood.

"Enjoy your soak," he said and left.

Damn him!

Despite her frustration, she soaked for a while longer, wrapping up in a drying cloth when the bath water chilled. She had only just begun to finger-dry her hair with her bound hands before the window overlooking the gardens when the door latch behind her made that familiar click.

A smile of welcome on her face, she spun 'round to greet the man who maddened her alternately with excitement and exasperation.

Exasperation won this round.

Her owner had not returned to her alone. At his side stood a stranger.

Another test of my love, Sarah thought and kept the smile stoically in place.

Nothing he could do or say would prompt her to draw this thing between them to a close. Like a small, grieving lad, an orphan boy, he pushed against the limits of her love to see if the perimeters would break.

They would not!

"Please forgive my dishabille," she said graciously. "Had I known to expect company, I would have properly attired myself for the visit."

Her patron performed the introductions. "Sarah, may I present an artist friend of mine, Gerard Philips. He is here to make preliminary sketches of you for a series of paintings I have commissioned."

The artist gave a formal bow.

She dipped her head cordially in reply. "I have never before sat for a portrait." She looked to her owner. "Sir, which gown shall I wear?"

"Your gowns are not what this gentleman is here to sketch." His smile was hotly possessive. "These are private paintings, meant for my eyes only. Now, if you would be so kind as to lower that cloth."

Many penetrations too late to claim modesty, still she did blush. This latest chipping away at propriety was positively scandalous.

"Gerard is a professional," her owner remarked, much too nonchalantly for nonchalance. "What is more, he understands the meaning of discretion. There is no need for embarrassment. And I really would like these portraits done of you. But the matter is entirely in your hands."

"If portraits are what you desire, then portraits are what you will have." She undid the tucked-in portion of the drying linen. "How much cleavage must I show?"

"All," Mr. Turner replied.

He turned to face the painter, offered as an aside. "The lady possesses the most extraordinary nipples. When excited, their elongation is nearly as great as my thumbs. And the shade! A color unlike any I have ever seen. I tell you, she takes my breath away."

Her patron had just discussed the merits of her female body with a strange man, and an artist at that. She, who had never felt worthy of any praise, was now the recipient of blatant compliments.

Quite beyond the pale.

Needless to say, here, her excitement nudged out her exasperation.

In truth, Mr. Turner's possessive tone made her knees go weak. His rough voice, dripping with desire, made her want to swoon.

Drugged on his lavish praise, buoyed on the knowledge that he lusted for her, resolute in her decision to prove there was naught he could do or say to drive her away, she lowered the linen.

And fully revealed her bosom.

Her nipples, sharp as knives, pointed directly at her owner.

"Come here," he growled.

She went to him bare-breasted and bound. And totally confident. Glowing, in fact, under his unmasked admiration.

Lids slumberous, her owner kissed her cheek.

While she clutched the linen at her waist, the gentleman assigned to paint her portrait surveyed her face from every angle before his gaze dropped to her bare breasts, his attention concentrated on her nipples. "Sebastian, my friend, you spoke the truth. Her nipples really are quite extraordinary. Look at that hue! A glorious shade of magenta! I can scarcely wait to pick up my brush and paint pots."

"She is lovely," Mr. Turner agreed, "and so much more. One day, the lady will become a famed horticulturalist, whose name is known far and wide."

And with that testament to her abilities, her champion said, "I will leave you two to your work," and walked away.

In a panic, her gaze flew after him. "But where are you going?"

"Not far. Just here, against the wall." Turning back, he gave her a jaunty wink.

One briefly closed lid, and her enjoyment had returned. All of this was so deliciously naughty. Charcoal and paper. Two admiring men. And a life model who felt no shame.

She assumed the suggested pose, and the artist took up his pad and pencils and began to draw.

He quickly rendered a sketch. Though she enormously enjoyed being the center of attention, still impatience gnawed at her nerves like a squirrel at an acorn, and his brevity prompted a sigh of relief. Soon, she would have her owner all to herself!

Her lover returned to her. "Sarah, I think you should know, these paintings I have commissioned are nudes."

Nudes?

The shocking idea took her aback.

And thrilled her at the same time, her exhibitionistic side rising to the forefront.

Mr. Turner looked at her intently, trying to read her expression, no doubt. "I would like you painted in a palette of pinks and rose," he said. "My pastel torment."

Her breasts, as they always did in her owner's presence, had turned achy. The nipples hurt. As the artist had only just related, the pigment of the areola had also darkened, taking on a red, animalistic tone—

If she was his torment, so too was he hers.

"Kiss me first," she demanded.

Her lips clung to his, and somehow the drying cloth disappeared.

As did Gerard.

The artist receded from her mind, no longer a third presence in the chamber. There was only one man in the room. She gave a private posing only for him.

To her dying day, she would never know how it was that she ended up atop the bed. Nude atop the velvet coverlet, she wildly and uninhibitedly kissed her co-conspirator in pleasure.

Placing another demand on him, a wordless one this time, she opened her thighs.

"Sarah, no!" he said in strangled protest. "Gerard!"

But lost in her partner, she no longer cared about extraneous details like a sketching artist. Throwing caution to the winds, she recklessly reached out to her owner as she had never before reached out to another soul. "I need you so."

Would he refuse her?

He did not. The bed dipped under his weight.

And everything and everyone disappeared. There was no one in the room—no one in the universe—save them.

A kiss on her throat, and he was sliding easily into her vagina. Up. Up. Higher again. His hands on her body gentle, he tempered his thrusts with a rigorous forbearance. As usual, he saw to her pleasure first. Only when certain that her climax was imminent did he allow himself to ease up on his restraint to seek his own satisfaction.

They came together, on a shout of mutual release.

While the artist sketched away with his charcoal, her owner continued to make love to her. Romantically. Sweetly. Privately.

For all that they were not alone.

Chapter Thirty-Three

Sprawled amidst the wreck of the bedding, too weak to cover her nakedness, too satiated with fulfillment to particularly care how abandoned she must look, simply smiling there on the bed like a complete ninny, Sarah conceded that what they had just done together surpassed even her most erotic dream. In fact, she felt so drained, lethargic, and *happy* that she continued her sprawled position without a thought to propriety.

Lying there, still and silent and content, she began to think—always a dangerous pastime—and came to a most startling conclusion. Mr. Turner's proprietorship of Clearbrook was no mere happenstance. Coincidence had played no part in Sebastian Turner's purchase of this, her childhood home. He had bought the furnishings, the horses, the carriages, everything—including her—for a specific reason. But what? What part did she play in his madness?

Her mind exhausted, unable to puzzle out a solution, she slipped back into the healing balm of sleep.

A shallow stroking awakened her sometime later.

"I thought you had left me," she whispered sleepily.

Her owner reiterated the rules of their engagement. "Ask me to remove your restraint, and I do it. Ask me to leave, and I go. Say my name, and everything stops."

Why would she ever wish him to leave, to stop? She had even grown accustomed to the leather tether about her waist...

"Are you tender?" he asked, inserting a finger into her vagina.

After indulging in protracted carnality during her portrait session, she had passed *tender* several occasions ago.

"Not at all." She prevaricated, her compromised truth necessary because he would use any reason to draw their excess to a close. And she was just as determined to give him no such excuse. In fact, she was determined to run him to ground. She would lance whatever was bothering him now, on this carnal battlefield. If they both came away bloody and torn, so be it. She was prepared to accept the consequences. Was he?

"Up for another?" she challenged.

"We should wait."

"I care not a whit about waiting."

"I do care."

Hope flared. He *cared!* Finally, an open admission that she meant something to him.

She pushed. "If I wish this to end, I have only to say your name," she reminded him as he had just reminded her. "Up until then, I demand we continue."

"You mean, continue to have intercourse?"

Her chin hiked to meet his gaze. *Intercourse.* A word as cold as it was clinical. Considering his point of view, little wonder he chose it. She would have preferred he call it fucking. Or warfare. Now, that term would have made sense.

She met his gaze with her eyes blazing, prepared to take no prisoners. "I demand you treat me as you would any of your previous whores."

"What do you have in mind? And please, remember my sensitive my ears."

Damn him for making light of this! The man possessed no sensitivity whatsoever.

"From the back," she suggested.

"Ah, I see. A rear-flank approach."

"Exactly," she retorted. *No white flag of surrender for me!*

"I am surprised you have not yet requested sodomy."

She would not back down. "All in due course," she said breezily. "I am leading up to it. Incrementally. One needs to deliberate before jumping into the more unconventional practices."

"And I suppose you will expect me to oblige all your prurient curiosities?"

"Of course."

"I suppose, after a period of such deliberation, you will demand I satisfy all your appetites, including perversion?"

"Naturally." She crossed her arms under her bosom, shelving her breasts so that they stuck out at a jaunty angle, a move done to capture his attention.

"Too bad," he rejoined, his gaze directed precisely where she wished. "I was hoping for somewhat less deliberation and somewhat more spontaneity." He walked to the door.

"What!" she screeched shrilly as he turned the knob. "You cannot retreat now!"

"Not a retreat. Merely a regrouping." The door opened and closed behind him.

He did not stay gone long. She knew he would not. This carnal obsession ran both ways.

"You will need to go to the edge of the bed," he told her as he reentered the room, sounding a tad grim.

During his regrouping, she had taken to prowling the chamber, her confinement to a single room beginning to grate. But at his directive, she stomped to the bed and then stupidly stood there, not sure of how to proceed.

A finger, just one, tickled down her spine. "Bottom outward, over the edge," he told her.

"Not joining me?" She looked around her shoulder.

"I find the superior position more enjoyable."

"Far be it for me to limit your enjoyment," she muttered, her voice raining sarcasm as she knelt on the bed, crouching at first, then fully bending, the extension of her hindquarters over the edge both lewd and utilitarian.

A cough from behind her. "For rear entry, I prefer the female on hands and knees."

She arranged herself to his specifications, in the universal pose of female receptiveness, arms straightened out before her, back straight, legs open for ease of penetration. Though her hair was short, the front strands had fallen into her eyes, the blindness locking her in on herself, intensifying her feeling of aloneness, of abandonment.

To break his apartness from her, Sarah rolled her shoulders.

With a groan that spoke volumes, he reached beneath her, caught a breast, and squeezed.

Purring at his touch, she next rolled her hips.

"Insatiable miss," he had the temerity to say, before spanking her bottom, and not at all playfully, which made her purr all the more.

"Stay still," he said.

"Wiggles count?"

"Yes." He chuckled, his free hand walking down her belly to the curls between her legs.

"Mmm," she murmured as he fingered her.

To urge him on, she hiked her hips high.

When he kissed down the length of her spine to the small of her back, sent his wily tongue inside the cleft, back to front, it was next to impossible not to wiggle then.

Both hands gripping her waist, he brought her buttocks back against his loins.

His *clothed* loins.

Her owner still wore day clothes, immaculate in their press and style. He was so well groomed he could easily take his leave of her and attend one of his many important business meetings in Manhattan.

She heard the adjustment of those fastidious clothes, felt the enormous head of his penis butt between her splayed legs, sliding back and forth, sawing across the pudenda.

So good. He felt so good there.

But he could feel better.

"Please hurry." This time, she spoke in supplication rather than demand.

A request he refused. Making her crazed, he continued to make repeated shallow forays across, but not into, her vagina.

Her vaginal wetness sounding like sloppy splashes in the quiet room, she pounded her fists on the mattress. "Do not torture me!"

She had cried out for a deeper connection, only to buck when he pressed his suit.

Everything stopped.

"Is my attention unwanted?" her owner asked

"No. Pleasure alone accounts for my jolt."

"Pleasure or not, it appears a large dollop of lubricant is in order."

"Surely a man of your vast and varied experience must have some on hand?"

"As a matter of fact, I do. Although, if you must know, far from a libertine, I am usually a conservative in the bedchamber."

"But not with me?" she asked.

His face dragged back and forth along the slope of her slightly elevated bottom, the sensation of whiskers somewhere between a tickle and a scratch. "But not with you."

The bed-stand drawer creaked open, slammed closed. His fingers ministered to her with a fragrant cream—gardenia, she thought—then began to widen her passage.

"I suppose I should be honored that for me you have elected to stray from the straight and narrow."

He chuckled some more. "You have a sharp tongue, Miss Winslow."

Her mouth twisted ruefully. "So sorry. Though I do believe you might eventually come to appreciate that quality in me."

Silence.

Well, at least he offers no denial!

Smugness escalated to spite, and she ground her pelvis into the coverlet, her bottom lifting and lowering.

"You move as though born to this," he told her.

"Born to whore?" she asked caustically.

"Born to seduce. Of all the acts men generally request, rear-entry intercourse is seconded only by sodomy."

"Its popularity would have nothing to do with the male's eternal quest for dominance, I suppose?" she asked, her face smothered in the feather pillow.

"Why? Are you feeling submissive, Miss Winslow?"

"I am feeling only concerned, as should you."

"Pardon? Concerned over what?"

"Over these damned pillows. Continue to tarry, and the feather stuffing is liable to send me into a sneezing fit at a most inopportune time."

He withdrew the pillow posthaste and immediately afterwards returned to his stroking. Would he never take her?

Employing subversive tactics, he did everything in his power to make her body open to him, despite her swollen state. Metered-out kisses. Orchestrated compliments. Drugging touches.

She was sick of it! "If you do not make your move, I swear I shall throttle you with my bare hands."

"My demanding Sarah," he muttered, the head of his penis dipping ever so gently into her vagina, back to front.

"Tell me you want this," he whispered.

Oh, I do, I do, she thought, owning her carnality completely and absolutely, without even a smidgeon of genteel reservation whatsoever.

Showing him rather than telling him, she pushed back against the male hardness that would please, *please* enter her. Why did he delay, when she welcomed this latest test of her love like a warrior welcomes the first thrust of the sword?

No thrust here. He penetrated her slowly. Steadily. When it came to pleasure, her owner never rushed.

She moaned—surely even seasoned warriors must moan—but she was long past flinching, either physically or emotionally, from certain acts. But a sob did escape her lips as the last of her romantic notions about courtly love fell about her like ripped pages of poetry. As far as she knew, no bard had ever sung the joys of rear-entry intercourse; not one sonnet had she ever read about the need for vaginal lubricant or about the pleasure of pain. Carnality was not always about hearts and flowers and pretty sunsets. Sometimes, being with a man involved getting up on all fours, bottom wagging in the air.

She would not back down. Full advance...

Until her owner fell under the might of her love. Until she owned him just as surely as he owned her—a reciprocal and equal loss of self.

Two strokes later, she came on a breathy scream. And this time, when she reclined on the bed, she was not alone. Removing his gentleman's clothes, he held her close as they both drifted off to sleep.

Chapter Thirty-Four

Sarah had fallen asleep on her belly where he had placed her for the last round of intercourse. While she slept on, he smoothed a hand down her tapered back, straight and delicately toned from the hard labor of her gardening, before letting his palm drift over her round bottom and down her long, muscled legs. When he took a narrow foot in each hand and spread her legs wide, scissoring her open, she moaned restively into the pillow.

He disregarded her unspoken complaint. He had one last act to get her accustomed to before letting her go to another.

While she slept on, he pushed two oiled fingers up inside her anus.

She awakened with a start. "Sir?" she said into the darkness of the room.

He removed his two digits to light the lamp beside the bed—*better to see your pretty ass, my dear*—and whispered, "Come on up on hands and knees now, Sarah." He could more easily control the depth of the penetration—and her—in an all-fours position.

With his instruction obeyed, he sent his tongue inside her ass, rimming that dainty hole he intended to make his own.

She squealed like a little piglet, but other than that, made no protest. Not when he patted her seductive bottom, and said, "Bring this up some more," and not when he judiciously moistened the port of entry with his saliva.

He drew back, his palm still riding the fullest part of her buttock. "Move your hips up and down."

When her pretty ass started to roll, he pushed his fingers back into her again. Deeper this time, more definite about what he wanted, what he expected.

The rolling motion of her hips jerked to a stop. "Sir—?"

"Keep moving your hips," he said severely, harshly. No kindness letting her believe she had a choice, when she had none. He wanted this from her, and so he would have it. He would take the last holdout of her innocence. He would own her ass, which meant he would own her, all of her.

"Oh," she gasped, grinding her pelvis into the coverlet, her bottom lifting and lowering, trying to escape the intrusion, the violation, when there was no escape.

Save one.

"Say my name if you want an out," he told her again.

When she remained mute, he widened the unnatural breach. "When you move on from me to a gentleman, whoever he might be, whatever his esteemed position might be in the community, he will routinely take you this way. Courtesans are expected to provide what patrons enjoy."

"Do you *routinely* take your partners this way?"

"I told you," he said uneasily, "I reckon you could call me a conservative in the boudoir."

"So you have never—"

"Sodomized a woman?" he completed when her voice stalled. "Yeah, I have. Upon occasion. Ain't nothin' I ain't done upon occasion, honey."

"And did you enjoy doing it to a woman?"

"Yes," he admitted, though the conversation was getting a mite too personal for his tastes. "I did."

"The lure of the forbidden has its own distinctive charm," she said thoughtfully.

He could tell Sarah enjoyed a walk on the wild side, too—pussy moisture dribbled down the interior of her legs, giving her carnal appetite away, giving proof to her insatiable hunger.

Seb played his own excitement closer to the vest.

As she rubbed her derriere against his hand, against the unforgiving callused flesh of his palm, he said, "Go on, sugar, you do what you need to do."

She started clawing at the sheets, whimpering deep in her throat; despite her hot nature, Sarah was finding this hard going, and not only physically.

Sodomy was the first step into depravity, a side journey from the primrose path few society ladies ever took. Once she allowed anal, she had to know there was no going back to the strictly polite missionary ever again.

He kissed the small of her back, already beading up with perspiration. "Shh," he crooned, trying to settle her down. "The first time is always the most difficult. After this, sodomy will become second nature to you."

In her bravado, Sarah had told him she wanted this done. Specifically, she'd called for him to do it, but she was obviously having a heap of doubts now.

Any lady born would have. This was unnatural intercourse, after all, condemned by Church and government alike, not to mention ladies' sewing circles. The initial trespass concerned him the most. That first inch assigned anal to either heaven or to hell.

"This will make me a seasoned whore," she whispered, her voice tight with apprehension. And shame.

"You know how to stop it. Otherwise, it gets done tonight."

"I understand. And I prefer it to be you, not someone else."

Some whores refused to take a man whole, and so to be polite, he asked, because he had to know now rather than later. "Ten inches in, or just the head?"

She shivered. "I want all of you."

"If the lady says so." The blunt end of his cock sprang free. He quickly lubed up and then allowed the purple head to root at her buttocks.

"Ah," he groaned at the sight of his hardness sinking into her soft bottom cheeks.

And then he was there. Against the puckered back opening. Not forcing it, just pressing the head against the rosebud.

She started to weep, the sound of her tears subdued and polite.

He hardened his heart against her upset. She had an out—up to her if she used it or not.

"Kiss me," she sobbed and angled her head so he could reach her lips.

He tasted salt as he opened his mouth atop hers and made the fateful push, catching her scream as he entered.

This was a make-or-break moment. If Sarah really wanted him, her body would show him.

Sarah showed him, all right. Her body sucked him right in—

And Seb spun out of control.

He climbed over her, on top of her, mounting her, his body flattened on top of hers, the flat of his hand pressed to the crown of her skull, unable, unwilling, to wait, frantic to make her his, his need for her consuming him.

In a garden gazebo, a snobbish young miss had spoken in romantic generalities about love. Knowing she would never apply that eloquently expressed notion to him, he had remained unconcerned.

The reverse had not held true.

Since her infancy, Sarah Winslow had molded the course of his life. Her existence had shaped him like a hunk of wet clay. Now he was dried-up and brittle, and the lady could break him with a single word.

Because he loved Sarah Winslow.

Shaken and shaking, he rode her hard, sodomizing her in every sense of the word, his ejaculate exploding into her on a violent stream at the end.

He threw himself from the bed—the only way he could bring himself to leave her—and paced the floor. "My lawyer will draw up the papers for your financial settlement."

Sarah was still flattened on her belly; she spoke half into the pillow. "P-pardon?"

"I got what I wanted from you, and now I need to pay up."

"I see." With a pained grimace, she settled cross-legged on the bed. "The campaign is finished."

He frowned. "What campaign?"

She shook her head. "Silly me. I misspoke. I should have said our arrangement is finished. At any rate, I shan't accept money from you. I am already in your debt."

"I reckon you just paid off your debt and then some." He fisted his cock. "That was one mighty fine ass fuck, better than any whore in a cathouse could have given me. You really know how to put out, gal! I see a long and lucrative career ahead of you."

Sarah dropped her gaze. "There is no need for crudeness."

"Well, I guess crowing is a sight crude. But how can I help but brag? I never got it in that deep before. And with a lady, too. Woo-hee. You got some hot tail there, sugar. The least I can do is pay you for it."

Her small, pointed breasts lifted and fell as she sighed. "No, thank you. That will not be necessary."

"Well, then—allow me to help you find a situation elsewhere."

Her lips turned pale. "When you say situation, you mean *protector*. Another man."

"Yep," he replied.

He could not love Michael Winslow's daughter! His obsession with Sarah had to end. What better way to end it than to arrange for her to become another man's mistress?

"Very well," she agreed and looked away.

Bile rose up in his throat. Seb forcibly swallowed it down. "As soon as I locate a suitable candidate, I intend to ask for Eleanor Cabot's hand in marriage. Until then, I can put you up in a hotel."

She rose from the bed. "No hotel, sir. Our arrangement remains in place until I have a new patron. Until then, I remain your whore." She made her way to the tall chest of drawers, her hips gently swaying, and folded her elbows up on top, her tousled dark head pillowed on her arms.

She spread her legs wide. "Until then, I have a debt to repay."

He narrowed his eyes on the flare of her ass. Semen rolled out from between her buttocks, and his cock surged at the sight. God help him, for there was no helping himself.

"It gets better each time," he rasped, walking up behind her. He clamped his hand on her fine ass, and a thumb slid inside.

What she did to him! His lungs were burning with what she did to him. And his cock! Jutting straight out, the head was already prodding for more forbidden delight.

"Afterwards, I got a plug you can wear," he grated out. "All the whores use them."

"Then, of course, I must wear one too."

That all neatly decided, he took her narrow hips in his big hands.

She pushed back against him, making it easier for him to get it in. All the way in. He buried himself deep inside her, until his wiry black hair had all but disappeared, and as he drove up deep inside her, pounded up deep inside her, he told himself, in time to the pounding rhythm, that he did not love Sarah Winslow, did not love Sarah Winslow, did not love Sarah Winslow.

Chapter Thirty-Five

"You look beautiful tonight," her owner said as they walked together in a small, walled garden.

Sarah tugged at her neckline. "I have never before showed so much décolletage. The bodice is so low, I fear one deep breath will cause me to spill out."

Sensuous lips quirked. "Chelle did get a mite carried away, though you really do look fetching. Good enough to eat."

Shrugging the compliment aside, she bent to inhale the fragrance of a yellow rose.

"The flower matches your gown," he offered. "I like you in yellow." His sigh filled the empty space. "This garden is a sight more manageable than the one at Clearbrook. You can start planting right away."

She looked up at him. "Are you trying to tell me something?"

He filled his pockets with his hands. "Sarah, this gentleman is interested in an immediate liaison. He wants to sleep with you. Tonight."

"What did you tell him?"

"I told him yes."

"I see." She'd assumed he would find her a new protector in the city, but there were benefits to having a local patron—about twenty of them.

The orphans.

If she pleased this gentleman, she could continue her work at the orphanage. The children needed her!

Though, at times, she thought Mr. Turner needed her far more.

While they strolled through the roses, he loosened his striped ascot and then the top button of his pristine white shirt.

The man at her side had set out to marry a pedigreed lady and beget pedigreed sons so that they might in turn suffer the tedious boredom that was New York society. But like the shirt he wore, the gentleman's life would gradually choke him.

Of course, he refused to acknowledge that slow death anymore than he would acknowledge that he hated wearing tight, starched collars. But he could not hide his true self from her.

Her owner brought her close against his side. She could tell he fought the urge to kiss her, refused to give in to what he perceived as his weakness. He might very well snap in two from the rigidity of his posturing, but he would never relent. No going off the course for Mr. Turner. No deviation from his plan. Others might succumb to the desires of the flesh, drown in corporal sensations, wallow in pleasure, allow love to waylay them from their goal. Not he. He was above such petty needs of the flesh. Of the heart. Only ambition ruled Mr. Turner.

Ah, but he did lust after her!

This past week, unease had strained their conversation. Aware their liaison would soon end, they had done very little talking.

But they had fucked endlessly. In fact, Mr. Turner had shown himself quite unable to keep his hands off her.

Or his cock out of her.

Of course, she had refused to make his desertion of her easy. Making him suffer pangs of withdrawal had given her life meaning...

"You need some fresh air," he told her early one evening and then proceeded to strap an odd belted contraption around her waist—a leather harness of some sort—as if she were a poodle requiring a walk.

She pulled back her shoulders. "May I at least wear a cloak?"

He eyed her breasts, which she had deliberately thrust forward. "No."

Determined to make him pay, she infused her walk with a rolling undulation, which matched the rolling undulation of the front lawns where he paraded her. Soon, in favor of walking by her side, he dropped the leash, leaving the narrow leather to trail behind her like a devil's tail. Appropriate, she'd thought, considering her devil-may-care attitude.

Walking beside her had progressed nicely to foreplay.

As she had intended, his hands wandered all over her. Breasts first, next belly, then bottom.

He stringently avoided the area between her legs, though he did look.

"You must be weary," he said abruptly.

She was as strong as an ox; it would take more than a walk to tire her.

Still, she gave a shrug, which made her bare breasts bounce, a shift he had not failed to notice, even in the fading light.

"Over there on the bench," he said, the directive as strained as the front ten inches of his trousers.

She took a seat, ankles neatly crossed, as a lady ought, even if the lady wears not a stitch of clothing.

He stood across from her, his face wearing a pained expression. "What did I tell you?" he rasped.

She pretended to think. "Why, I seemed to have forgotten."

"You know what I need to see, Sarah."

Yes, indeed she did.

She parted her knees.

Soon, her companion grew remarkably restless. "We need to get back now, Sarah. Right now. Right this very instant."

For the return trip, his touch had remained concentrated on her back. In particular, on her undulating derriere. He smoothed his palms over her, cupping her buttocks, sliding his fingers in between like a greedy little lad.

They never made it back upstairs to the bedchamber. He had her right there in the front parlor, rounded appropriately over the back of the love seat...

Yes, he certainly did lust after her, Sarah mused.

Which explained his rash decision to wed Eleanor Cabot sooner rather than later. Desire had wrinkled her owner's fine, gentlemanly tailoring, and he wished it ironed away.

Sarah straightened her resolve with her spine. "Shall we go in now and get the introduction over and done?"

"No need to hurry. The evening is still young."

She took a deep breath. "No point delaying the inevitable, is there?"

What they had done this past week could not be alluded to in polite company. Sadly, though she had lain naked in Mr. Turner's arms until but a few short hours ago, they had never been one person, one body seeking the completion of orgasm. Her owner had always maintained separateness from her.

He lifted her chin onto the crook of his finger. "Sarah, I am not a total cad. I realize this may be awkward for you."

"What would possibly be awkward about leaving one man's bed and going directly to another within the space of the same day? All whores do the same."

She paused, giving him the opportunity to call an end to this farce. To tell her he loved her, to tell her the idea of sending her away to another man was utter madness.

He admitted to nothing.

Instead he said, "If you please this gentleman tonight, you will stay in this stately townhouse and live the life of luxury. Apart from the occasional visit from him, you will have your independence."

Their garden stroll completed, they made their way back to the house. As they walked down a road from which there was no retreat, he added, "Would you like me to stay?"

"Pardon?"

"A threesome," he explained. "This gentleman is highly regarded in the community, but he is a total stranger to you. You might feel more comfortable if I stay."

Her brow puckered. "Is that done?"

"All the time."

"Goodness! Three abed! Someone might topple off the edge."

He coughed. "Certain precautions will be taken to avoid that result."

She looked at him sideways. "Then, yes. Do stay." She would hold on to him as long as she could.

Regardless of what had brought them here tonight, Mr. Turner nevertheless wished to protect her, shelter her from a whore's hard lot in life. Less altruistically, he sought to end his growing feelings for her. He could live with lust, but nothing deeper would he allow.

Mr. Turner feared love. Which explained why, she supposed, he believed Eleanor Cabot would make him the ideal wife. No chance of loving or being loved there!

Sarah snorted to herself. Were they not the clever pair?

She loved this troubled man. Deep down, he loved her. And neither of them would own up to a blessed thing.

He escorted her into a darkened bedchamber on the second floor of the townhouse. He did not light the lamp.

She immediately guessed the reason. "I take it this new protector wishes to retain his anonymity?"

"The parish is small, and he has his reputation to consider. He leased this residence for a week, on a trial basis. A quiet retreat from the rigors of the city."

"Of course. I quite understand. If I fail to please him this evening, he will walk away, his reputation and identity intact. If I do please him, he will simply extend the lease on the house and set me up here until he grows weary of my company."

Her heart cried out to the warm and caring boy-child locked inside the man's body. *Come out, come out, wherever you are!* To the conflicted adult, her heart held a different plea—*Remove your mask before we reach the point of no return, before it is too late for us!*

He handed her a black silk scarf. "To protect his good name, your suitor insists on a blindfold."

"What an exceedingly careful gentleman!" She tied the scarf in place.

When the sound of a heavy door closing echoed through the house, her owner said, "That must be him now. I'll return to you shortly, new benefactor in tow."

Do not go! Stay. Tell me you love me! Tell me what has hurt you so... But he left her alone in the strange bedchamber, and her false courage drained away. How would she ever to go through with this?

A dismal laugh rose up inside her. She asked herself the question as though she had a choice! Only gentlemen and ladies of independent means had choices.

One day, perhaps, after serving as mistress to a succession of wealthy gentleman, she might then have the financial wherewithal to determine her own destiny.

And even then, one troubled man would still own her.

Door hinges squeaked; footsteps approached.

She tilted her head, listening to the heavy silence. "No one is speaking."

The quiet in the bedchamber lengthened.

"So soon in our relationship to run out of things to say," she said. "We really should try to converse, you know, for how else will we learn each other's foibles?"

She gasped at her faux pas. "That is not to say you *have* foibles, anonymous sir. And most assuredly actions do speak louder than words. However, on the flip side of the coin, one might..." Her inane chatter drifted off, the thought left unfinished. What was she doing here?

Lips claimed her.

Her prospective patron's lips.

His kiss, though pleasant, moved her not at all. Only because he would expect it of her, she opened her mouth to the unfamiliar tongue and offered her tongue in return.

Not her heart, though. Never her heart. Only one man claimed her heart.

An exchange, then, one mouth replacing another.

To her dying day, she would recognize this man's kiss.

She clung to him, melded her mouth to his, gave herself over to him. He did the same. Not since their kiss that night in the gazebo had they shown each other such all-consuming passion, such lack of restraint, such honesty.

Tears seeped into the binding covering Sarah's eyes, the salty wetness absorbed in black silk. He loved her! And she loved him.

And even now, they would not speak of their feelings.

Why, why, why? Why did it have to be like this?

No matter how many men came after him, only he would touch her. She would go with him anywhere. To the ends of the earth—

The backs of her knees connected with velvet.

The bed. Wide enough to fit three.

During their embrace, her owner had danced her across the floor. That he had willfully manipulated her during a vulnerable moment came as the last crushing blow.

Sarah determinedly forced herself to feel nothing.

Well practiced in keeping her emotions inside, she would show none of her despondency, her disappointment. Up until the present moment, she had never believed he, too, would abandon her.

Fingers moved deftly behind her. Her fasteners were undone in short order and the gown drawn down over her shoulders, slipped over her soft-tipped bosom, to drop over her hips to the floor. The loosely laced corset was readily dispatched, the rest just as quickly, and she was left nude, apart from silk hose, gartered at the thigh.

The sound of disrobing then, as two men went about the practicality of shedding their clothes. The weight of two male bodies settled on either side of her on the bed. Firm lips tugged the lobe of her right ear.

Mr. Turner had always played with her earlobes.

Her thighs were splayed, the action, courteous and careful, originating from the left—her prospective patron.

Mr. Turner had chosen well, and she was grateful. She should not have liked to have been grabbed and groped and greedily touched. But this was nice. Pleasurable, even. And perfectly acceptable. Her cushioning detachment fell away.

Two palms, each coming from opposite directions, met in the middle. On her mons. Her pubic hair was combed and patted and twirled. And she moaned, if not in abandonment, then not in revulsion either, as the space between her knees was widened.

Hands, then. Four palms. Roaming her nude body, plucking at her nipples, smoothing over her belly, sliding beneath to cup her buttocks, gaining access to the most private parts of her. Unfamiliar fingers, dry and analytical, examined her vulva before a deft insertion was made into the outer lips of her labia. Those anonymous fingers claimed her, deeply invading that most personal part of her woman's body. Though considerate and gentle, the touch failed to touch her heart. Only one man would ever touch her heart.

But her body was a different matter entirely.

"Mmm." She sighed, unable to help her response. Riding a crest of intense physical pleasure, shaking and writhing, her body malleable to both men, she hit the summit and orgasmed.

Afterwards, limp with satiation, she was placed on her side and her knee was raised.

Up until that point, the two men had simultaneously curried her favor; now her prospective patron flanked her rear whilst the man who owned her heart took up her front.

Her back opening was massaged, her clitoris caressed. She grew very wet.

Rather nice, finding oneself the focus of attention from two suitors, she mused.

An exotic perfume spiced the air. The scent was no less appealing than the gardenia-tinged lubricant Mr. Turner preferred, only different.

And then the formalities had finished. An erect penis replaced the massaging finger at her anus, her new protector at the advance.

Taking the future into her own hands, she rolled into a tight ball in anticipation of sodomy, as her owner had taught her to do this past week, submitting her bottom for penetration. No sense making things difficult, no sense playing the coy maiden; the gentleman expected anal intercourse from her, and to serve her best interests, she must try to please him.

Though a groan did escape her lips as the head of his penis began to delve her, a groan in acceptance of sadness. For the owner of her heart. For herself, too.

They might have had everything; they might have had it all. And in that sadness, she reached out to the man she loved, needing to touch his face in those few brief remaining moments whilst she still belonged only to him.

"Sebastian," she whispered.

Chapter Thirty-Six

If a man learns by his mistakes, then Seb figured he must rightly be the most learned man in all of New York state.

He had made every mistake in the book with Sarah, mistakes that would haunt him for the rest of his life. He hated himself for what he had done to that proper young miss from a garden gazebo, detested each and every revengeful step that had culminated with Sarah blindfolded in a strange bedchamber, wedged between two men. He would never forgive himself for his low-down, mangy, double-dealing treatment of her. Now that it was too late, his head finally accepted what his heart had known all along: Sarah was an innocent, every bit a victim of Michael Winslow as he and his mother had been.

Seb looked out the window onto the back garden. There was Sarah now, giving a lesson in botany to the rapt and attentive children who surrounded her.

Sarah had declined returning with him to Clearbrook, requesting instead that he drop her off at the rundown orphanage at the edge of the village center. There, she had remained for the past eight weeks.

Apart, that is, for Thursday mornings.

On Thursday mornings, Sarah transported every last child from the orphanage to Clearbrook.

Dear Mr. Turner, she had written. *Might you possibly agree to receive my class for an outing on Thursday mornings?*

Agree?

He lived only for Thursday mornings.

At the conclusion of this Thursday lesson, while Sarah gathered up her supplies and the children raced for the wagon for the return trip to orphanage, Seb left his watch by the window and hurried outside.

By the towering grove of hemlocks, he gave a formal bow. "Good day, Miss Winslow."

"Good day, sir."

"Sebastian," he said, bravely. "Please, if you would be so kind as to call me by my given name."

"Sebastian." She smiled. "How do you do, Sebastian?"

"I do miserably," he replied, his answer totally honest.

"And why is that?" Looking alarmed, she sought his eyes. "I do hope it is not your health."

"It is, in a manner of speaking. My conscience, which I thought long dead, has suddenly been resurrected. The pangs hurt like hell. So, here I stand, making my confession. I do so not to seek forgiveness, but to set things straight."

He took a deep breath. "Sarah, you once told me you felt as though you had spent your whole life wearing a mask. I have always felt the same. Only you removed your mask with me, and I lacked the courage to remove mine with you."

She reached for his hand. "Remove it now."

No use delaying, he tore the disguise away. "Before you stands a bastard and a thief."

Her eyes never fluttered; her hand stayed put in his palm. "Is that all?"

"You mean to say, that is not bad enough?"

"Well, tell me, when did you begin to steal?"

"During my mother's illness."

"And for what purpose did you use the ill-gotten gains?"

"What does that matter?" he blustered. "Stealing is stealing."

"I wish to know the full extent of your crime. So, since this a confession, for what did you use the money you stole?"

"Food. Medicine. The rent. Everything."

"Oh, dear. That *is* reprehensible. Choosing to eat rather than starve!" She shook her head. "Of course, since I myself chose to whore rather than starve, I am hardly the person to stand in judgment over you."

"You are mistaken."

"Pardon? Mistaken in regards to what?"

"Choosing. You had no choice. I made that choice for you." The words came rushing out then, spilling out, lest he lose courage. "For years, your father, Michael Winslow, was my mother's protector. As a lad, I lived here at Clearbrook. I called the house my home and its owner 'Father.'"

Blanching, Sarah swayed like a wilted rose.

Seb caught her before she fell. "Shall I stop?"

"No, please continue."

A few yards away, an Italian marble garden bench caught the shade of an oak tree. He led Sarah there, pressed her into a seat. He paced before her. "When Michael Winslow threw us on the streets in favor of a new bride, my mother turned to prostitution to support us. As a result, she came down with consumption. When she lay dying in a tenement room in the Bowery, I returned here to Clearbrook to beg help of your father."

Seb ground his thumbs into his eye sockets to prevent the unfamiliar onslaught of tears. Usually, when he thought of how and why his mother had died, rage consumed him. The anger was gone now, and the onslaught of grief surprised him.

A few moments later, control regained, he found that Sarah held his hand again, this time in both of hers.

He continued. "When I went to beg at Michael Winslow's door, I met you, a newborn swaddled in a pink blanket. You held my finger."

"Did you meet my mother also that day?" Sarah searched his face. "Can you tell me something about her? Anything at all, no matter how small and insignificant. What she looked like. The color of her hair. Do I resemble her? There are no portraits, and I cannot remember her face, but perhaps if you described her features to me—"

"The housekeeper held you, not your mother."

"Mrs. O'Sullivan." Sarah nodded. "She was very kind to me. She was the wife of the gardener, you know. But she died when I was little more than a toddler, and then I was placed in the care of—"

Sarah tsked. "Will you listen to me? Here I am holding center stage when this is your story to tell. Please, do go on."

He did, leaving out none of the details, sparing himself nothing. "I hated you."

"A baby? You hated a baby?"

"A baby? No. You were never a baby to me. To me, you were the reason my mother lay dying."

"And the reason you became a thief."

"After my mother's passing, I stole and conned and lied and cheated for the pure pleasure of it. I was good at it, too. When the authorities got after me, I headed out West. I made my fortune there. Explosives," he explained, as he had explained to her that first night. "I met Molly in a mining town. She was a madam in a saloon."

"Oh, I see—"

"I became part owner of that establishment. Basically, so I could have whatever whore I wanted, whenever I wanted her. And I did, Sarah, sometimes two and three whores at a time. Anyway, when I had enough money put aside, I wrote to my childhood friend Leonard Dutton back in New York—"

"Oh, God, no," Sarah said, squirming on the bench, but still holding his hand.

"I told Len to purchase a gaming establishment on Park Avenue, a front for a high-class whorehouse. He did, we became partners, and my plan was put in motion."

"My father frequented those gaming tables?"

"He did. In fact, he lost his shirt."

"A set up?"

"No. Fair and square. No rigged tables, Sarah. I might be low, but I ain't that low. Your father lost his fortune without any help from me. And when he needed a loan to continue to gamble, I told Len to give him enough rope to hang himself."

"Now you may stop. I think I know the rest." Letting his hand fall, she stood. "I must go see to the children."

Seb called at her retreating back. "Sarah, are you carrying my baby?"

She turned. "Why? Was that part of the plan, too? Did you wish me to conceive a child? Was abandonment of that child to be your final revenge?"

Her raised hand prevented his denial.

She squared her shoulders. "I am not with child, a circumstance for which I am past grateful. A child should be conceived in love. Obviously, you have no grasp of that word's meaning."

"Sarah, wait," he called again. He would see this through! "I found the man who assaulted you in Eleanor's stables the night of the charity event. He confessed the attack was unprovoked." At which point, Seb had beaten him to a pulp. "I was jealous."

"No need. There was only ever you. Even in that townhouse bedchamber with the prospective patron, there was only you."

His chest burned; his heart slammed against his ribs; tears scalded his eyes. "Sarah," was all he could say.

"Sebastian, I never asked you—that night, why did you stop it?"

He looked down and away. "You said my name. I told you, if you said my name, everything would stop. That my name would keep you safe."

"Yes, your name," she said. "I had quite forgotten. I thought, perhaps, you might have stopped it for another reason. Well, I really must gather the children together and return to the orphanage."

He yelled after her. "Why return to the orphanage? You can still see the children every day. I promise to stay out of your way. Why not stay here, in your home?"

She burst out laughing. "Oh, Sebastian!" she said with a half-turn back toward him. "You could not possibly be any more mistaken about Clearbrook. This house was never a home to me. Truly, I felt only relief when the house and contents were sold at auction. You see, I have always hated the house."

This time, he let her go. What more could be said? Now that it was much too late, he realized he hated Clearbrook, too. He hated the damned mansion he had schemed and lied and stolen and ruined Sarah to possess.

Epilogue

Two months later

Sebastian let the brass doorknocker fall on Clearbrook's front door.

Sarah, looking beautiful in her plain gray schoolmarm's gown, answered the summons.

"Sebastian!" she exclaimed, throwing the door open wide. "What a coincidence! I was just thinking of you."

Stunned, he blurted out, "Why would you think of me?"

"I have yet to thank you for giving Clearbrook to the orphans and for providing a yearly fortune for their care. Because of your support, many new teachers and caregivers have been hired." She laughed. "I am no longer needed here."

"No thanks necessary. I only came to tell you goodbye." Another blurted sentence. After which he hovered uncertainly on the threshold, not knowing what else to say. When he needed it the most, his facile tongue had deserted him.

Sarah reached for his hand, held it tight. "Goodbye? Why goodbye?"

Her hold on him gave him courage. "The last time we were together, you said I had no understanding of love."

"Oh, Sebastian. That was most unkind of me. I spoke out of anger and hurt—"

"No, you were right. And...and...I reckon I need to learn the meaning of that word because...because when you get right down to it, love is the only thing that counts."

"Sebastian, you were only a boy when you lost your mother. When the man you thought of as your father rejected you, naturally you became embittered." She paused, then said, "I think you should know—I went to see Len Dutton—"

"Len? You saw Len?" He shook his head. "That club is no place for a lady like you."

Sarah laughed. "I am not the same priggish snob I used to be. And what a tremendous relief it is to no longer be a lady." She laughed again. "In answer to your question, I went to the club to ask about my father. Interestingly enough, Mr. Dutton informed me that you had bailed my father out of his financial difficulties. Otherwise, the men he owed money to would most likely have killed him. Mr. Dutton also told me that my father not only lost at cards at your gaming tables—he lost at cards in every gaming establishment in this state. Because of your intercession, instead of coming to a gambler's violent end, my father died in his own bed with me at his side."

She was letting him off the hook, and he wanted no part of her charity. "Make no mistake, I set out to destroy my mother's killer."

"Yet, when you had the opportunity, you resisted the impulse. You stepped in and made my father a loan. Why?"

"Strings came with that loan."

"Why, Sebastian? You tell me why you kept those men away from my father!"

His voice rose. "Because that heartless maggot was all you had!"

Sarah looked him right in the eye. "I might as well tell you something else, too. I know about the wet nurse. Mr. O'Sullivan told me the story many times. If you hated me so much as a baby, why send that woman to nurse me?"

Seb felt his face overheated. "You were such a pretty little thing. How could I have let you starve? If it had been possible, I would have nursed you myself."

She laughed full out. "I think you know all about love, Sebastian Turner."

"Maybe once, but I lost sight of the true meaning somewhere along the way. I need to relearn it. Not here, though. Not making business deals, wearing fancy clothes, trying to make the right impression, being somebody I never was. I need to start over right from the beginning, from scratch. I can do that out West. No place to hide, under the big ol' sky out there. Out West, you realize how small you are. Damn humbling. Speaking of which—" He fell at her feet.

"What on earth! Get up at once, Sebastian!"

"The bands. I need to undo these damn blasted gold bands," he muttered and got busy keying the locks to free her. Hard to do with only one hand, seeing as she still held the other.

"I should love to see the West," she might have said then, but too intent on finishing his planned remarks, he kept rolling along.

"Sarah—from the very first, from when I first clapped eyes on you, I loved you. I never loved anyone but you. And I am so sorry for destroying you."

She sighed. "Oh, Sebastian. You have always thought me such a puny weakling. Do I look destroyed to you?"

He glanced up into her glowing face. "If not for me, you could have had everything."

"I might still have everything, if you would just see it. Now get up at once, before I am forced to use a severe measure to get you up."

Gaining his feet, Seb undid the locks on the gold bracelets around her wrists. After saying everything he wanted to say, doing everything he needed to do, there was nothing left to keep him.

He whispered, "Goodbye, Sarah," and tugged at his hand to free it from her grasp.

She refused to let him go. No matter how hard he tried to extricate himself from Sarah Winslow, she hung on to him, her tenacious grip holding him like a vice.

Even as a baby, her fingers had been mighty strong.

No way could he break the connection without hurting her, and he would never hurt Sarah again, not if he had to stay on the threshold, neither out nor in, for the rest of his natural life.

"I love you," he sobbed, tears raining down his face. "I love you so much. It feels like my heart will burst with it."

"Oh, Sebastian—"

"You once told me you believed in love. After everything I've done, after all you've lost on account of me, I hope you still have faith in that belief."

"My faith is as strong as ever. Perhaps even stronger, now that it has been tested." To prove her strength, she yanked him close. Pulled him right into her arms. And in her arms, at the front door of the house that had started him on a path of destruction, her forgiveness surrounded him, giving him absolution. The mercy of her love gave him the courage to plead for a second chance.

"Marry me, Sarah. Let me show you the West. Let me put a baby in your belly. Let me love you for the rest of my life."

Trusting she would not refuse him, he asked the same question he had asked at this same door once before. "Please, come with me now?"

She stroked his tear-wet face. "Yes."

It was the word he had waited eighteen long years to hear.

THE END

Louisa Trent

I am a writer raised in a family of storytellers. My earliest and fondest memory is of my Irish Nana relating a mystical story of a man looking in a window upon a beautiful lady whose long silvery hair swept the floor as she walked. With a simple telling, my grandmother drew me into her tale. A man. A woman. A forbidden love that wouldn't die. From opening word to shivery conclusion, I lived that story with her. Many years later, I'm still awed by the spell of the fantasy world she created with only the dip and swell of her voice.

There's power in words. Hope in love stories. Joy in a happy ending. I'm proud to carry on my family's storytelling tradition.

Visit Louisa on the Web at www.louisatrent.com.

Printed in the United States
75385LV00009B/13-18